Stylecroft

M. V. Hanna

R. Hanna

Miriam and Bob Hanna

AuthorHouse™ UK Ltd.
500 Avebury Boulevard
Central Milton Keynes, MK9 2BE
www.authorhouse.co.uk
Phone: 08001974150

© 2009 Miriam and Bob Hanna. All rights reserved.

No part of this book may be reproduced, stored in a retrieval system, or transmitted by any means without the written permission of the author.

First published by AuthorHouse 4/3/2009

ISBN: 978-1-4389-6938-1 (sc)

Printed in the United States of America
Bloomington, Indiana

This book is printed on acid-free paper.

Characters.

Christopher Kelly	Reverend.
Margaret Kelly	Wife.
Elizabeth Kelly	Eldest Daughter
Rose Kelly	Elder Twin.
Ruth Kelly	Younger Twin.
Rev. B.A. Hughes	Margaret's father
Mabel Whittam	Best friend to Margaret
Bob Whittam	Husband in Home guard.
Tom Hargreaves	Owner of Beckside Farm.
Eric Denson	Corporal in the Home Guard.
Mrs Walton	Parishioner.
Dick Robbins	Proprietor of the Red Lion.
Wolfgang Rumfler alias Joseph Kaminski	German Pilot.
William Williams	Tramp.
Mrs Hardy	Parishioner.
Mr. Smalley	Farmer.
Mrs. Smalley	Farmers Wife.
Mrs. Green	Shopper.
Mrs. Jean Pye	Headmistress.
Bill Bentley	The Verger
Bill Turner	ARP Warden.
Donald Hodges	Corner Shop Owner.
John Bish	Dutch representative.
Captain Parkinson	Home Guard.
Major Blackburn	R.A.F. Top Brass.
Burt	Lorry driver.
Pete	Lorry Driver.
Beryl Stagg	Student.
Madge Cunningham	Cleaner.
Mrs. Russell	Teacher.

Edward Grimes .... Owner of Field House Farm.
Mabel Grimes .... Farmers Wife.
Jessie Lambert .... Post-lady
Sir Harold Parkinson
Lady Parkinson.................... Local Gentry
James Wood .... Doctor
Bishop of Blackburn

Prisoners of War.
Kurt Fuhrmann.
Rolf Flohr.
Martin Dieter.
Jutta Piper.
Wolfgang Rumfler.

Special Operations Executive. (SOE)
David
Peter.
Jack.
Captain Pierre.
Marcel. Henri.
Madame Louise.   Martin.
Joseph Hammond. Alex Gregory. Captain of the Maid of Honor.
Marie Hammond. Robert.
Claude.   Madame Beauchamp.
Susan
Betty
Doris
John
Colin

This is the BBC news from London
On September the 3rd 1939.

This is a radio address by Neville Chamberlain the Prime Minister.

"I am speaking to you from the Cabinet Room at 10 Downing Street.
This morning the British Ambassador in Berlin, handed the German Government a final note, stating that unless we heard from them by 11 O'clock, that they were prepared at once to withdraw their troops from Poland, a state of war would exist between us. I have to tell you now that no such undertaking has been received, and that consequently this country is at war with Germany".

Christopher Kelly entered the church. There was silence. The pews were empty. He walked slowly down the central aisle to the chancel steps, knelt down and prayed. He brushed away a tear with the back of his hand. Slowly he stood up and made his way to the vestry.

'Good morning Christopher.' The vicar beckoned him to sit down. 'Have you made your mind up?'

'Yes I have. I'm going to join the army.'

'But, you've just been appointed Curate of this Parish and you are exempted from Military Service…..and what about Margaret and the children?

'I shall speak to Margaret today.'

'Think about it Christopher, it was bad enough when my daughter Margaret lost her first husband.

'Your daughter is strong and I love her and the children very much.'

'I know you do. But to leave them now, surely you will talk it over with Margaret and not just say you're going to join the army. That wouldn't be fair Christopher. You must discuss it with her.'

Margaret saw Christopher coming up the path and went out to meet him. 'What's the matter Christopher you're looking rather serious? Has daddy been giving you a hard time?

'We've been chatting about the war and me being curate at the church. I've a hard decision to make and I'd like your help.'

'There's a better way to chat and be useful at the same time, let's give 'Betsy' a clean.'

'I think our Austin Seven has had more washing and polishing than the King's Rolls Royce.'

'I've already washed it down for you.'

'That's kind of you Margaret. Have you any old cloths we can use for polishing?'

'Lots of soft ones for our 'Betsy' – muslin from the butchers ideal for polishing.'

'Just the job.'

'Now Christopher what is bothering you?' I know there's something wrong.'

'With many of the young men in the Parish joining the forces, I think I should too. I do not think I should wait for my 'call up papers' to arrive in the post.'

'I suppose my father has been trying to tell you to wait, because his only daughter and granddaughters need you. Of course we need you, we love you and we don't want to lose you. You're your own man Christopher. Go with what you feel is the right move.'

'Come here my darling.' Christopher gave his wife a big hug. 'You have helped to make the old car look her best and you've helped me to realise what I must do. I'll be back shortly. I just need to make a trip into town.'

Although the Recruitment Office in Oxford was on a side street, it was well sign-posted. Once inside, Christopher glanced up at the high ceiling, it gave the room a sense of space. Although there were many men in the room, it didn't feel crowded. There were several desks marked alphabetically. *Ah, G to K that's where I go.* Christopher joined a short queue of men. *They all look younger than I do.*

A young man came to stand behind him. 'You been here long mate?' Christopher turned to face the young man. 'No, I've just arrived.'

'I queued up over there, I didn't realise until I reached the desk that I was in the wrong queue.'

'What's your name?'

'Chris Green.'

'Well, you're in the correct queue this time. I'm a Chris too, Christopher Kelly.'

'Look like we're moving.'

'Next,' called the sergeant. 'Name?'

'Kelly'

'Christian name?'

'Christopher.'

'Age?'

'Thirty-five'

'Married?'

'Yes'.

'Children?'

'Three girls'

'Three?'

'Yes, one 15 years old and twins of five.'

The sergeant wrote down all the details on a form. 'Any qualifications?'

'I've recently finished at Oxford University gaining a B.A. degree.

The sergeant looked at Christopher raising one eyebrow as he did so. 'Studying what?'

'Divinity – I'm the Curate at Holy Trinity Church.'

'Really, and have you any other qualifications?'

'When I left Grammar School, I completed a year's course in French Studies in Poitiers. Recently, at Oxford University I did part time training in the Army Cadets.'

'Now that is interesting. Would you care to take a

seat at the back of the hall? Listen for your name being called, you won't have long to wait.' Christopher walked to the back of the room and sat down.

'Christopher Kelly '
'Yes.'
'This way please.'
Christopher entered a room at the end of the Recruitment Hall.

An army officer with several pips on his shoulder held out his hand. 'Pleased to meet you Kelly. 'Je suis a la recherche de talents inconnus.'
'What kind of talents are you looking for?'
'Well, you can obviously understand French. I would be pleased to send you for special training with the S.O.E. Sign your name here.'
'Who or what is the S.O.E,'
'The letters stand for 'Special Operations Executive'. I'm not at liberty to divulge any more information. I am going to send you this address.' He pushed over a slip of paper on which was printed *'82, Baker Street, LONDON.'* 'You're in the Army now.'
'What do I say when I get there?'
'Just give your name. They will be expecting you.'

Christopher made his way to a telephone box. He lifted the receiver, pushed two pennies in the slot and dialled.
'Oxford 4340, Margaret Kelly speaking.'
'Hello, Margaret its Christopher.'
'I thought it would be you, how did you get on?'

'Well, I'm in the army now – so they tell me.'

'I hope you're coming home.'

'I've to report to an office in the city and when I've been interviewed and hopefully accepted, I understand that I'll be given a 48 hour leave, then I start my training.'

'Only 48 hours, that's not long, but we'll make the most of it. I'll get daddy to look after the children.'

'Does your father know what I've done?'

'Yes he does and his only comment was he thought you would join up.'

'That's surprising, anyway I'll be on my way now and I'll see you later this evening, TTFN'

'TTFN'

Christopher put down the telephone. Once back on the street he made straight for the railway station and took the train into London. Outside the station there he made his way to the nearest bus stop. There was a long queue and as luck would have it there was a man who could help him.

'Excuse me Inspector, can you tell me which bus I need to take for Baker Street?' The Inspector took off his peak cap and pulled out a route map. After a short pause for thought he looked Christopher up and down.

'If, I were you reverend I would walk as far as the traffic lights at the end of this road, turn left and after about one hundred yards, take the next right – that's Baker Street.'

Within ten minutes Christopher stood outside a tall building. He looked up the wide stone steps that led to a large glossy black door. The number 82 was painted on the stone pillars on each side of the door. There was a brass sign stating – 'Inter-Services Research Bureaux'

This must be it.

Now, feeling a little apprehensive Christopher pushed open the heavy door and entered a reception area. A woman sat working at a table. He moved with some reticence towards her.
'Excuse me, Miss.'
A pair of piercing blue eyes looked up at him.
'Yes sir, can I help you?'
'I wonder if you can. My name is Christopher Kelly, I was advised by the Army Recruitment Officer to report here.'
'Well that's a nice way of putting it – most of the recruits tell me they were 'ordered' to come here.' She lent forward, picked up the telephone, pressed a button and spoke into the mouthpiece. 'Yes sir, he's here now.' She put down the receiver and turned to Christopher.
'Please go to room 312 on the third floor.' Her smile never reached her eyes.

Christopher was a fit young man following his Army Cadet training at the University. But after climbing three flights of stairs breathing became difficult. He knocked on 312 and waited.
'Come in.' A woman's voice called out.
Christopher entered. A dark haired woman looked up from her typewriter.
'Hello, my name is Vera, I'm Colonel Buckmaster's secretary. Please take a seat.'

He slipped into a leather armchair, crossed his long legs and tried to look relaxed.

'The Colonel will see you in a moment.' She continued with her work.

After several minutes of silence, a buzzer startled Christopher.

'He's ready to see you now. Just go through into his office.'

'Thank you Vera.'

Colonel Buckmaster sat behind his desk, directly opposite the door. He looked up as Christopher entered.

'Take a seat young man.'

'Thank you sir.'

'Now, I expect you are wondering exactly why you are here,' he glanced down at his paperwork.

'Yes sir.'

'I am particularly anxious to find anyone British or Canadian who can speak French fluently and pass for a Frenchman. Parlez vous francais?'

'I gained a distinction in French HSC level whilst at Grammar School, attended Poitiers University for one year. I spent most of my holidays in France.

'Excellent, I understand you are now a Clergyman and serve as a Curate at Holy Trinity Church in Oxford.'

'That's correct.'

'Well, what I am about to say to you at this moment Kelly, may take you by surprise.'

'I'm intrigued Colonel.'

'If you join my group Kelly you will be a volunteer. We, that's the S.O.E. aren't ordering you to take part in this unconventional warfare, but we're offering you a chance to do something more interesting for the war effort than simply drive lorries or fly planes. If you want to take the job, it will be entirely up to you.'

'Can you give me any more details about the S.O.E.?'

'Not until you have signed the "Official Secrets Act." You will be sent on many missions dealing with sabotage. Are you comfortable with that?'

'Yes sir.'

'Then sign here. Welcome to the S.O.E. Vera will give you your instructions.' Colonel Buckmaster shook hands with Kelly and wished him well on his 72-hour leave period especially as he was only expecting to spend 48 hours with his family.

'Here you are Christopher.' Vera handed him railway tickets and advance pay for his first week in the S.O.E. 'Your orders are in this sealed envelope and are for your eyes only. There's a gift for you from Colonel Buckmaster. All his agents receive a gift; the men a pair of gold cuff links the ladies a gold compact.'

'I don't know what to say – but please give the Colonel my thanks, it's like Christmas. Thank you Vera. Maybe we will meet again?'

'I certainly hope so, but you will be hearing from me soon'

Christopher made his way back to Oxford.

'Darling I'm back.'
'Tell me all about it.'
'Where's Elizabeth and the twins?'
'They're with their grandfather, we've got the whole

evening to ourselves, and I've booked a table at the Romany Restaurant.'

'Well done Margaret.'

'Now, how did you get on?'

'Well, I've been given 72-hour leave. Tomorrow I should receive my instructions. And you won't believe this, but my Colonel has given me a pair of gold cuff-links.'

'No, whatever for?'

'Your guess is as good as mine, for my shirt sleeves I should think.'

'Can I see them?'

'I'll wear them this evening. Come let's get changed and we'll make a night of it'

'Thanks to Daddy.'

'How do you like my dress?' Margaret gave a twirl in front of the mirror.

'Hang on darling, you look great. Wait till I put my tuxedo on and my new white shirt, no dog collar.'

'Don't forget your new cuff-links.'

'Daddy's booked a taxi for us.'

'Smashing.'

'It's here already.'

Christopher opened the car door and Margaret climbed in. She looked radiant.

'The 'Romany' restaurant please.'

'All right, Governor.'

'Let's not mention the war Christopher.'

'That suits me fine. We'll enjoy the meal and there's a dance floor too.'

'It's not very big, but let's make a night of it.'

The taxi came to a halt. 'Here we are, that will be one

shilling please.'

'Can you pick us up at 11 o'clock?'

'Eleven o'clock it is then.'

The lady at the reception desk greeted Christopher and Margaret with a cheery smile.

'A table in a quiet corner if you have one please.'

'Are you the Kellys?'

'Why, yes.'

'Well I was advised you were coming and he did ask if we could make it in a romantic corner.'

'Who did that?'

'He gave the name Hughes – I believe you know him well!'

'Daddy,' smiled Margaret.

'This way,' said the waiter – 'a table for two.' He pulled the chairs out for Margaret and Christopher. The waiter handed them each a menu.

'We know what we would like,' said Margaret – 'fish and chips.' They both burst out laughing. It was a 'Fish and Chip' restaurant.

'You know Margaret, that I can't talk about what I will be doing now that I've joined up.'

'Yes, I can understand that.'

'Well, that's good of you – I was going to say, that I don't even know myself.'

They both burst out laughing.

'Christopher, I too have a secret but its not for telling yet.'

'Waiter – two glasses of Vimto please.'

'A toast – 'Secrets.'

'Well, we can't sit here all evening looking at each other, would you care to dance Madam?'

'Most certainly sir.' Margaret replied rising from her chair. Christopher was quick to hold the back of her chair and take Margaret's hand.

The small dance floor was just big enough to cope with the five couples stepping out a waltz, followed by a quickstep and then a fox trot.

'Ask them if they will play some 'old time dances.'

'I certainly will Madam. I can do a Saint Bernard's Waltz and a Gay Gordons.'

'Forget the Gay Gordons Christopher.'

'Well, let's see what they have to offer first.'

'Take your partners for the Saint Bernard's Waltz', called out the M.C.

'I think you'll be saved from the Gay Gordons.' Christopher whispered into Margaret's ear and then added 'The M.C. said the small dance floor was not suitable for the Gay Gordons.'

Margaret gave Christopher a cheeky smile. 'Oh what a pity.'

'Kellys, your taxi is outside.' A voice came from one of the speakers.

Christopher helped Margaret with her coat and they made their way to the exit. The Manager was standing close by. Christopher shook hands 'Thank you we've had a pleasant evening.'

'I hope you will come again.'

'God willing.' replied Christopher.

'You sound like a priest,' said Margaret with a giggle.

The taxi driver opened the cab door. The taxi didn't move. The driver, through his mirror, watched them kissing.

'Why aren't we moving?' Margaret asked.

'Perhaps we should tell him where we want to go,' replied Christopher with a laugh.'

Back home there was message left on the table.

'Looks like your father has called.'

'What does it say?'

'Not to worry about Elizabeth and the twins they're staying the night at the Manse.'

'Oh that's kind of him.'

'Well darling what about going to bed?'

They stood at the foot of the bed and removed their shoes. Off came Christopher's socks and he gallantly helped Margaret with her nylons. Then facing each other they kissed and began to undress each other.

'Did I feel something stirring?' whispered Margaret.

Christopher's trousers fell round his ankles. He fumbled to remove Margaret's bra. As it dropped away Christopher gently kissed her protruding nipples. Naked they crawled on to the bed and whispering words of love. Christopher poured a specially warmed body oil on to his hands and gently massaged Margaret's beautiful body. He played with her clitoris. Margaret took the oil and lovingly took hold of Christopher's penis. Their lovemaking went unhurried and their cries of pleasure were not curtailed with their children at granddads. The morning would come all too soon.

'Time to get up,' called Margaret.

Christopher opened the bedroom curtain and looked

out. There was a roar of a motorcycle as a despatch-rider pulled up. He took out a large envelope from his bag and knocked on the door.

'Special delivery for Cadet Christopher Kelly.'

'That's my husband,' said Margaret. 'Can I sign for it?'

'No marm, I have to hand it over the soldier.'

Christopher came to the door, 'I'm Christopher Kelly' and showed his Idenity Card.

'This envelope contains instructions for your eyes only.'

'I understand,' said Christopher.

Christopher took the envelope to his bedroom and read his instructions.

That goes in my wallet. There was a railway ticket for Inverness.

He read a typed message signed Vera.

'You will be met by an S.O.E. Agent, who would simply reply 'Silence is of the Gods. Only Monkeys chatter.' You should say – 'They would be better in a zoo.' Memorise this instruction. Now burn it.

'Well that's simple enough. I wonder what will happen next?' Christopher took out a match and set fire to the message and dropped into the fire-grate. He watched the directive curl at the edges then disintegrate.

'Breakfast on the table.' Margaret called out. 'What was that all about?'

'More secrets,' said Christopher.

'Two 'Shredded Wheats' for you then,' quipped Margaret, 'especially after last night.'

'It was a beautiful evening Margaret.'

'Enjoy your Shredded Wheat, *Britons Make It Makes Britons* so it says on the packet.'

'After breakfast, I'll pack what things I need and call on your father to say my good-byes to him and the children.'

'I know you have to go. Tell dad he can bring the girls home at lunchtime and I'll make lunch.

'That's a good idea.'

'If you can write to us and let us know how you are and I will write to you. Let's hope this war will be over soon. I've been invited to organise the collection of funds for the Red Cross – so that and the Mothers Union should keep me occupied.'

'Sounds like your father's car.'

The first to burst through the door was Elizabeth followed by the twins.

'Morning Elizabeth, Ruth, Rose – did you all sleep well at Grandad's? Is he not coming in?'

'No, he has some calls to make.'

'Were you all good for Grandad?'

'Yes, he read a story to the twins from 'Milly Molly Mandy' and he said he would be back with more bedtime stories,'

'That's good," said Christopher. 'I'm going to see him later.'

'Have you got everything packed Christopher?' asked Margaret.

'Yes, including writing paper and envelopes.'

'Is father going away?'

'Yes, but he'll be back, very soon.'

'Are you going to help end the war?' asked Elizabeth.

'I hope so. Be good for your mother, help her with the twins, say your prayers every night.'

'I will pray that you will be kept safe.'

'Thank you Elizabeth. Well, I'd better be off now.'

The door closed and Margaret turned to her daughters. There were tears in her eyes.

'Breakfast for you three, then off to school.'

'Can we take our skipping ropes for play time?' asked the twins.

'Of course you can.'

Christopher walked briskly down the street. He was still wearing the clothes of a clergyman.

It will please father-in-law. He found the Reverend Hughes tending his roses in the vicarage garden.

'Morning Christopher, have you received your call-up papers?'

'Well, you could say that. I received my instructions and I'm on my way to the railway station now. But, mum's the word.'

'Well, best of luck son, may God be with you. I'll keep my eye on things here.' They threw their arms round each other. After a few hugs they parted and Chris stepped out, he had a train to catch.

I'm going to be late.

Christopher checked his watch. He waved down a taxi.

'Railway Station please. As quick as you can.'

'Right sir.'

'Can you can step on it driver, if I miss the train for Scotland; well it does not bare thinking about.'

'Don't worry sir, I'll get you there with hopefully time to spare.'

The taxi pulled up at the entrance to the station.

'Well done driver, I've even time for a cup of tea.'

'What did I tell you sir. Have a good journey sir, thanks for the tip.'

Christopher made his way to the station café.

'Can I help you?' said the lady behind the counter.

'Tea please, no sugar.'

'That's good sir, we only have saccharine today.'

Christopher looked round for somewhere to sit. There were three tables occupied by gentlemen reading newspapers. One gent lowered his paper. 'Take a seat.'

'Thank you.'

'Going into the city?'

'Not today.'

'Any good at crossword puzzles?'

'Well, not bad, try me.'

'Silence is of the Gods. Only Monkeys chatter.'

Silence is of the Gods. Only Monkeys chatter, where have I heard that before.

Christopher sat there thinking for a moment. It was more like a pregnant pause.

'They would be better in a zoo.'

'David, there's been a change of plan. Can't say much here. As soon as you've finished your tea, meet me at the entrance to the station.' He left David gulping down the liquid.

Must remember I'm David from now on. Well here goes.

David picked up his bag and made his way out of the station. He could see the agent standing next to a Sunbeam Talbot he was holding the boot of the car open.

'Put your bag in the boot,' he said. 'Good, let's go.'

David jumped in the passenger seat next to the agent who was now moving off towards the A1 heading for Croydon.

'Now we can talk, my name is Sam.'

'Pleased to have met you.'

'We've a plane waiting for us in Croydon.'

'A plane?'

'We'll be in Scotland much sooner.'

'First we'll collect our parachutes.'

'Parachutes!'

'The RAF insists, but they will only be used if there is an emergency. Parachute training will be part of your training during your two weeks in Arisaig. It's up in the Scottish Highlands north of Fort William.'

'I've read about that area when Prince Charlie was there in the mid 1700's'

'It will be hard going David, it's a tough area.'

'Well, I've still got youth on my side, I'll do my best.'

'Sounds like you were a Boy Scout at one time'.

'I certainly was.'

'You'll have lots of exciting things to do. Apart from

your parachute training, you will given practice with firing pistols and other small arms, learning the Morse Code, unarmed combat, generally getting very fit, maybe deer stalking and fishing for salmon and lots more.'

'Can you tell me Sam what role you play in the SOE?'

'I'm a Physical Training Instructor.'

'It seems quite a lot to do and learn in six weeks.'

'Don't worry David the time will pass quickly and you'll wonder where the time has gone. There's no training book. It is assumed all our agents will parachute into an area at some stage, first you start in the gym, then we have a special high parachute frame to jump from and hopefully at least one jump from a plane.'

'And what about the other skills I'll need?'

'The rest is like being back at school with set periods for physical training, map reading, French conversation, how to make and use explosives, rope work, elementary Morse and semaphore signalling. Then plenty of outdoor lessons which will include Commando Training and silent killing, boating, pistol and machine gun firing, poaching salmon.'

'Salmon poaching!'

'Yes, that's great fun, but even better, you will be expected to raid the 'Officers' Mess for what drink you can steal from them.'

'You make it all sound like a bit of fun'

'Don't you believe it – especially if you are caught, then you'll find out what it is like to be interrogated.

Six weeks of highly secretive training the Reverend Christopher Kelly, now known as 'David' in the Special

Operations Executive, returned home to be with his wife and daughters.

'Christopher you do look well.'
'You're looking good too, have you put some weight on?'
'What with all this rationing. I don't think so.'
'Have you been good?'
'Yes father.'
'Good, then I can give you all a present.'
Christopher did not tell his daughters that he had acquired the large box of chocolates from the Officers' Mess. Margaret was about to ask, when Christopher put a finger to his lips.
'Remember, no questions, top secret and all that. You can all enjoy the chocolates. '

The week passed too quickly. They agreed 'no tears' but it was difficult for them not to show their emotions.
'Where is father going?' Rose asked.
'Why does he have to go?' Ruth pulled at her sister's pigtails.
'Don't do that.' Elizabeth reprimanded them.
'Girls please. Father has gone away for a few days. He's in the army now and it's his job.'
'Mother I don't like war. It's horrid.' Rose said tearfully.
'Don't cry.' Ruth put her arm around her shoulder.
'Come on, let's play out on our bicycles,' Elizabeth suggested.
The children ran outside, their laughter ringing in the afternoon sunshine.

Note SOE formed upon direction of WS Churchill, following appointment as Prime Minister and defeat in Europe in 1940 (after June 1940)

This is the BBC Home Service

Here is the 9 o'clock news on April 9th 1940

Germany invades Norway and Denmark.

That is the end of the news.

S.O.E. Agent David Dubois made his way to the railway station knowing that he might never see his family again. He had received his orders – 'Report to R.A.F. Station Tangmere.

A high winged monoplane, the Lysander, stood on the edge of grassed field, its engine barely ticking over. David stood outside 'Tangmere Cottage' on the edge of RAF Fighter Base Tangmere near Chichester. His instructions were – 'keep yourself anonymous'. He entered by the back door and quietly slipped inside.

'Hello, I'm David Dubois.'

Two men, drinking tea, sat at a square wooden table.

'Come and sit down and join us. I'm Lionel and this gruesome looking individual is Henry.'

'Dank you Herr Commandant.' Henry stood up, and clicked his heels together.

'Our local joker.'

'It's nice to know you can act about like a comedian.'

'If we didn't make light of it all, we'd be certified for a place in a lunatic asylum.'

'I can understand that even though I'm pretty new at this game.'

'We guessed that matey,' said Lionel.

'What gave me away?'

'Introducing yourself. Seasoned agents would just wander in and sit down.'

'I'll remember that next time.'

'Always hoping there will be a next time old chap.'

'Who's Lysander is parked out there?'

'You mean Bessie, she's mine,' Lionel answered. 'She's just finished having her undercarriage checked.'

'We hit some pretty rugged terrain on our last mission,' Henry explained.

'When do we go?'

'We're waiting for instructions from Air Liaison. But, the next full moon would be a good guess.'

'Have you received the aerial photographs from RAF Reconnaissance Unit?'

'Not yet, you'll be able to study them before your jump.'

'Thanks, I'll be interested to see if there are going to be any obstacles in the way.'

'What did you do before you joined this lot?'

'Let me say I knew a little about aeroplanes but more about angels.'

'Say no more, mum's the word Padre.'

'This Lysander of yours, it has a flying range of around 600 miles hasn't it?'

'More like 900 miles with recent modifications and bigger fuel tanks, that's at a cruising speed of 165 mph.'

'That's interesting, good to know I'm in good hands,' he leaned back into his padded chair.

The sound of a throaty motorbike drew up outside the cottage.

'Could be your instructions have arrived!' Lifting his heavy frame from his chair, Henry collected a large envelope and placed it on the table.

'Let's see.' Lionel ripped open the directive. All was silent as he read the instructions.

'We go tonight.'

The rest of the afternoon and the evening, the trio studied their instructions over and over again until they were clear in their minds exactly what they had to do.

'The flare path will be L shaped. We land by the first light and turn around between the other two, which will be 150 yards further on.' Lionel explained'

'How long will you be on the ground?' David asked.

'Only three minutes.'

'Blimey, that's not long.'

'That's providing everything goes all right chum.' Henry chipped in.

Lionel checked the instrument panel in front of him. He signalled for the chocks to be pulled away. The Lysander taxied slowly at first then picked up speed over the grass runway.

'Come on girl, up you come, up.'

They were airborne. Lionel banked her around and headed on the flight path for France.

'Right David, any questions?'

'What height would you be for a drop?'

'About six to eight hundred feet. I bet you're pleased we'll be making a landing on this trip.'

'How long will the flight take?'

'Just over the hour. That's providing the wind speed isn't too great.'

'What happens if the air current is high?'

'Blimey you do have a lot of queries, everything is going fine at the moment. But, to answer your question – we'd be blown off our course and I'd have to make adjustments – which is why I'm the pilot and not you. Sod it, I shouldn't have spoken. Look ahead.'

'What's wrong?'

'A bank of bloody fog. Would you believe it? It's no use; we'll have to turn back. I can't land in a pea souper.'

'Maybe it will clear a little further on.' David suggested.

'No, we have to clear the Loire River. It will be worse not better. Hold tight folks.'

The aeroplane banked around in a tight circle and they were on their way back home. It seemed ages before Lionel announced 'Not long now.'

There was a screech from the tyres as they hit terra firma. The aircraft swung to the left moving off the main runway and rolled to a stop about one hundred yards from the cottage.

'Let's pop down to the pub, I could murder a pint.' There was no objection.

'Jump in.'

Lionel revved up the Jowett Javelin. *[marginal note: !! Post-war car]*

'Ready lads, hold tight,' and with a roar from the exhaust the Javelin zoomed off towards the 'Dog and Duck.'

'There's not many people here this evening,' noted Henry as they entered the public bar.

'Three pints of your best bitter Landlord if you please.'

'Certainly gentlemen.'

'Bottoms up chaps,' invited David.

'No problem,' said Lionel.

'Three more pints please Landlord.' Called Henry.

'Celebrating?'

'No just thirsty!'

'This beer is really good' Christopher wiped his mouth with the back of his large hand.

'Better slow down lads, we should be off early in the morning,' cautioned Lionel.

'Going far?' asked the Landlord.

'Just there and back, to see how far it is,' replied Lionel.

Back at Tangmere Cottage the trio slept well. The morning and afternoon they spent in preparation for their second attempt on their assigned mission. It was dusk when the three men climbed into the aircraft. The take off went well. The first hour passed quickly.

'The French coast ahead,' called Lionel. He pulled back the joystick and the aircraft responded gaining height as flack peppered the Lysander.

'No problems,' called Henry, 'we're clear.'

'The Loire river ahead chaps!'

'Where?' David made his way into the cockpit.

'There. See that ribbon of light. That's the reflection of the moon.

'I didn't realise it would be so clear.'

'We need to see the landmarks.'

As the Lysander lost height it banked around.

'Sod it, I can't see it.'

'See what?' asked David.

'White Morse code letter 'S', Ah there it is. Hang on. In we go.'

David grabbed the arms of his seat almost losing his balance. The wheels of the plane hit the ground and bounced unevenly, but Lionel had the plane under his control, landed in a straight line, then rolled to a stop.

'Best of luck David.' Lionel held out his hand.

'Thanks Skipper. See you in two night's time.'

'That you will my boy, that you will.'

David turned and shook hands with Henry, climbed out and ran well away from the plane as it circled and took off.

Safe journey old boy. Best be off before any Germans arrive.

He hurried across a ploughed field as best he could with his sack of plastic explosives and detonators.

David's first port of call was a 'safe house' where he had to make contact with a radio operator. Once clear of the field he could see the farmhouse against the skyline. He approached with caution and feeling all was well, he knocked at the door. It opened slowly and there stood a young lady.

'En quoi puis-je vous servir?'

'The Condor flies high.'

The door opened wider. 'Come inside quickly, I've been expecting you.' David looked at a pair of bluest of blue eyes he had he had ever encountered.

'David?'

'Yes'

'I'm Marie your radio operator,'

'Pleased to meet you. Have you any specific instructions?'

'We go tomorrow. So enjoy your meal and get some sleep, there's a bed there for you in the corner. I'll inform London you're here.

David opened his eyes. It was still dark outside. He could hear movement in the kitchen. He dressed quickly and with the smell of freshly baked bread tantalising his nostrils, he wandered into the kitchen.

'Ah, you're rested? Good, fancy ham and eggs?'

'Do I? I should say so. Thanks.'

Marie busied herself cracking eggs into the frying pan. David sat himself at the table and looked around.

It's small but it's certainly well equipped'. He tucked into his breakfast.

'Thanks I haven't eaten like this for a long time.'

Marie watched him while he buttered more toast.

'Coffee?'

'Please.'

Marie joined him at the table and they both sat dunking their bread into the coffee.

'It's unusual seeing a woman radio operator.'

'Believe me, there's plenty of us. Sadly many have lost their lives. We change our locations quite often as a precaution. The Germans, in their detector-vans, patrol the area constantly listening out for our signals.'

'Yes, I know it is dangerous work and we couldn't carry out our operations without your help.'

'Help me clear the table and we'll take a look at the map.'

Marie pulled open the table drawer, took out a chart and opened it up.

'This is where we are and there's Figeac.'

'How are we getting there?'

'I've a motorbike outside.'

'But, I don't drive.'
'I'll soon show you how, if you want to!'
'Thanks. That'll be something else to master.'
'No time like now then.'

David followed her into the yard. Marie sat astride the motorbike, tickled the carburettor and kick started the engine.

'Climb on David.' She revved the engine and David placed his sack between his legs and held on to Marie.

'All right.'

'Here we go then. Hold tight.'

The narrow roads, they had chosen, took them ever closer to Figeac and they came to the outskirts of the town and stopped.

'The Maquis will be here soon.'

'How many are coming?'

'Two.'

'Good, that should be enough. Do you have anymore details?'

'No, they will tell you more when we get there.'

'Let's sit down on the grass verge, there's no point in standing up.'

'David.' The voice came from behind him. He turned, 'John-Paul?'

'Greetings mon ami.' They shook hands and embraced. 'How are you?'

'Very well John-Paul.'

'It's the Ratier factory we're after David.'

'Yes, I understand that, but I need more details from you.'

'Well, they make variable pitch propellers for the Luftwaffe, around 300 each week. It's quite a busy works and production needs to be stopped. That's where you come in.'

'That's nice to know you are wanted and that's what I've been trained to do.'

'You have to destroy their machine tools, which are irreplaceable. It will put their production out of action.'

'Is the factory guarded?'

'Oui, four on and four off duty.'

'I understand.'

'Follow us. We'll take care of the German guards and leave the rest to you.'

'I see there's a railway track next to the factory.'

'Oui, it is an essential part of the plant to transport the propellers to the airfields.'

'We'll soon put a stop to that.' Christopher pulled the sack of explosives on to his shoulder.

They made their way into the factory. John-Paul's men took the lead.

'Wait here David, I'll give you a signal when it is all clear.' A few minutes later David heard footsteps ahead, he slipped behind a milling machine. The figure drew level. It was John-Paul.

'Is the area clear?'

'Yes, it is, but be aware, we only dealt with three of the German guards. There should have been four.'

'I'll be careful. I'll lay the charges here. Then I'll go over to the railway.'

'Take care.'

'I will mon ami.'

David made his way into the interior of the building the smell of industrial oil hung in the stagnant air. He carefully picked his way between the machines.

Now what apparatus would cause them real problems?

He pushed the blue prints aside, opened up the sack he carried and emptied out its contents on to the metal table; black tape, plastic explosives and detonators. He surveyed the scene before him; he picked up the plastic explosive and squeezed it between his fingers.

Now which machines, once destroyed, will be the most damaging?

Having made his mind up, he ripped off several strips of black tape, sticking the end of one strip on to the worktop. David worked carefully ever mindful of his surroundings. From the plastic explosive, he fashioned a sausage shape, took a couple strips of tape and wrapped it around the legs of the milling-machines; inserted the detonators and set the timers for thirty minutes. Next he taped the explosives on to several hydraulic lifts, turret lathes and horizontal grinding machines.

Retracing his steps, he gathered up the rest of the explosives and made his way over to the railway tracks. Cautiously he moved towards the sidings, hesitating for a moment by the Workman's Hut. He stopped to listen.

That missing guard. I wonder where the hell he is?

Sweat trickled down his face; he impatiently brushed it away on the sleeve of his jacket. Then, listening all the time, he moved away in-between a bogie wagon and a flat bed.

I could do with a pint of cool Guinness right now.

He peered out between the rolling stock, checking left and right. The way was clear. He dropped to his knees, emptied the contents of the sack on to the damp ground.

What was that?

He thought he had heard the crunch of footsteps on the gravel. No it was all right. Just nerves getting the better of him.

He placed the dynamite with the deftness of a seamstress and connected each charge together with wire, then set the timer to go off in a single blast.

He crouched low, and remembering the missing German guard, made his way to the factory perimeter.

'Everything all right David?' John-Paul enquired.
'Yes,' he looked at his watch. 'Two minutes to go. Keep low everyone.'
Conversation stopped.

I hate this delay. It makes my stomach churn and I feel sick.

There was a loud explosion. Flames surrounded the black silhouette of the factory building licking up into the dead of the night.
'Let's go..... There was a look of great delight on all their faces. Au revoir mes amis, 'till we meet again.'

David shook hands with Jean-Paul and waved good-bye to the Maquis. Marie sat astride the motorbike and opened up the throttle. David held on tight as the machine leapt forward disappearing into the darkness.

Back at base they enjoyed a meal of strong horsemeat and potato stew with chunks of homemade bread, which they washed down with a carafe of red wine.
'I'll contact London. Get some sleep, you need it.'
'Thanks I'll do that.'
 Marie left the cottage and entered the outhouse. She dragged out an old suitcase and placed it on top of a bench, opened it up and attached an aerial to her transmitter. She tapped out the message – 'The Condor flies.' Listening for a short while on her head- phones the reply came. Just one letter – 'R'.

Confident now that the message had been received and understood, Marie quickly detached the aerial and put the machine away. She was well aware of the danger that the German military frequently monitored the area listening for signals.

She left the building and returned to the cottage where David was sleeping soundly. She smiled on hearing his rhythmic snores.

Should I creep in bed beside him? It would be much warmer.

She hesitated at his door and slowly turned the brass knob.

It was mid morning when David rose from his sleep.

'You shouldn't have let me sleep on Marie.'

'Why not. You've needed it. It was a wonderful night.'

They ate a cooked breakfast together and David sat down on a comfortable wicker armchair.

'Are you based here Marie?'

'Now David, you know the rules, no tittle-tattle'.

'You are right, I shouldn't ask such questions.'

Marie busied herself clearing away the breakfast things.

Better help her. I wonder what her full time job is?

The afternoon ticked away. David sat around reading, eating and drinking mugs of black coffee.

'The weather will be clear David. So we will rendezvous with the plane at midnight as planned.'

'Good. I like things to go smoothly.' He grinned showing his white teeth.

Eleven o'clock, Marie and David stook their seats on the motor bike. David gave it a kick- start.

'Ready?' shouted David.

'Ready.'

The smell of the exhaust fumes was very strong.

'Hold on, here we go.'

He opened up the throttle and the bike leapt forward. The throb of the engine gave him great pleasure with Marie holding him tight. It was another first in his life. This time he was the driver of the machine.

The road narrowed as they arrived at the appointed place on the edge of a large field. They checked their watches; they were in good time.

'Thank you for all you've done Marie.' David looked into her sparkling blue eyes. 'This mission could not have been accomplished without you.'

'You must have kissed the Blarney Stone David, as well as me,' she smiled looking at him with true affection. A rustle from the undergrowth warned them, they were not alone.

'Condor.' It was just a whisper.

'It's the Maquis,' Marie explained.

'That's a relief.'

Three figures approached from out of the darkness.

'Glad you made it in time. The plane is due soon.'

The French Resistance trio took their positions in the field, fanning out into a 'L' shape whilst Marie continued to listen. They waited...... Time ticked by.

'Listen, I hear them.'

Marie took her torch and flashed the signal 'C' towards the on coming plane. The drone of the engines grew louder. Then through the gloom of the darkening skies a giant shadow zoomed towards them. The plane touched down on the first red light and taxied between the next two red signals.

'Take care David,' called Marie.

'And you.' The two friends hugged. David ran for the plane and hastily clambered on board.

'Thanks mate, you don't know how pleased I am to see you.'

The Lysander bounced over the rough ground and gathered speed. David looked out of the window hoping to see Marie. Only then to his horror, he saw Marie with her arms raised. German soldiers surrounded her. There was nothing he could do about it.

Oh my god. What have I done?

If I hadn't delayed her, she would have been well on her way to the farmhouse.

What can I do?

He could not do anything.

This is the BBC Home Service
and here it the 9 o'clock news
on May 10ᵗʰ 1940
Winston Churchill replaces Neville Chamberlain
as Prime Minister in Britain.
of

That is the end of the news.

Completely exhausted from his many missions Christopher made his way back home to Oxford, tormented in his mind with recollections of his dangerous exploits. His head ached and no matter what he tried to gain some relief, it did not work.

Maybe I do need to be checked at the hospital for 'post traumatic stress'. I think that's what they called it. After all I have been told that they will lessen gradually.

Tired and weary, he dismissed it from his mind. Taking another large gulp of whiskey from the bottle. *All I want to do now is sleep.*

When he arrived home, Margaret was appalled at his weight loss and his haggard appearance. Even the girls recognised that something was not right with their father.
'Play quietly,' advised their mother. Your father needs a bit of peace and quiet for a while. Don't worry, he just needs a rest.'

For a while Christopher was in a depressed state. His doctor helped as much as he could. He chatted with Christopher on his visits and was able to convince him drinking whiskey was not the answer and that time would be the greatest healer. And so it was.
As time went on, with his wife, family and friends supporting him, his headaches did lessen and much to the delight of all, he became more like his old self.

'Margaret, I've received a letter from the Bishop. He

has offered me a living as Vicar at Holy Trinity Church in the village of Stylecroft in Lancashire.'

'That's good, but how do you feel about it darling?'

'I think I need a new challenge. It would do me good. But, what do you think?

'Well, it sounds like an answer to my prayers.'

'It would mean the girls would miss their friends and would have to start at a new school. Do you think they would mind?'

'Well, let's ask them.'

They called the girls into the kitchen.

'Sit down girls, we've something to you.'

Christopher sat at the kitchen table. His daughters listened attentively.

'I've been offered a living at Holy Trinity Church in Stylecroft in Lancashire.'

'What's a 'living'? Asked Ruth.

'It's the word the clergy use for an appointment or a job if that makes it easier for everyone.'

'When do we go?' asked Rose. There were tears in her eyes.

'I like it here,' Ruth said stubbornly, her face wrinkling up into a pout.

'What about our friends?' Rose brushed away her tears with the back of her hand.

'You'll soon make new friends,' said Margaret.

'Stylecroft is in the middle of the countryside, there are hills and mountains with lots of sheep, cows and horses and ponies,' said their father.

'Now that will be nice won't it girls, I'm sure you will like it there?'

'I won't.'

'Now, don't be awkward Ruth. It will be good for your father and he'll be with us all the time.

'When do we go?' asked Elizabeth.

'Very soon.'

'Could we learn to ride a pony?' asked the twins.

'I don't see why not.'

Ruth's smile lit up her face, her sulks all forgotten.

'Would we make new friends?' asked Ruth.

'I'm sure you will,' said her mother.

'So, everyone is all right about the move?' Questioned Christopher.

Everyone nodded and it was agreed the move would go ahead.

For the next week they were packing up their belongings in wooden crates and cardboard boxes. The front room was crammed full with boxes almost to the ceiling.

They had all been carefully labelled – 'SITTING ROOM', 'LOUNGE', 'BEDROOM', 'KITCHEN'

'Have we enough room for Teddy?' asked Ruth.

'Of course we have. You can take him with you on the train,' said Margaret.

A large removal van pulled up outside the cottage. Two men made their way up the garden path and knocked on the door. Margaret's father arrived to supervise the removal.

'Leave it to me, I'll see that everything goes and the cottage is left tidy.'

'Grandad we're going on a train to Lancashire.'

'I know Ruth. Are you and Rose looking forward to this new adventure?'

'Yes', piped in Rose, 'And we'll be able to have riding lessons on a pony.'

'Well, don't forget to write to me and tell me all about it.'

'I'll make sure they don't,' said Elizabeth. 'We'll all miss you Grandad, but maybe you can come and stay with us for a holiday.'

'That would be nice, but I'll let you settle in first, so make sure you tell me what Stylecroft is like.'

'We will father,' said Margaret. 'I'm sure Christopher will be inviting you to give the sermon whilst you are with us.'

'That's a great idea,' said Christopher. 'It will give me a chance to have a rest on that Sunday.'

'Have a rest? Said Elizabeth, 'I thought clergymen only worked once a week!'

They all laughed.

'Come time to go.'

'Now, now let's behave children,' urged Christopher.

'All aboard,' shouted the railway guardsman, his red and green flags tucked under his arm as he closed a carriage door. 'Hurry along.'

The family hastily climbed on board and wandered through the carriage until they found four empty seats. Within minutes after a few doors were slammed. The guardsman waved his green flag and the engine driver had the train moving, slowly at first, but with a joyful whistle the train picked up speed. Gradually the city of Oxford became a memory and the excitement of going to live, in a part of England that was completely new to them, raised a few questions from the excited girls.

'Do you think the people in Stylecroft will be friendly?'

'Of course they will. They will be pleased they to have a new vicar again.'

'I don't know about that Margaret,' chipped in Christopher.

'They will father,' the twins said with glee.'

'Thank you girls, I feel much happier with your support.'

'Look,' said Elizabeth, 'it's raining.'

A few spots of rain appeared on the windows and ran down in criss- crossing streams whilst Ruth and Rose playfully followed them with their fingers.

'I hope the rain stops before we reach Stylecroft, its no fun unloading furniture in the rain.' Margaret's voice took on a despairing tone.

'We've a few miles to go yet. The weather can change again. It could be snowing,' quipped Christopher. The twins looked at him in horror.

'He's only joking,' said Margaret.

They arrived late afternoon. The train pulled into Ulverston station.

'Come children, pick up your things, this is where we get out.' Christopher stepped on to the platform and helped his family with their luggage.

'Reverend Kelly?' Chris turned to a smart army officer holding out his hand. Christopher grasped it.

'I'm Captain Parkinson. I've come to give you a lift into Stylecroft.'

'Well, that's great Captain. Meet my wife and children.'

'Pleased to meet you all, I expect it has been a tiring journey. My car is just outside the station door.'

'Thank you very much Captain Parkinson. We were wondering if we had to find a taxi or something.'

'Let me have your luggage. I'll put it in the trunk.'

'You can't have my teddy.' Ruth said clutching her toy close to her.

'Of course not young lady.'

'I'm Ruth.'

'Very well Ruth. Get into the back of the car with your sister and we'll be on our way.' Margaret, Elizabeth, Ruth and Rose squeezed on to the back seat whilst Christopher sat in the passenger seat next to the Captain.

'Lovely car. What make is it?'

'A Wolseley, my pride and joy.'

'I can understand why, she's beautiful. Christopher ran his fingers across the highly polished woodwork. All the seats were leather and so comfortable.'

'It won't take us long to reach Stylecroft, and you can see we have arranged for the sun to come out to brighten up your day. Enjoy the scenery, you are in the most beautiful part of England, well that's what I think,' said the Captain with a chuckle.

The car drew up outside the vicarage.

'Oh, how quaint,' said Margaret, 'look a little wooden gate, ivy climbing up the stonework. Perfect.'

The family stood looking at their new home. The Captain pulled out the cases from the car-trunk.

'Thank you so much.' Said Margaret.

'I think it best if I leave you all to explore your new home, so I'll be on my way.'

'Well, thanks again Captain Parkinson, as soon as we have settled in, you must come and visit us, you'll be welcome anytime.'

'I'll do that and I'll bring my wife too.'

'That would be great, we'll look forward to seeing you again and your wife.'

The Captain gave a wave and drove off down the Village Street.

'What his is wife called?' asked Margaret.

'Sorry dear, I forgot to ask.'

'I think the street through the village is called Broad Street,' said Christopher.

'Well, it is certainly wide enough. It looks like there are a few shops.

'But, have you noticed our nearest neighbour?'

'How could I miss that – the village pub, look its called the 'Red Lion.'

'It all looks very peaceful,' Christopher observed.

'It certainly does' Margaret agreed. 'It's so quiet.'

The silence was broken. 'Come on – let's go inside our new home.' The twins ran ahead and pushed open the door.

'How did you manage that?'

'It wasn't locked.'

'Maybe there's someone inside?'

'Hello, and welcome,' a voice came from the hallway. 'I'm Mrs Whittam from the Mothers Union, I've just made up the fire for you, and left something for you in the fridge. I'll leave you to explore the vicarage and hope we'll meet later in the week when you have settled in.'

'That's kind of you Mrs Whittam. Maybe I'll meet you and others at church tomorrow!' Said Christopher. 'But first – meet the family.'

'Believe me I'm pleased to be the first to welcome you all, but I know you'll all be excited to explore. So I'll leave you to it. Ta tar.'

'Daddy what is 'Ta tar?'

'I think that is what they say for 'good-bye'.

'Come on Ruth, let's explore.'

'All right Rose. I'll race you up the stairs.' The twins tore off at a pace.

'Will they ever learn to calm down?' asked Christopher. He wiped his forehead with his hand.

'Give them time darling, they will. Let's have a look to see what rooms there are.'

From the hall a door opened into a sitting room. Next was the office. To the left a large kitchen.

'This looks more like your domain Margaret.'

'Thank you Christopher. It certainly looks a cosy place. Let's put the kettle on for a cup of tea.'

Upstairs, the twins were arguing as to which bedroom they were to have.

'Mother come and look. I think we should have the room at the back of the house.'

Margaret wearily climbed the steep stairs. 'Now girls please behave. Everyone is very tired. Now what is the matter?'

'Don't you think we should have the biggest room?'

'No, that's enough, you heard me.'

Downstairs, Christopher had gone out into the garden.

The back garden needs some attention, but it won't take too much work to get it straight, Margaret will be pleased about that.

'What do you think Christopher?'

'We're all together in our new home, what more could we want?'

Margaret rested her head on his shoulder. 'Do you think you can cope with this new parish?'

'Well, the doctor told us it's the best thing that could have happened, moving to a place like this. We're in the country, wonderful fresh air. What could be better?'

In the fridge was a meal all ready made and all they had to do was to heat the vegetable stew.

'So that is what Mrs Whittam had placed in the fridge. I'll put it in the oven and heat it up and we can have it later.'

'Good idea, I can hardly wait.'

'But mother, we're hungry now,' said Ruth.

'I know my darlings. Mrs Whittam has made this for us. So you find the spoons and set the table, then we'll eat just as soon as it's ready.'

'I'm going to like it here,' said Rose.

'We're all going to like it here.' Christopher ruffled his daughter's hair.

Sunday morning Christopher was up early. He had his first sermon for his new congregation. He knew what it would be. Christopher had being thinking about it ever since he had been told of his appointment.

The first person Christopher met was the Verger.
'Good morning Reverend Kelly, I'm Bill Bentley the Verger.'
'Pleased to meet you Bill, I'll be depending on you for sometime before I really get to know this Church and its congregation.'
'Leave it to me Reverend, I'll see you are all right.'
'Thanks Bill, at the end of the service you must stand next to me and introduce everyone to me as they leave the church.'
'I'll do that Reverend. It's a pity I can't ring the church bells in welcome. I'm the lead bell-ringer, but we don't want everybody to think we're being invaded with parachutists.'
'Quite right Bill, now what keys do I need to have?'
Bill handed him two keys. 'The large one is for the main entrance to the church and the smaller one for the Vestry, and that's where we'll go now, if that's all right?'

Inside the vestry Christopher met the twelve choirboys and three choristers. Verger Bill Bentley introduced them.
'We used to have twelve choristers, men and boys. Most of them are now in the forces.'

The first part of the church service went well. The church was full and the singing was remarkable. Christopher sensed all eyes were on him. So he too sang with gusto.
During the singing of the second hymn Christopher

made his way to the steps of the pulpit. There was spiral of seven steps to climb. He arrived at the top, placed his prayer book and notes in front of him on the book rest provided and looked up to face his congregation. There was total silence.

His first duty was to read a list of the men and women of the parish who were serving in His Majesties Services, then, with some solemnity, he read a list of those who had be killed whilst fighting for their Country. Christopher could sense that all eyes remained on him. The villagers were inquisitive. They were eager to know what he was going to say to them.

Next came his sermon.

The verger met Christopher at the large oak doors at the back of the church under its tower. Mr Bentley introduced to the vicar the members of the congregation as they left. Even Mr Bentley was surprised to find some of the villagers he had not seen in church for some time, if ever.

Thank God that is over I don't know when I last felt so nervous.

'Thank you Bill, for introducing everybody. You don't mind me calling you Bill?'

'Not at all Vicar, the villagers call me 'Bill the Verger'. There are a few Williams and Bills in the village.'

'Right, Bill the Verger how about coming with me to the church hall?'

'Can't do that at the moment Vicar, I've to check through the church to make sure everything is in order, that the hymn and prayer books are back in place and there are no lights left on. And if you don't mind me saying Vicar would you like to know how much the Sidemen collected in the offertory?'

'You are right Bill, here am I forgetting to see how the Churchwardens are coping with all the collection. I'd better go first and give them my apologies.'

The Church Wardens, Mr Todd and Mr Grimes, were busy finishing their count and were about to place it in the safe, when Christopher joined them.

'Good morning gentlemen I'm pleased to meet you and I'd be grateful if you could join me at the Church Hall and perhaps you could tell me more about the church and the village.'

'We certainly will. Everything is in order now.

Christopher felt much more at ease when he walked round to the church hall where everyone had been invited for coffee.

'Is there any problem with the supply of coffee?' asked Christopher.

'Not for this occasion,' replied Mr Grimes giving a wink.

Margaret, Elizabeth and the twins joined them.

'Hello dear, you've beaten me to it.'

'Yes, I've introduced myself and the girls to lots of people. They are all very nice.'

'Hello Vicar, Mrs Kelly and girls. I'm Mabel Whittam?'

'Yes Mabel, thank you for the supper you made for us – it was very thoughtful of you.'

'A pleasure. I thought you'd been travelling all day and would need something.'

We certainly did. The family was starving.

' I was wondering what I would cook for them when we arrived.'
'Then it was a nice surprise? Good.'
'I'm sure we're going to be good friends Mabel.'
'That would be great Margaret.'

This is the BBC Home Service

And here is the 9 o'clock news
on June 13th 1940
Churchill flies to Tours for crisis talks
with the French Premier Paul Reynard.

That is the end of the news.

What was that?

Reverend Christopher Kelly, dressed in his best black suit, stopped in his tracks. He turned around pushing back his thinning hair with his hand, shielding his eyes against the brilliant afternoon sunshine. He squinted at the horizon, his brown eyes searched along the skyline.

I thought I had heard something.

Christopher's three daughters chased one another in the long meadow grass. Their laughter carried across the fields, disturbing a flock of black crows into flight.

Margaret called out to the girls 'Don't go too far,' she pushed her blonde hair back into the restraining felt hat she wore at an angle. Her green eyes were dancing with merriment as she watched her daughters at play.

From out of the peace and quiet, a low drone invaded the still air. The girls stopped their game and turned to see a low flying aircraft approaching
'Look,' Rose pointed in its direction. 'Give him a wave'. She stood there energetically waving her arms.
'It's a German aircraft!' Christopher shouted a warning.
Automatically the girls dropped to the ground, peering between the buttercups, as the Henschel passed overhead. They lay on the grass sobbing, terrified at the noise and the fear of the unknown.

The machine coughed and spluttered as a vortex of

black smoke streamed from its engines.

'It's crashing,' screamed Elizabeth.

Rose and Ruth scrambled up and ran to their mother seeking protection, wrapping their arms around her skirted knees.

'There, there,' she tried to comfort them. 'Don't worry it will be all right.' She gathered them to her, into the circle of her arms and held them tightly.

Please God keeps the children safe.

The crash was ear splitting. The twins screamed in terror as the thick sooty fumes belched up into a cloudless sky. The air was filled with acrid burning fuel.

'Mother, what's happened? Why has the plane crashed? Ruth asked.

'I expect he was caught in the crossfire of our aircraft.'

'It's horrible, horrible.'

'War always is my love.'

'Go with Mother,' Christopher shouted as he charged across the ploughed field and headed for the wood. The dark cloud of smoke still hung over the tops of the pine trees.

'Mother will Father be all right?' Rose looked up into her worried looking face.

'Of course he will,' she stroked her daughter's frizzy hair' He's the vicar.'

'Can't we stay here and wait? Father might need us.' Pleaded Ruth pulling at her mother's silk blouse.

'All right,' she agreed.

God I hope I'm doing the right thing.

Their attention was focussed on the thick undergrowth – expecting goodness knows what to emerge. There was no sound, no clue as to what was happening. All seemed at peace on that summer's afternoon.

Breathless, Christopher pushed his way through the bracken and barbs of the blackberry bushes, slashing into them with his walking stick like a Samurai with his sword. He ignored the deep scratches on his arms and legs as he made his way to the stricken aircraft.
The sight he came upon was horrific. The aeroplane had almost burned itself out. The bracken surrounding area was scorched and the heat from its embers was still too intense to approach. He stepped forward and quickly stepped back shielding his face with his hand. There was nothing he could do. He assumed the pilot had lost his life.

War! The futility of it all, and the senseless waste of life.

'Mother'. Margaret turned her attention to her eldest daughter. 'Do you think 'Father's all right?'
'Of course he is,' she replied with an assurance she didn't feel.

What if I'm wrong and he needs my help.

'He could be burnt and laying on the ground', Ruth

chipped in.

'Now, you're letting your imagination run away again, young lady,' said Margaret.

'But he's only just getting over his experiences in France.'

'Don't fret Elizabeth. Now he's here in Stylecroft, he'll soon be feeling a lot better, Dr Wood has assured us he would.'

Rose and Ruth made themselves busy by making daisy chains, which led in to an argument as to which was the longest. In the end the two girls fell on to the ground fighting and pulling at their gas masks.

'Don't do that, girls, they're not our property. You'll not be able to use them if you damage them and where would you be if the Germans dropped gas on us?'

'We don't want to use them, they smell horrid.'

'Yes, they stink.' Ruth agreed.

Christopher pushed his way back out of the wood, brushing aside the bracken and thick undergrowth.

'Father, we were getting worried.' Ruth was the first to reach him. He gathered her small hand in his.

'You're all scratched and bleeding. Look at the blood.' Elizabeth pointed out.

'What happened?'

'By the time I reached the aircraft Margaret, it was completely burnt out. There was nothing I could do.'

'What about the pilot?'

'There was no sign of him, he may have perished in the crash, or he could have bailed out.' Christopher shrugged his shoulders unable to explain the situation.

'Come on let's go home.'

The family abandoned their walk and returned to Stylecroft to report the incident to the police station.

'Are you going to leave the aeroplane Father? Elizabeth asked.

'Yes, there's very little we can do.'

.

This is the BBC Home Service
and here is 9 o'clock news.

The Mechelen Incident.
Bad weather forces a German aircraft
to land at Mechelen in Belgium.

On board was an officer
with the plans for Hitler's
projected spring offensive in the west.
The Belgium's pass copies to
the French High Command.
This leads to Hitler and Von Mastein
to develop an alternative plan.

That is the end of the news.

David (Christopher Kelly) focussed his eyes on the light above his head. His stomach tightened like a discarded piece of unwanted paper. He watched the pilot as checking the aerial photographs provided by the RAF Reconnaissance Unit. The plane flew over the Channel at a low altitude.

'Why so low skip?'

'I'm hoping to avoid detection'

He rose to 1,500ft to get a clearer indication of the French coastline. Then dropped to 1000ft. After a hundred miles the pilot levelled off at 800ft.

'The dropping zone will be any time now'

He banked to his left anxiously searching for signals from the Resistance Group.

'Ah!'

He saw three red lights forming the triangle, this is what he was hoping to see, then the white light beaming out the coded message.

'Sod it. It's the wrong bloody group.' He pulled back on the joystick bringing the aircraft back to 1,000ft. He turned again flying over the red lights, still looking for the correct agent's signal.

Flack filled the night sky as the pilot journeyed on, vulnerability showing on his tired granite face. A pungent smell of smoke, coupled with burning aviation fuel filtered into the Lysander aircraft.

'We've caught it in the tail skip,' the navigator shouted above the noise of the engines.

David could feel his chest tightening, panic wasn't far from the surface.

Keep calm, breathe in -, out, in, out, David tried to regulate his breathing.

'Hold tight we're nearly over the dropping zone.'

'But skip.'

'I didn't come all this bloody way to fail. Get ready. Where's the bloody light? He flew on, his eyes desperately searching the area. Ah there they are,' relief sounded in his voice. Then he switched the cabin light from white to red.

David found he couldn't take his eyes off the mesmerising signal that seemed to pulsate to the rhythm of his heart. It was getting harder to breathe as the smoke thickened. There was a stinging pain in his eyes. The dispatcher fastened the paras' parachutes to the static line. Then they waited. The light turned to green.

'Jump,' came the curt instruction.

He felt a slap on his left shoulder as he sat over the dropping hole. David froze. His sweaty fingers clutched at the cold fuselage his white knuckles exposed to the night air.

'Jump,' the instruction was repeated, accompanied with a hefty shove between the shoulder blades. He was free falling through the freezing wind, pulling at his face, stretching the skin to its limits. Frantically he pulled at the ripcord.

To think I volunteered for this.

The rushing air filled his camouflaged parachute, snatching him backwards until the multi-coloured canopy was fully extended. He looked back up to the tiny aircraft, the maelstrom of smoke trailing from the back of it.

God I hope they make it back home safely.

He glanced across at the other Paras. The pilot glided the plane on its silent path down to earth.

I hope this mission is successful.

The darkness felt claustrophobic, not a light to be seen anywhere. He recalled his instructor's words of advice. 'Feet together and roll.' He sensed he must be close to the ground now. His large feet hit the top of a tree; he slid down through its branches. The parachute entangling itself, leaving him swimming in mid air.

'Oh bugger it. That's all I need.' He punched repeatedly at the release clip of the restrictive harness. Finally he fell from its grip on to the hard ground. He lay there for a few seconds looking up at the winking stars. Tentatively he moved his arms and legs, thanking the Almighty that there was nothing broken. He scrambled to his feet, still keeping low.

Where the bloody hell are they?

The French Resistance was supposed to meet them. Still nothing. Desperately he tugged at the silk canopy, slashing out with his knife, until it billowed down around him. The snap of a twig halted his efforts in hiding the evidence of his unauthorised entry into France. He held his breath, not daring to move.

Is it the paras? The Resistance, or the Germans?

He listened, straining to hear anything, the blood pounding in his ears. The hairs on the back of his neck went rigid. He tried to regulate his uneven breathing.

'Tread carefully.' The whisper sounded from his left.

'As softly as I can,' replied David.

A figure loomed out of the darkness and an outstretch hand grabbed his hand. They shook hands.

'Je m'appelle Marcel.'

'David.'

'Follow me. Are all your men here?'

'We're here,' said Peter.

'We certainly are,' Jack confirmed.

'Bon, come, I've a lorry parked at the other side of those tall trees.'

The four men stealthily made their way over the ploughed field to the line of Poplar trees. On a dirt track a lorry loomed up out of the half-light and stopped. Marcel lifted the thick sacking covering the back of the truck. The saboteurs climbed in. With a jerk they were one their way.

'We have a 'safe-house' at Clermont-Ferrand. There we'll make our plans for 'Tread Careful,' yes?'

'Good idea Marcel.'

An hour later they arrived at a stone built farmhouse. Marcel jumped down from the truck.

'We have been given the use of this building for a short while David.'

'The last time I heard, they were in the United States

of America. This way.'

He unlocked the heavy door and entered into the darkness. As his eyes became used to the gloom he was able to locate a kerosene lamp.

'Make sure all the curtains are pulled. We don't want to attract any unwanted guests.'

The men sat down around the kitchen table whilst Marcel boiled a kettle and made a large pot of fresh coffee. He placed newly baked bread on the table and a hunk of strong smelling cheese.

'Help yourselves mes amis. I went shopping for you earlier.' The men ate heartily, consuming the wholesome food in a matter of minutes.

'Let's get down to business.' Marcel pulled out a folded map from the drawer in the table. He opened it and smoothed out the creases, then placed a mug on each corner to hold it down.

'Now, the Michelin Factory is guarded closely.'

'Do you know how many?'

'Yes, four have been counted doing their tour of duties.'

'Is that twenty-four hours?'

'No, at night it's reduced to two guards.'

'Not expecting any trouble then. They're in for a surprise,' said Jack.

'According to information, carefully gathered by my agents, the factory is divided up into five departments. Each dealing with special operations in the manufacturing procedure.'

'Good Marcel, now let's have a look at the map.'

The men studied the plan of the factory and the

surrounding area. They noted the river, main roads, railway sidings, in fact anything that could be of help to them on their mission.

'We'll make a move tomorrow evening. This will be the best time,' Marcel advised.

'Great, it doesn't do to hang about too long.' The whistle of a train interrupted their conversation.

'That's the midnight express to Bordeaux. Time to sleep mes amis.'

David handed each of them a sleeping bag. The four men settled down for the night.

It was early morning, the mist drifted slowly across the fields. The men were already eating breakfast.

The day seemed to pass by slowly. They played cards, chatted about this and that, but their thoughts were about their imminent mission.

'It's time to go over our equipment.' The group moved into action.

'Explosives – check, detonators- check, black tape- check.' David was satisfied that they were now ready.

Cautiously, Marcel opened the farmhouse door, surveyed the surrounding area and gave the 'All Clear'. The men made their way to the rear of the building. Their transport lorry stood waiting for them.

'Climb on board,' Marcel ordered. A turn of the key, the engine stated first go and they were on their way. The group sat amongst a load of sacks filled with potatoes. It was a bumpy ride across a ploughed field before they reached a narrow track leading to the road.

Picking up speed Marcel called out – 'With a bit of luck we'll reach Clermont-Ferrand without any trouble.'

'That we would all appreciate, wouldn't we chaps?'

'You can say that again.'

'That we would all……..' and there followed a chuckle from the rest of the group.

'It should still be dark when we reach our target area. The guards will be despatched first.' Peter reached for his knife.

'Put it away – you'll cut your finger,' quipped Jack. Peter made no comment; he knew what he had to do. The lorry slowed down.

'Here we are,' mes amis.'

'Quiet men. Signals only from now on, Give us one hour Marcel'

'Bon chance.'

Quickly the men jumped out of the lorry on to the grass verge. They crouched low, keeping in the shadows as much as they could. Treading cautiously they approached the Michelin factory from the east. A large brick building was silhouetted against a darkened sky, its shadow gave them more cover.

David stopped and signalled with two fingers pointing towards his eyes. Jack shook his head, then brought his finger to his lips.

'What?' David whispered.

'Music.'

'Are you sure?'

'Do you think the guards have settled for the night?' Peter whispered drawing out his knife. As they crept forward the music became louder. A wooden door stood ajar. They glanced into the room. Two guards were sitting at table playing cards. David signalled with three fingers, two fingers and then one – go. They guards had hardly moved when they were despatched.

'Right, that leaves us with a clear run, but keep alert there may be other guards that we are not aware of. Peter – deal with the Water Cooler; Jack the Ovens I'll put the rail link out of action. Rendezvous with Marcel in one hour – check your watches.'

One hour it is. The three men went their separate ways.

David moved off in the direction of the railway track. *Let's hope we're all successful. There are a few hundred tons of existing tyres here. The explosions should have them all burning.* He made his way towards a hut. All was quiet – it was empty. Stealthily he crept along the railway line and chose a spot to place the explosives. He dropped down on to his knees, pulled the explosives from his sack, set the detonators with meticulous care, taped the dynamite to the rail and set the timer for half an hour. *Great that's my job done, now to get back to Marcel and see if the others have had success.*

Jack and Peter had placed separate charges in different areas of the factory. Peter made his way back to find Jack placing his last charge.

'All right Jack?'

'Yeah, sweet as a nut.'

'Let's get going then.'

David signalled to Marcel. He could hear the sound

of footsteps approaching. Jack and Pete loomed into view.

'We'll done lads, all set?'
'Five minutes to go.'
'Come – we'll move off now.'

The men clambered back into the lorry and it moved slowly away. David glanced at the wrist-watch – 'A minute left.'

The first explosion cracked into the night, then a second and a third. A red glow spread across the dark sky. Black smoke curled its way upwards obliterating the full moon. The red glow of the burning factory with more black smoke belching into the night sky told the story of success.

'Let's return and pass on the news – 'Tread carefully' has been successful.' Marcel said.

This is the BBC Home Service

Here is the 9 o'clock news on May 26th 1940

The evacuation of British and French troops from Dunkirk begins.

Over 330,000 soldiers return to England.

That is the end of the news.

After informing the police of the crash, Rev. Kelly waited for them to arrive from Ulverston. The Home Guard and the police joined forces in the search, led by the Vicar. They were armed with sticks, forks and other farming implements each held in a defensive manner. The searchers called noisily to one another, their voices could he heard several fields away, interspersed with long blasts from the police whistles.

Unfortunately there was no trace of the missing pilot. The speculation in the village was rife and rumours travelled as quickly as a forest fire.

'I heard the Germans have invaded.'
'We'll all be killed in our beds.'
'Did you hear it? It was a dreadful noise.'
'I see it go over. Made my blood curdle.'

The search continued for a considerable time. Then, on a given signal everyone returned to the village hall where several villagers were waiting for news.

'What happened?'
'Did you find anyone?'
'Was anyone hurt?'
'What's going to happen now?'
'Please, please,' implored the Reverend Kelly. He held his hands up to quieten the crowd. 'There's nothing to report. The pilot could have bailed out. Be on your guard.'

The crowd dispersed and the Reverend breathed a little easier.

A Major from the Army Camp in Ulverston, twitched his braggadocio moustache, stood up on a crate provided by Dick Robins, the proprietor of the Red Lion, and addressed the crowd.

'Men!' his whiskers twitched as he spoke. Then he coughed as he had noticed a group of land-girls eagerly waiting to see what was to happen next.

'Men! And ladies.' He nodded towards them. 'You've all helped to search for the pilot, sadly without success. An Army squad will comb through the forest. Other groups have been alerted. There is a possibility that the jerry could be injured, but it would seem unlikely or we would have found him by now. But, you must remain on your guard. So be sensible and don't be afraid to report any sightings. Thank you for your help. If he's not found before morning, a larger sweep will be made to cover the fells. If you are free to join in the search meet here at ten o'clock. Thank you!'

The Major stood down from his improvised rostrum and disappeared into the public bar of the Red Lion. The crowd dispersed. Several villagers stood in a group discussing the situation.

'What do you think?'
'Do you believe he jumped?'
'If you asked me...he's a goner.'
'I reckon they've no idea what's happened.
'If he's dead, the crows will find him.'

Captain Parkinson of the Home Guard ordered two of his men to take a four-hour surveillance of the crashed German aircraft. The men selected were older soldiers from World War I, they took their guard duty very seriously, and. marched with rifles slung over their shoulders. Corporal Eric Denson advised his comrade.

'First we'll examine the plane, then knock off any souvenirs worth having.'

'Are you sure we should be doing that?' Bob Whittam, who was younger with only one stripe on his sleeve, rolled a cigarette and put it behind his ear for later.

'Look,' Eric placed two fingers across the chevrons on his tunic. 'I'm corporal here and I'll give the orders. Come on, let's see what we can find.'

The two men made their way into the forest. The trees had been planted in lines so progress was reasonably easy. Looking ahead they could see an area where the sun shone through on to the forest floor. There was an acrid smell of embers and gasoline.

'There it is.' They spoke in unison.

'Steady,' said Eric.

The burnt trees, left standing, resembled a Petrified Forest. The aircraft's nose was buried into the earth, with one broken wing leaning at an awkward angle.

They climbed on to the shattered wing and looked into the cockpit. The charred joystick had been pushed forward and the seat had all but melted away. Bob wiped the blackened dials with his fingers.

'Sod it.'

'What's up now?'

' I've cut my finger.'

'Trust you, you'll have to get that fixed'.

Bob thrust his finger into his mouth, pulled from his trouser pocket a handkerchief and bound it around the cut.

'Ah, mummy will see to you when you get home. Look here, there's a belt of cartridges. We'll remove those for safety,' he winked at Bob.

'Quite right we don't want any schoolboy souvenir hunters getting hold of them. We'll have 'em'

Eric strapped the canvas belt around his waist under his tunic. One of the plane's dials was hanging loose from the control panel. With one tug, Bob removed it and placed it inside his gas-mask case.

'Nothing else worth taking,' said Eric. They were just about to make an inspection of the crushed wings and fuselage when they heard a rustling in the undergrowth. They lifted their rifles to their shoulders.

'Halt, who goes there. Stand forward to be recognised or I'll shoot,' shouted Corporal Eric Denson. The two men stood still. Their narrowed eyes moved slowly, searching the scrubland.

'Stand forward and be recognised.' The order was given again.

The face of a fox appeared from the undergrowth. The two guards fell about laughing.

'Cor! I need a clean pair of under-pants.'

'Time for a break, nature calls. You guard the aircraft. I suggest you march around it a few times, so don't let me catch you napping'.

'All right Eric.'

'All right Corporal.'

'All right Eric.' He made a show of sloping arms, then presenting arms, finally sloping arms again, before goose stepping around the burnt out wreckage. Eric could see that Bob was taking his guard duty seriously and decided to go for a rest and a smoke. He walked away and, delving into his tunic-pocket withdrew a small leather pouch. Inside it contained a packet of green Rizla papers and the makings for a cigarette. He carefully placed a meagre amount of tobacco on to the thin paper, then rolling it expertly with his thumbs and forefingers; he then licked the gummed edge. He cupped the flame with his hand and lit the cigarette, drew hard on it until the smoke filled his lungs. As he exhaled, he formed smoke rings into the night air.

'Put that light out!'

Eric hastily pinched out the end with his fingers and stamped on the glowing ember.

'Blimey mate, you needn't have done that.'

'You silly sod, fancy doing that.'

The two comrades sat down on a fallen log and discussed what they should do next to complete their stint of duty.

During the next hour they roped off the stricken plane and set a few booby traps that would give them a warning if anyone approached the area.

'What do you think happened to the pilot?'

'Oh I reckon he bailed out miles away.'

'Stands to reason he's not going to sit in a crippled aircraft till the last is he?'

'I suppose not, but it is a possibility.'

'Anything's a possibility. But my gut feeling is he jumped miles away.'

'You could be right.' Bob nodded. 'When do you think we'll be relieved. I'm starving. I didn't get time to grab an sandwich.'

'You and me both. We'll have to stay here though until someone comes.'

About half a mile away from the crashed plane, William Williams, known to most villagers as the 'Old Man of the Wood' lived like a hermit. His unkempt appearance and strange behaviour frightened many young children. The more brave, poked fun at him, whilst their parents either ignored him or handed out clothes they no longer needed. For William, he counted it as a really good day if, in exchange for small services, like cutting a hedge – he was given food and maybe a mug of tea. Now, for him, that was a good day.

If the truth were known, William was a sad character. He had lost his wife and unborn child in an air raid. He had been living in Manchester at the time. The family home had taken a direct hit. William was out on the streets doing his tour of duty as an A.R.P. Warden. Following the loss of his family and home, William moved to Stylecroft. It was a village he had visited before in his youth. Happier times whilst camping with a troop of Boy Scouts.

Now, thirty years later he shunned company. He preferred to live away from the village and he had built himself an underground shelter in the forest! The entrance to his 'home' was through dense undergrowth, a labyrinth of tunnels and a bolthole, gave him peace of mind. At fifty years of age and with a long unkempt beard his appearance earned him the title 'Old Man of the Woods'.

Unknown to William the German pilot was heading

in his direction.

William Williams snatched a hurried look behind him, making sure that none of the village boys were following him, as they had a habit of doing so. Dusk was falling as he crossed the stream. He could have crossed it blind-folded. He clambered up the bank. Then he made his way into his secret dwelling. He delved into his pocket for his lighter and struck the metal wheel and with the flame lit the wick of the lamp. A soft glow spread over the meagre furnishings. The old rocking chair stood by a well-used table, the only two pieces of furniture that reminded him of better times. A camp bed was placed towards the back of his dugout giving him a clear vision of the entrance. In the centre of the bed was a pile of clothes. William grinned as he sorted through them. The jumble sale had come up trumps. *These will come in really handy. He lifted up the clothing a piece at a time. Not bad at all. Should help keep the cold out. It was nice of Mrs Kelly to put these aside for me. You don't meet too many decent people these day's folks seem to always be looking out for themselves, especially since the war has started. A really kind person is Mrs Kelly.*

This is the BBC Home Service.
Here is the 9 o'clock news.
On May 21ˢᵗ 1940

The British succeed in decrypting
the Luftwaffe Enigma Transmission.

That is the end of the news.

!! Ultra was never the subject of 'News'

Wolfgang Rumfler struggled at the controls of his stricken aircraft. Black smoke was filling the cockpit and he pushed back the overhead Perspex canopy, gasping fresh air into his lungs. He pulled off his goggles, his eyes were stinging and he wiped them with the sleeve of his flying jacket, trying to clear his vision.

Luck's travelling with me, there aren't any flames yet.

He looked down over the side of the aircraft, a patchwork of fields passed underneath him.

I've no idea where I am. I remember the dogfight with the Spitfires over Barrow. I'll have to ditch her soon. I can't keep her flying much longer.

He braced himself, for the inevitable. His breathing quickened and his pulse rate rose as he struggled with the controls.

There's people in the field.

With superhuman effort he pulled the joystick back. The aircraft faltered, almost hovering in flight, then engines failed and the plane nose-dived. The aircraft hit the treetops. Wolfgang lost consciousness as he was thrown forward. The heat and the crackle of flames pierced his unconsciousness and he opened his eyes.
Get out you idiot, get out.

Adrenaline rushed through his veins, he wrestled to lift himself out of the cockpit and on to the wing and with unsteady legs jumped on to the ground. His jacket was burning; he pulled it off and stamped the flames out.

I'll have to get away quickly. I reckon those people will be here shortly. I must avoid capture at all costs.

His eyes still stinging, he stumbled his way into the wood; his breath coming in short gasps. He stopped at a brook, knelt down and splashed his face with the cold water. He sat back on his haunches, feeling in his pocket for a packet of cigarettes. Wolfgang was about to light up when he heard a rustling sound only a few yards away. Instinctively he flattened himself against the dense bracken.

What the hell was that?

He peered through the fronds and was astonished to see a man crawling from out of the undergrowth. The man stood up, looked around and then covered the gap over with branches. Within a few seconds he had completely vanished from sight.

I must be dreaming; perhaps the crash has affected me more seriously than I thought.

He waited for several minutes. Then confident that it was safe to move he approached the mysterious hole. Wolfgang cautiously pulled aside the branches and entered. He took his matches from his pocket and struck a match. The flame lit up the area, he could see a neatly dug out shelter. A bed in one corner, boxes that seemed to serve as a table. Here he found some candles. He quickly lit one as the flame burnt closer to finger and thumb. He dropped the spent match and ground it into the earth with the toe of his boot. He looked around fascinated.

A well constructed hideaway, or maybe it's an air-raid shelter?

Props were placed at strategic points shoring up the roof.

Someone who knew what he was doing built this. I mustn't hang about here too long, he may come back. I wonder who he is?

His gaze fell upon a neatly folded pile of clothes.

Now these would be useful.

Wolfgang picked up a jacket, trousers.

I could use these.

They fit.

Right, let's hope my luck stays.

He blew out the candle and retraced his steps Wolfgang then put the branches back in place over the entrance and set off down the hill slope towards a stream and followed it into a wood. As he walked along the trees they became less dense and finally opened out on to a field. He sat down and looked around. Here he had a feeling of peace and tranquillity. Wolfgang recalled the time he had visited England for a holiday, just before the hostilities began. He remembered how friendly the people had been towards him.

(I have fond memories of my visit to England. But, that was before Hitler had changed everything. I am now one of the enemy.)

His thoughts snapped back to the present.

No use thinking of the past. Einen kuhlen behalten. How am I going to overcome this situation? Yes, I must stay cool. Could I pass myself off as a friendly foreigner? My English is fairly good. It could work; it would take plenty of nerve, but it's worth a try. Well, here goes.

He started walking again. There were dry stone walls everywhere separating one field from another. In the distance, nestling in the trees, he saw a church steeple.

It's time to find out if I can pull this off.

Wolfgang climbed over a stone stile on to a concrete road. There was a church in the distance. He could see two men chatting. As he came closer, he saw one of them had grey hair. A tall man wearing a black shirt with a round white collar.

Must be the priest.

The other one was wearing a black helmet with a white 'W' painted on it.

Hmm, I reckon he's the Air Raid Warden.

Wolfgang approached them.

Steady now, take a deep breath, be confident and don't hesitate. You can do this if you keep your nerve. Here we go.

'Good afternoon.'
'Hello, I haven't seen you before. I'm the Reverend Kelly.' Christopher offered his hand in friendship.

Wolfgang grasped his hand and pumped it vigorously up and down.

What do I say now?

'Good afternoon. Kaminski, Captain Joseph Kaminski – Free Polish Airforce on extended leave and looking for work.'

'Where did all that come from? There now, I've done it.

He paused and waited for a reply. None came, so he carried on.
'I look for work Father. Work for bed and keep I think you say.' His confidence grew.
'Polish Air Force you said?'
'That is right.'
'Have I seen you somewhere before?'

'I think so not.'

'Well, there are plenty of jobs to be done in the rectory and the church.'

'You say rectory, this is like factory?'

The reverend threw back his head and laughed, his eyes twinkling with merriment.

'Forgive me for laughing Captain Kaminski. No, the rectory is the vicarage, the big house behind me where I live with my wife and three children.

'Perhaps I can help – yes? I am to you very thankful'

What luck? It seems too good to be true.

'Come with me then and meet the family. My name is Christopher by the way.' He led Joseph along an alley, through a rustic gate and up to the front door of the vicarage.

'Take a seat Joseph, I'll find Margaret.'

The house looked comfortable and lived in. The smell of home baking permeated the kitchen. Small fairy cakes were cooling on a tray, two heavy iron pots sat simmering on the stove. There was a large pine table with six chairs. He pulled out one of them and sat down.

Now, this wouldn't be a bad place at all. Home cooked meals, a roof over his head, somewhere to sleep. He couldn't want anything better.

'Margaret, Margaret we have company. Ah there you are. Come and say hello.'

As they entered the kitchen, their guest stood to attention.

'Hello Captain I'm very pleased to make your acquaintance.' She wiped her floured hands on her pinafore.

'Madam, it gives me great pleasure.' He shook her hand and almost clicked his heels together.

Christopher introduced his daughters.

'This is Elizabeth, our eldest daughter, and our twins Rose and Ruth.'

All three girls shook hands with Joseph. Elizabeth studied him closely and liked what she saw.

'If we all agree, how about letting Joseph stay here for a while, we can find work for him.' The family nodded in agreement.

'Fine, Elizabeth take Joseph up to the attic and show him where he's to sleep.'

She smiled at him, her face flushed.

'This way please.'

They climbed the steep stairs to the attic. Elizabeth stood just inside the doorway, giving Joseph enough space to enter the sparsely furnished garret. He smelt the freshness of her as he passed close to her.

The Reverend Kelly lifted up the telephone and informed his Bishop of their new arrival at the Vicarage.

It will be nice to have another man about the house.

I've missed the camaraderie of the S.O.E. agents. Being in a household of women, sometimes I feel overwhelmed just to have a man to man talk, all the joshing and to have someone on my side for a change. Yes I'm really looking forward to him being around. He'll be able to do the little jobs that need attention and to help in the garden. He'll be able to relieve me of the mundane work, while I get on with my church duties.

As he looked through the window he could see in the distance William Williams striding up the hillside returning to his home.

.

This is the BBC Home Service
and here is the 9 o'clock news
On the 9th of August 1940.

The Battle of Britain begins.
That is the end of the news.

In the attic, Captain Joseph Kaminski made himself comfortable.

Washing was basic. There was a large earthenware bowl and a jug in one corner of the room. Next to the attic door, in a recess, was a toilet and wash basin. There was just enough space to place the large jug under the only tap. He filled the jug with water. It was cold water. He then carried it into his room, poured the water into the bowl and washed himself.

The view from his window was breathtaking. Brown and green fields lay before him, where sheep were grazing under a cluster of small trees. A road snaked its way through the countryside disappearing into the distant hills bathed in a mauve haze.

This is just perfect.

Having made himself more presentable and feeling refreshed, he went down the stairs into the kitchen. The smell of home baking assailed his nostrils making his mouth water with anticipation.

Joseph, the new handy man, joined the family for the meal.

'You don't look very old.'
'Rose! Whatever will you come out with next.' Margaret scolded her wayward daughter.
'That's all right Mrs Kelly.'
'Margaret, call me Margaret, you're part of the family now.'
'Yes, we will have to introduce you to village life. As

most of our young men are in the armed forces, you'll not be short of work Joseph.'

'Thanks Christopher. I can't tell you how much I appreciate all this.'

'Think nothing of it. When we've finished eating, I'll show you around.'

The two men rose from the table and walked out together into the early evening.

'Hello vicar, out for a stroll?'

'Jessie let me introduce you to our new handyman Joseph Kaminski.'

'This is our postlady Jessie Lambert.'

'Nice to meet you.' Said Jessie.

They shook hands and Christopher and Joseph continued on their way.

'Broad Street runs through the centre of the village.' Christopher indicated the way. 'We have a corner shop and a pub – the Red Lion. There's a butcher's, newsagents, ironmongers, not bad for a small village, but if you require other things it's a long trip to Barrow. It's about twenty miles away. It's very quiet. Nothing much happens. Of course there are the Air Raid warnings. The Jerries are more interested in the docks at Barrow, but we get a few stray aircraft flying over the village. It's a lot worse in London.'

'I hear a German plane crashed near here.'

'Yes, I was out walking with my wife and daughters. The plane was in flames when it crashed.'

Scheisse, I saw them in the field before I crashed.

'Was the pilot killed?'

'We're waiting for reports, the army is dealing with it. I don't mean to be rude Joseph, but I've just remembered a phone call I need to make. You have a walk down the street and I'll catch up with you later in the Red Lion here's a florin to keep you going.'

'Thanks,' said Joseph, with a look of bewilderment on his face.

'You'll be all right,' smiled Christopher, who turned and hurried back to the vicarage.

Donald Hodges was stood outside the Vicarage.

'Reverend Kelly!'

'Hello Donald are your coming in?'

'No thank you vicar. I just called in the off chance that Joseph could pop over and put up a shelf for me, in the shop.'

'Of course, I'll send him along. I've just left him walking down Broad Street, you might be able to catch up with him. If not you'll find him in the Red Lion.'

'Thanks vicar, see you later.' With a wave Donald turned and retraced his steps, back towards his general store.

Christopher went in doors and picked up his phone.

As arranged Reverend Kelly caught up with Joseph at the Red Lion. He brought with him a brown canvass tool-bag and passed it over to Joseph.

'Finish your pint Joseph then make you was to Hodges Village Store, he needs a handyman to help him out and the job's yours.'

'Thank you, 'Hodges Village Store' you said. Yes I remember walking passing it.'

'On your way then Joseph and I'll see you later back at the Vicarage. Landlord, I'll have a pint of your Best Bitter.'

'Certainly your Reverend.'

'Just Vicar if you don't mind,' replied Christopher.

Joseph was already striding out, carrying his tool-bag towards the Hodges Store.

He pushed open the door of the Store. His tall frame filled the opening as he entered the well-stocked shop.

Donald was serving a customer. Joseph stood to one side and waited.

'Thank you Mrs Green,' he said wiping his hands down his overall. 'Take care.'

She carried her purchases in a wooden trug, gave Joseph a smile as left the store.

'Good morning.' Thank you for coming so quickly,' greeted Donald. ' I need a shelf put up, along the wall here. But, can you make sure that the door doesn't knock on to it. I'm afraid I'm no handyman, myself.'

'Good, or there would be no job for me to do.'

Joseph went about his business, trying not to interfere with Donald's customers. He drilled the holes into the wall to take the brackets. He reached into his brown bag and pulled out a handsaw. He balanced the wood on an old chair, knelt down on it and proceeded to saw.

'Sorry about the mess. I'll clear it up shortly.'

'Don't worry about that Joseph. I will sweep up. I'm just pleased you can do the job for me. My 'Odd Job

Man', usually helps me, he's been called up for Army service.'

Joseph nodded and continued with the job. Assembling shelves was easy for him. Handling tools was something he was used to and for a moment he had memories of home in the Fatherland helping his mother.

'You've done a good job there Joseph,' Donald tested it by giving it a good shake.

'You'll not shift zat'

'Wait a minute. I'll get your money for you.' Donald wandered off towards the till and struck the cash register's drawer which popped open with a ping, he pulled out some money and passed it over to Joseph.

'Thank you.' He walked out into the brilliant sunshine and bumped straight into Elizabeth. 'And vere are you going to young lady?'

Flustered she stammered 'Ba..ba.. back home.'

'I'll keep you company then,' he gathered her arm in his and they walked together towards the vicarage. Elizabeth snatched a quick look at the good-looking Captain striding at her side.

I wonder if he knows how I feel about him? I doubt it. I don't think he thinks about me like that. For me it has been love at first sight. I suppose I must keep it all to myself. I can't even tell Mother. No, it's best I keep quiet about it.

'Here we are,' he disengaged her arm and stepped aside allowing her to pass into the house. She had an overwhelming desire to snatch a quick kiss on his cheek, this she did and ran laughing into the house. Joseph touched the side of his face with his long fingers, deep in thought. He knew she'd noticed him, her blushes told that and when he spoke to her. Then it hit him like a punch on the jaw; Elizabeth really liked him.

How am I to handle this? She is a lovely young woman.

He tried to push his thoughts to the back of his mind, but it was impossible.

It can't last much longer, or can it? I'm amazed how I've managed to socialise with the villagers. They've accepted me as a Polish labourer. Without any official papers they will soon find out who I really am. What shall I do? My time here is limited.

Joseph undressed and reached for the pitcher of water and poured into the china wash bowl. He washed and then slipped into his pyjamas.

I hate all this deceit. But, it's expected of me to avoid capture. I should be making an attempt to return to Germany. But, I like it here. I like Elizabeth too. I like Stylecroft and the people in the village. I love this place, everyone is so friendly. It's so different from my days in the Hitler Youth, the Air Force and being a fighter pilot.

He pulled back the sheet and blanket, then climbed into the narrow camp-bed. Stretching out, he lay back and looked at the moonlight shining through the skylight. Diamond shaped shadows rippled across the walls, then disappeared when a cloud skated over the moon's rays.

I remember, before this hateful war, watching the moon shadows back home on the farm. Mutter, Father and Gunter working in the harvest fields, such happy days.

A tear fell on to his pillow, sadness filling his whole being as he remembered his family. He reached up and pulled the blackout curtain over the window. The room now was in total darkness. He closed his eyes waiting for sleep to come.

The heat of the sun warmed them as they walked up the green hills of the Fatherland, a woman by his side.
Dear Elizabeth, would it become reality, the two of them together.

The vision accompanied him into a restless sleep.

THIS IS THE BBC HOME SERVICE
AND HERE IS 9 O'CLOCK NEWS ON MAY
THE 26TH 1940
OPERATION DINAMO CAME INTO FORCE
TODAY.
UP TO 1,000 SMALL CRAFT SET SAIL FROM
MARGATE TO DUNKIRK, TO RESCUE OUR
STRIKEN
SOLDIERS FROM THE BEACHES OF
DUNKIRK

THAT IS THE END OF THE NEWS

It was a busy day in the Kelly's household. Margaret looked at her watch. It was time for her to go and have a chat to Mrs Pye, the headmistress of the school. There were the final details of the jumble sale to be discussed.

I don't like sorting through cast-off clothes. Still Jumble Sales have their uses. If the truth be known, I do not particularly tem, But, being the Vicar's wife it's just one of my duties and more important I'm helping to raise funds for the War Effort. Besides it's expected of me.

With a sigh Margaret pulled on her blue cotton dress and wriggled into her navy coat.

After her meeting with Mrs. Pye she dashed along to the hall and busied herself with opening up the hall. She snapped open her handbag and delved inside it for the key.
'The big key for the big place,' she mumbled to herself.

The village hall was large. At one end there was a stage. Long red velvet curtains were drawn across it. There were tables and chairs stacked along two walls of the hall. Then on the wall opposite the stage was door leading to a fully equipped kitchen. The toilets were at the rear of the building.
Mabel Whittam, Margaret's best friend, was first to arrive. She dragged in a large canvas bag.
'They say donkeys go best loaded. Now I know how they feel. Am I too early?'
'No not at all. I'll be pleased for your company. Here

let me help you.'

The two women lifted up the heavy bag on to a table.

'Do you know, I have been collecting this bric-a-brac since the last sale. No wonder it's weighty.'

'Couldn't Bill have helped you with this? It's far too heavy for you to manage on your own.'

'He has Home Guard duties, or he would have helped. He's guarding the plane that came down. Still you know more about that, don't you?'

'It was so frightening. The girls were petrified.'

'It must have been terrible for you all. What happened next?'

'Well, it crashed in to the woods and Christopher dived in after it.'

'Weren't you worried?'

'That's an understatement.'

'No sign of the pilot then?'

'We didn't see him. He could have jumped out earlier.'

'Strange don't you think?'

'It's worrying.'

Other members of the Mother's Union arrived in the hall and the serious work began. As the morning went on, more villagers called in, dropping off their unwanted jumble of goods. The job of sorting out took up most of their time. The mens' clothing was placed on one table. Ladies apparel was piled up high on several trestles. Shoes were placed neatly in a row. Handbags were put into a corner. Another table for children's clothing, toys and jigsaw puzzles. The 'bric-a-brac' stall was full with unwanted items; vases, pictures, books, fishing reels, tea caddies, spoons, boxes, watches, small pieces of furniture and lots more.

It was two o'clock when the door was pulled back and the eager bargain hunters paid their entrance fees. The 'Jumble Sale' was open! Pandemonium prevailed people elbowed their way in through into the hall. They all seemed know which table had the goods they were looking for. Garments, were pulled from out of the numerous piles, many discarded. Some clutched with delight. There were two ladies who managed to take each end of the same garment
'I had it first.'
'No you didn't.'
'I did.'
'Just let it go.'
'I won't its mine.'
'I'm not letting go.'
One of the organisers rushed across and tried to iron out the trouble. In the end the item was withdrawn from the sale.
'How do you like this one Margaret?' Mabel had chosen a red pillar-box hat, with black lace hanging limply around it.
'I can't see where your hair ends and the hat begins.'
'Blow it. I was going to wear it on Sunday.'
'It might look better on the side of your head. Look at this.' Blowing away a stray feather she flung the boa around her neck.
'It's seen better days Mabel.'
'Are you going to serve me Margaret Kelly?'

'Sorry Mrs Woods. We must have a laugh now and again. Not much to laugh at these days. That will be tuppence, please.'

'Your prices are going up every month,' She grudgingly passed over the coins for the brown skirt and stuffed it in her leather shopping bag.

William Williams came into the village hall, pushing his way to the table with gents clothing. He picked up a pair of grey flannel trousers and a jacket to match it. Margaret offered it to him for sixpence. He held them up in the air to look at them with some scepticism, he didn't really think they would be any use to keep out the winter's keen winds.

'Thank you Mrs Kelly, but I'll leave it this month,' and left the hall without making further comment. He still felt uneasy about the theft of the clothes from his hideaway, so he decided to go and see the Vicar and tell him of his suspicions.

Could it be that Joseph was the pilot from the crashed plane? If so then he wasn't an ex Polish pilot as he claimed to be. Now if I've got it all wrong, I'm blackening his character for no good reason. Was it possible? The village had accepted him without question.

'William! Have you got five minutes? Donald Hodges the shop owner called out. 'The lawns need cutting, would you have the time to do them?'

William raised his hand in acknowledgement. Still deep in thought he made his way towards the vicarage.

The jumble sale was a success, all the funds helped towards the war effort. 'Salvage and Save' was the war cry, since clothing coupons were introduced it seemed right to recycle everything. Margaret and her friends started to pack away the items ready for next month's sale. The items were put in large cardboard boxes, to keep them dry, and given to the verger to store away.

'Look at these Mabel. I think they would do for Joseph. I'll take them home with me.' She held up a shirt and a pair of trousers, placed the clothes into a shopping bag and dropped a few pennies into the kitty box.

Tables and chairs were re-stacked up against the wall. Margaret thanked everyone for helping and making sure that no one was left behind, she locked up the hall and dropped the keys into her handbag.

Mabel and Margaret walked along Broad Street.

'Well, that was successful this month.'

'The more money we collect, all helps the war effort.'

'What are you having for dinner tonight Margaret?'

'Meat and potato pie. Not much meat though. Our weekly rations are nearly used up. What are you having?'

'Spam fritters and vegetables from the allotment.'

'Are you finding it a job to manage on these rations?'

'It's a headache every day. I mean 4oz of bacon and one and tuppence worth of meat, doesn't go far at all.'

'I find only 12oz of sugar is hardly enough. Christopher has a very sweet tooth. He misses all the cakes and sponges I used to make, and the eggs I sometimes get a few from Mrs Malley, otherwise I have to use the powdered stuff.'

As they approached the vicarage, Joseph was

making his way along the street carrying a ladder on his shoulder.

'What an asset Joseph's been, since he arrived here.' Mabel said.

'I know, I don't know what we'd have done without him. He's obviously helping someone out. Do you want to come in for a cup of tea?'

'I shouldn't really.'

'Oh come on, Bill will wait for his tea.'

'All right then you've persuaded me.'

The friends turned into the vicarage, up the garden path and into the building.

'Make yourself comfortable.'

'Thanks.' Mabel seated herself at the kitchen table. 'It certainly went well today. I reckon our village raises more money than any other village.'

'Unfortunately we've no means to check that. But I think maybe you're right.'

'Any more news on the burnt out aircraft?'

'Not to my knowledge.' Margaret shook her head.

'Bill was at the plane doing his stint of guard duty and he cut his finger on the wreckage.'

'Not too badly I hope.'

'No, just a bit more than a scratch'.

'That's all right then. You know what men are like. If they have a cold they are dying.'

'You never said a truer word.'

Margaret heated the teapot first then placed two teaspoons of tealeaves into it. She stirred the boiling water into a rich brown tea and poured out the brew into the cups through a strainer.

'Sorry there's no sugar left until next week rations,

you can take a saccharin?'

'Don't worry, I'm getting used to it not being sweet'.

'Any more tea in the pot?' Christopher walked into the kitchen.

'I'll be off then,' Mabel said.

'Don't go, I'm not staying. I have to write a sermon for Sunday. So I'm straight back to the library.'

Margaret poured out an extra cup of tea and passed it to him and Christopher turned on his heel 'Nice to see you Mabel' and headed towards his office.

'I saw Elizabeth and Joseph walking together the other day. They make a nice couple too.'

' Now don't you go matchmaking Mabel. They are just good friends.'

'If you believe that, you'll believe anything. Haven't you noticed how your daughter looks at him? You must have.'

'No, I'm sure your wrong Mabel. She would have mentioned it to me.'

'Maybe, but there's definitely an attraction there. Perhaps she's too shy to tell you. Anyway, I must say cheerio, Bob will be wanting his dinner, see you later.'

'Bye Mabel.'

Is she right, are they becoming attached? I'll have to have a word with Christopher when he has five minutes. She's only seventeen; she's still too young

No, I'm sure Mabel's wrong. She's reading too much into it. She hardly knows him. Now I must get the dinner on the go, or it won't be ready for when the twins come in from school, starving.

THIS IS THE BBC HOME SERVICE
HERE IS THE 9 O'CLOCK NEWS
JULY 10TH 1940
THE LUFTWAFFE BEGIN WIDESOPREAD
AIR ATTACKS ON CHANNEL SHIPPING
AND
ON SOUTHERN ENGLAND

David had been summoned to Baker Street.

As he entered the office, raised voices could be heard. He looked at Vera the secretary who put her finger to her lips. The door to Buckmaster's room stood ajar.

'I tell you, we need more radio operators.' Buckmaster bellowed.
'But, it's not a woman's place.' The voice was unknown to David.
'I'm telling you they are able to do this job just as well as any man.'
'But sir.'
'No, I'll have my way with this one Major.'
'You can't expect….'
'Major, have more women put on the programme and that's an order.'
'But.'
'That's my last word on the subject. Thank you.'
The door was flung wide open and an officer marched out his face red and screwed up in anger.
'Well now that little episode is over, I'll see if Colonel Buckmaster will see you.'

I hope his temper will have improved by the time I get in there.

'He'll see you now David.'
'Is it safe to go in?'
'Of course.'
Buckmaster was sitting at is over large desk. He looked up as David entered.

'Ah David close the door.'
'Sir.' He did as he was bid.
'Sit down.'
'Thank you sir.'
'Now we have a huge problem. The Germans are transporting heavy water stocks through France into Germany. The route they are taking will be the ferry crossing on Lac Leman. It has to be destroyed David. We can't allow them to use it for an atomic bomb.'
'I see sir.'
'Vera will give you the entire details, money and cyanide pill.'
'Thank you Sir.'
'Best of luck my boy.'
'Thank you Sir.' David lifted himself up out of the padded chair and walked into the outer office.
'There's your instructions David, the monies are in the envelope and the pill box.' Vera handed over the packets. 'Good luck David.'
'Thanks I'll need it.' He walked out into the busy London Street.

Back at home David ripped open the envelope and read the information carefully.

This is going to be a job and a half.

'Margaret I'll be away for a few days. I'm sorry I can't give you any details.'
'I know my love. You take care of yourself.'
The two stood locked in each other's arms.
'Look after the children,' he whispered in her ear.

'I will. Make sure you come back to us my darling.'

David picked up his suitcase and left Margaret crying into her handkerchief.

The train journey to Tempsford was non-eventful. David caught up with much needed sleep. A whistle blast awoke him. He stretched his legs, pulled down his suitcase from the rack, and as the train came to a halt, pushed open the heavy door and stepped down onto the platform crowded with lots of Service personnel.

'Sir, the daffodils are beautiful this year.'

'Wordsworth would be pleased.'

'This way Sir. The car is parked just outside.'

'Thank you corporal.'

It was a short drive to the aerodrome and hardly a word was exchanged between him and the driver.

'Here we are Sir; through the door over there.'

'Thank you corporal.'

He slammed the car door and walked briskly towards the building.

'Reporting for duty sergeant.' David placed the directive on to the table.

The sergeant picked up the envelope, opened it with a paper-knife and pulled out a document which he studied with great care.

'Hut 2B, back through the door you entered, turn left and you can't miss Hut 2B.'

'Thank you sergeant.'

The sergeant was right. A hut directly in front of him, with giant sized letter and number, was about fifty yards away.

'Good afternoon.' As he entered, three women, not in uniform, greeted him.

'Afternoon,' I'm David.

They introduced themselves as Susan, Betty and Doris.

'It's our first mission, so we would appreciate any guidance you can give us regarding any special procedures.'

'I'm sure you are all well trained. Try not to worry – it's all teamwork and we'll all help each other. Main thing is not to worry, I know that's easy to say, but stay focussed.'

A Royal Air Force Officer entered the building. 'All present and correct. Good. Take off is at 11.30. Someone will come for you. Relax, there are magazines, books, jigsaw puzzles, playing cards, tea, coffee, biscuits – just help yourselves.'

'Where's the lavatory?'

'At the back of the hut. There are two blocks of buildings, one for men and one for women.'

'Thanks.'

'Good luck,' the officer turned and left.

'Anyone for a game of cards?'

'How about whist, there's four of us?'

Time passed slowly. A delivery of ham sandwiches and a sliced sponge cake went down well. David checked his watch.

I'll be glad when we take off. It's driving me mad all this waiting around.

The door flew open.

'This way please.'

The group gathered up their belongings and followed

the airman towards the waiting Lysander. The propellers were already turning.

'Do we meet the pilot?' Betty asked.

'No I doubt it. Usually the crew and agents keep themselves apart.'

'Why's that.'

'It doesn't help to get too friendly with anyone. Loose talk and all that.'

'I see.'

The drone of the aircraft lulled David off to sleep.

'I don't know how he does it sleeping now before a mission.'

'Perhaps he's used to it.'

'He's very good looking isn't he.'

'I wonder if he is married?'

There was a change in the sound from the engine.

'Feels as though we're gaining height.'

Betty looked out of a window. ' I think I can see the French coastline.'

'It's about another three quarters of an hour flying to our destination.' David struggled to sit upright.

'Thanks. Have you flown on many missions?'

'Many.'

'A seasoned agent then?'

'You could say that. But, it is not up for discussion.'

'No, of course not. Any comment on how the pilot lands the plane at night?'

'The crew watch for a signal. The pilot is guided in either by fires or lights from torches.'

'Three minutes to touch down.' The co-pilot called out.

The chatting ceased.

'Hold on tight we could be in for a bumpy landing.' Called the pilot.

The Lysander touched down, rose up off the ground and dropped again. The whole plane vibrated as it travelled over the uneven ground.

'Goooood lannnndding.' David complimented the pilot.

The pilot only grunted in reply. The plane jerked its way to a halt. The co-pilot threw open the side door, let down a ladder for the agents to disembark. One by one the women climbed down followed by David. The ladder disappeared and the door closed and the plane turned ready for take-off.

'Those lads don't hang about do they?'

'Come ladies we've a gentleman to meet.'

Quietly they slipped into the cover of trees. 'We'll wait here.'

'How long?'

'Are we putting ourselves in danger waiting here?'

'Risky, but our contact should be here any moment.'

'Bon soir David mon ami.'

David turned to see his old friend appear.

'Jean-Paul.' The two men embraced and vigorously shook hands.

David turned towards the ladies and introduced them.

'Mademoiselles, you will travel south with my compatriots. David and I go east,' said Jean Paul

David shook hands with the ladies, 'Bon chance, safe journey'

'And you David.'

The two groups disappeared into the night.

'Now mon ami, how are you?'

'Very tired Jean-Paul. I'm hoping this will be my last mission. Is there are news about Marie? I know she was taken by the Germans, but ....that's all I know.'

'Ah, the lady with the blue eyes. Yes, I know whom you mean. She was taken to the local police station for questioning then taken by the Gestapo, but the Maquis attacked the building and your lady escaped but has not been seen since.'

'Let's hope your friends have her then.'

'That, I cannot be sure.'

A lorry stood by the roadside. A light flashed.

'That's our signal, it's our transport.'

On reaching the lorry two men shook hands with Jean-Paul and disappeared into the night. Jean-Paul and David climbed into the lorry.

'We'll make our way to the safe-house at Challes and rest there.'

'Good, I could do with a few hours sleep.'

'How are the English coping with the air raids?'

'There's been no let up with the bombing.'

'I understand Manchester has been a target.'

'Yes, it was bad enough but nothing like the blitz on Coventry.'

'That's the news we've been hearing.'

'Coventry's situation is grave, but how are things here?'

'Pretty grim. The German grip grows ever tighter. So many people are arrested and never seen again.'

'Give me a nudge when we reach Challes, I'm going to try and take a nap.'

'All right mon ami, sleep if you can.'

The lorry trundled on its way along straight narrow roads passing through lines of tall trees. A few houses stood in darkness by the roadside. There was not a single sole to be seen. An owl hooted. The clouds hurried across the blackened sky and covered the moon and now it was only the dim lights of the lorry that lit up the sign 'Challes'.

Jean-Paul drove the lorry around the back of a detached isolated house. As he turned off the engine David woke up.

'Follow me David.' He pulled a bunch of keys from his pocket and jumped down on to loose stones. David joined him and they entered the house together.

'This house belongs to friends of mine.'

'Very kind of them I'm sure,' said David.

They made their way into the kitchen. David was pleased to see that not only had they been give the use of the house, but also they had left plenty of food and drink.

'These friends of yours Jean-Paul are good friends.'

'Very good friends. Red or white?'

'Red please.'

Jean-Paul opened a bottle of red wine and filled two large glasses.

C'est la vie!'

They sat at the table drinking wine and eating freshly baked bread with a choice of strong cheeses.

'We make our way to Lac Leman in the morning. What are your plans David?'

'Well, I'm hoping to take a trip on the ferry and make

a study of the area before we make a move.'

'Good idea. When is the heavy water timed to be transported across the lake?'

'Two days time mon ami.'

'Cognac before bed?'

'Then sleep is next on the agenda'

'I see the beds are already made up.'

'Thanks I can always rely on you Jean-Paul.

The two men slept well until the crow of the cock.

The smell of coffee and David was awake. They were soon dunking chunks of bread in their hot morning drink.

'C'est la vie.'

'It certainly is,' agreed David.

David cleared away the breakfast dishes leaving everything tidy, then made his way to the yard where he found Jean-Paul starting up the engine of the lorry.

'Let's go.'

David climbed into the passenger seat and off they went. They travelled along the back roads keeping away from roads used by the German army vehicles. Soon they reached the approach road to the ferry at Thonon. There was another farm lorry ahead of them and what appeared to be a German military car. The ferryman beckoned the car forward. The lorry was directed to a parking area and a German soldier checked the driver's papers and cargo. There was a small kiosk where another German soldier stood guard. Jean-Paul drew level with the kiosk, a man held out a ticket.

'Deux billets si vous plait,'

'Ca va.'

'Does your friend wish to inspect our lorry?'

'He is no friend of mine.' He spat on the ground. 'I think they have found what they are looking for.'

They glanced across at the parked lorry to see the poor driver being forced to kneel on the ground.

Jean-Paul moved his lorry forward onto the ferry and pulled up behind a German Staff-car. The ferryman removed the mooring ropes and the boat drifted away from the jetty. The gap of water grew wider as the small steamer chugged out into the lake. The Captain gave a double hoot on his whistle giving the signal they were on their way.

The scenery was wonderful and peaceful only the chug chug of the diesel engine disturbed the idyllic scene. But now it was time to check out the boat.

'There's no room below deck for storage it could be they intend to use the decks. Don't you think so Jean-Paul?'

'Yes, I agree mon ami.'

'Good we'll sit back and enjoy the scenery.'

At that moment a German Officer came and stood beside them.

'Je parle francais un peu.'

Jean-Paul rattled off a french poem he had learnt as a child.

Looking a little bewildered the Officer blurted out – 'Verzeihung,' and walked away.

'Better not be too friendly with the enemy.'

As the engines throbbed under their feet David and Jean-Paul reconnoitred the ferryboat.

'Looks as though it will be brought on board and left on the deck. Don't you think so Jean-Paul?'

'There's not much room here at all. Yes, I agree mon ami.'

'Let's sit down, we may as well enjoy the crossing, enjoy the scenery and work things out.'

'Good idea. I think it will be safe to chat.'

The hour-long sail ended back in Thornon. In their minds the trip had been a success. The Operation 'Cuckoo' would go ahead. They would not have long to wait.

Soon after their return to Challes, there was a knock on the farmhouse door.

'Are you expecting anyone Jean-Paul?'

'Non. I will see who it is.'

'Bon jour monsieur.'

'C'est le facteur…David.' Jean-Paul called out.

'Poste.'

'Merci.'

Thank God for that I didn't expect any visitors.

'Are you all right David?'

'Sorry Jean-Paul. I didn't realise I was getting a bit edgy'

'I'll make a coffee with a drop cognac and we'll make our plans.'

'That's a good idea Jean-Paul, thank you.' He opened out the map on the table.

'Now, the cargo is expected to arrive in Montreux by early morning. They will have everything in place on the deck of the boat for a mid-day crossing.'

'We'll wait till we are in the centre of the lake. Then

woof!'

'What about any passengers David?'

'It's almost certain the German Military will not want any passengers on board.'

'In the event of any casualties, and there will be some, can we plan a rescue?'

'The ferryboat will sink slowly. The cargo will sink. I'm hoping for no loss of life and there will be other sailing craft in the area to go to the rescue. This is included in the plan.'

'What about setting the charges David?'

'I will place the explosives on board the ferry the night before.'

A heavily guarded German truck made its way towards Montreux. The roads were quiet. The driver glanced at his watch.

'Another fours hours before our expected time of arrival we'll make a stop and stretch our legs.' There were grunts of approval from the back of the truck. The small convoy of three trucks and two motorcycle soldiers with machine guns slung over their shoulders, pulled to the side of the road.

Several other soldiers climbed down from the leading truck, lit up their cigarettes and had a pee.

'Sergeant,' called an officer.

'Yes, Captain?'

'Give me the map.'

The Sergeant pulled the map out of his tunic and handed it to the Officer. The Captain spread the map out as the Sergeant lit a match.

'Thank you Sergeant. Yes, I see where we are.'

The peace of the night was disturbed when the sound of bombs exploding could be heard. The map was quickly folded and put away.

'Back to the trucks,' called the Officer. 'We need to move on.'

As the trucks pulled away from the back of the leading truck several machine-gun muzzles were sticking through the sacking cover ready for action.

'I don't think the bombers know about our movements, but the sooner we reach the ferry the happier I will be.'

'Shall I drive a little faster?'

'No, take it steady we have a precious cargo to deliver.'

'What are we carrying?'

'It's an important cargo from Norway.'

The officer looked to see if the soldiers, in the rear of the truck, were occupied.

'It is a highly secret project. I understand it is Heavy Water for use in nuclear experiments for a new type of bomb.'

'I'll drive more slowly.'

'No, continue as you are. We must reach the ferry by noon.'

David crept down the steep stairs to the lower decks. The toilets were to his left. He looked left and right making sure there was no onlooker. He stepped quickly inside the cubicle, locking the door behind him. He breathed a little easier as he unbuttoned his coat. Buckled around his waist was a belt holding the explosives. He took out a screwdriver from his coat pocket and squatted down in front of a wooden panel opposite the toilet bowl. He quickly unscrewed the panel, removed it and placed it to one side. He then pushed the dynamite and detonators between the lead piping. Setting the detonator to the appropriate time, he picked up the four screws and replaced the panel. He made sure that everything was as it should be. He pulled the chain that flushed the toilet, unbolted the door and walked back up the steps to the upper deck and rejoined Jean-Paul. The ferryboat was steaming towards Montreux.

'Are the explosives in place David?'

'Yes, I hid them well, but don't use the toilet facility on the return trip.'

'Excuse me gentlemen can I check your tickets?'

'Certainly.'

The ferryboat man inspected the tickets carefully.

'Did you plan to stay on board on reaching Montreux?'

'Yes.'

'There could be a problem.'

'What problem is that?'

'The Germans have reserved the whole of the upper deck.'

'What no lorries or foot passengers?'

'Only German transport, maybe a few locals. You may have to take a later ferry.'

Jean-Paul and David walked on to the upper deck.

'We should have expected this when they refused the lorry drivers to board at Thornon.'

'Don't worry Jean-Paul, I'll make sure I'm on board, leave it to me.'

'What is your plan?'

'Can't say now, but the mission will be accomplished.'

Jean-Paul looked worried. He could only hope that David would not do anything foolish.

It was ten minutes to twelve when the ferryboat steamed slowly into Montreux.

'Everybody must leave the ferryboat.' Came a message over a loud speaker.

'Come,' said David, 'don't look so worried.'

They walked on to the quayside with the other foot passengers and watched the convoy of three German lorries drive towards the ferryboat.

'Surprised there are only three vehicles,'

'I guess the heavy water is being carried in the second lorry, I was expecting something bigger,' said David.

As the third lorry drove over the ramp, several soldiers with rifles climbed out and moved quickly into position circling their precious cargo.

'So that's where the heavy water is,' David spoke and smiled.

'What now?'

'Wait Jean-Paul, the German officer is speaking to the ferryboat captain.

After a few minutes the captain came to towards the ramp and spoke through a speaker.

'All passengers with tickets may come aboard now, but please hurry.'

'Come,' said David, 'that includes us.'

One of the German guards inspected the tickets. There were a few others that boarded all of them French.

'How many do you make it?'

'I counted five men and two females,' said Jean-Paul.

'Agreed, we can cope with that.'

'Will passengers please note that they are free to stay on the top deck or take their seats below decks,' the captain announced over the speakers. Please keep clear of the German vehicles, thank you.'

'Well, that couldn't be better,' said David.

'When do we jump overboard?' John-Paul whispered.

'First I'll make sure our French passengers are not pro-German.'

'How are you going to do that?'

'Leave it to me.'

David made his way to chat with the French. There was a good deal of laughter coming from the group. When David left them they seemed happy enough.

'Did you tell them the ferryboat was going to be blown up?' asked Jean-Paul.

'Not exactly, but they will act quickly when the time comes....I hope,' replied David.

The ferryboat had almost reached halfway between Montreaux and Thonon.

When there was a shout - 'MAN OVERBOARD.'

The Germans and passengers all moved to the side of the boat. 'It's a woman.'

'Au secour, au secour,' she shouted.

'Is no one going to save her?' David turned to the German soldiers for help.

'She's French, you save her,' replied one of the German guards.

'Stop the boat,' called the other passengers.

'Can't do that,' shouted the German Officer.

There was no more shouting. David and Jean-Paul were the first to dive in and the French men followed. Within a few minutes they had joined their drowning lady – who was threading water quite comfortably. As the group of swimmers turned to swim to a nearby island, not two hundred metres away, there was a ear splitting explosion.

Just as David had predicted the precious German cargo could not be saved whether or not the Germans had perished would be known soon enough. Once back on dry land a friendly agent in a French Resistance Group arranged transport for all of them to safety, well away from Thonon.

In London the message was received – 'The Cuckoo has returned…..The Cuckoo has returned.'

'Thank God for that,' said Vera reading the de-coded script. She walked quickly into Buckmaster's office.

'The message reads – 'The Cuckoo has returned.'

'Well done. I knew he would be able to pull it off.'

'Any reply message Sir?'

'Just well done.'

'Very well sir.'

'A reply from London, David.'

'What's the message?'

'It simply says *well done*' said John-Paul.

'That's Buckmaster for you; short and to the point.

THIS IS ALVA LYDDELL
READING THE 9'0'CLOCK NEWS
ON SEPTEMBER 7TH 1940

NUGHT TIME RAIDS BEGIN ON LONDON
A FORMATION OF HEINKEL BOMBERS
WERE USED BY THE GERMAN LUFTWAFFE.
A DOG FIGHT DEVELOPED
INVOLVING OUR HURRICANES AND
SPITFIRES

THIS IS THE END OF THE NEWS

Reverend Kelly turned the wireless control to 'off'. The news was grim. Every time they listened, it was not good at all. With a sigh he returned to his desk and sat down.

Now what do I preach about for Sunday? Thou shall not kill. No that's hardly appropriate. Something from the New Testament perhaps, he thumbed through his well-used Bible. *Ah this will be appropriate.*

He picked up his pen and began to make notes, he was oblivious to the passing time being completely absorbed in his task. Then the telephone rang.

'Stylecroft 469, Reverend Kelly speaking.'
'Hello Reverend, my name is John Bish from the Free Polish Forces, My office is in Todmorden and I've been asked to check on your visitor Joseph Kaminski'.
'Oh yes, how can I help?
' Sadly I can't trace any records of this man. Would it be possible for you to put him on the line so that I can speak to him? He may have more than one first name. These records are far from being perfect.'
'Well at the moment he's out working in the village. I'll get him to ring you when he gets back. Could you give me your number and I'll pass it on to him.'

Rev. Kelly jotted down the number. 'Does he ask for you personally?'
'Yes, John Bish – Records Office. Tell Joseph not to worry as soon as he gives me his service number, I will be able to trace his records and fix him up with

the appropriate documents. It's not surprising; we have dozens of Polish servicemen applying. I'll wait to see what he has to say. I'll be in my office for the rest of the afternoon. Hope to hear from him soon.'

'I'll give him the message, bye.' Christopher replaced the receiver back into its cradle, then scribbled a note and left it pinned to the family notice board.

His concentration returned to his sermon and after much thought he had decided Leviticus from the Old Testament, chapter 19, verse 18, Love thy neighbour, would be a good way to finish. He carried on with his notes and was exceedingly grateful when his wife popped her head around the door.

'Tea?'

'Lovely,' he sat back in the chair, relaxing as Margaret brought in the teapot, cups and saucers, milk and saccharin. She stirred the pot with a silver teaspoon, picked up the tea strainer and began to pour.

'No biscuits I'm afraid.'

'Come and sit for a few minutes,' he patted the chair beside him. 'How has your day been?'

'Oh busy as usual.'

'I had a funny telephone call this morning, about Joseph. It seems as though they need his service number. Now you would have thought he would have known that working in this country.'

'Perhaps there's been some sort of mix up?'

They heard heavy footsteps in the hall and Joseph appeared carrying two bags of shopping.

'Ah, Joseph. There was a telephone call for you. Come and join us in a cup of tea.'

'A phone call for me?'

'I'll leave you both to it, .. I've things to do.' Margaret left the room after pouring out another cup for Joseph.

'It looks as though you'll have your papers through soon.'

'Is that what the call was about? I read your notice.'

'Yes, a John Bish called and asked as soon as you got back, would you give him a call.'

A frown appeared across Joseph's forehead; he looked more than a little concerned.

Here we go. I knew it couldn't last much longer.

'You'll need to give the authorities your service number. I can't think why we didn't think of it when we first applied for the documents. Still it will soon be sorted out.' Christopher picked up the telephone. 'I'll get the number for you.'

Suddenly Joseph jumped up and closed the door.

'Don't do that.'

'What's the matter Joseph,' looking at him in complete astonishment.

'Don't do that,' he reiterated.

Joseph re-placed the telephone and looked at Christopher. 'I'm sorry. You've made me so welcome since I came here, almost one of your family. But, I'm not Joseph Kaminski; I am the pilot for the crashed plane. I realise you have to inform the authorities. I won't give you any trouble. I can only apologise again'.

There was a silence.

Good God, what have I done? How could I have been so stupid not to realise it before? He's such a nice chap. What about my poor Elizabeth? How will I tell her?

'What is your real name then?' Christopher demanded. His face reddened, and there was a hint of anger in his question.

'Wolfgang, Wolfgang Rumphler, I'm from Hamburg.'

Christopher lent back into his chair, folded his arms while digesting the news he had just received. After a long pause of silence he stood up. He walked round the room stroking his chin. Then following a few stampings of his feet, he regained an element of calm and returned to his chair and sat down.

'Well, Wolfgang, I'm annoyed and feel let down. You have deceived all of us. But at the same time I realise why you did it. However, you have put the whole family in a very awkward position. Stay where you are and don't speak. I'm sorry too about this Wolfgang, but I've got to, as you rightly said, phone the police and inform them of the situation.'

Christopher picked up the telephone again and reported that the missing pilot was at the Vicarage. Wolfgang could only sit and wait to hear what his fate was going to be. He sat in a chair, there were tears in his eyes. Christopher put down the telephone.

'My instructions are to hold you here until the authorities arrive. Wolfgang I feel so disillusioned, betrayed. We gave you a home here, our friendship. What do I say to Elizabeth? She has feelings for you, you know.'

Wolfgang nodded; he listened to Christopher's words; the tears rolled down his cheeks. He had grown to respect the Kelly family. He hated himself for all the deception he had woven to avoid becoming a Prisoner of War..
Elizabeth, Elizabeth, my words fail me.
He lowered his head into his hands, in despair.

'I'll come upstairs with you, and you can collect your belongings.'
Christopher stood up and walked towards the door. The two men climbed up the steep stairs together, knowing that this would be the last time that Wolfgang would enter his bedroom. Christopher had lots of questions he wanted to ask him, but time was too short.
'I want you to know Wolfgang that had things been different between us, you would have been welcomed here. Maybe, after the war, who knows? Trust is very hard to earn, when it's lost, it's almost impossible to re-gain it.'
Wolfgang listened in silence his head still bowed. Then he faced Christopher.

'I hated what I had to do. But I had to avoid being captured, surely you must see that?' He looked directly at him, tears glistened and he blinked hard to keep his emotions in check. He gathered up his clothes and returned with Christopher to the living room.
There was a knock at the door, Christopher moved to open it. Standing there was the Arresting Officer, flanked by two soldiers carrying rifles.
'Afternoon Reverend. This our man?' He nodded

towards Wolfgang.

'Yes.'

'Come on matey. Do I have to use these?' He held up a pair of handcuffs.

Wolfgang shook his head.

'Let's be away then.'

The four marched away to the waiting truck.

Christopher went back into his study. There were many mixed feeling rushing through his mind. He had never revealed to his own family his S.O.E. activities. Now, here he was now involved with having an escaped German airman passing himself off as a Free Polish officer. Buckmaster was right to return me to the Church of England.

Even at that moment one of the villagers was on his way to see him with some misgivings.

William Williams knew he had to go to see the Vicar and mention his uncertainties regarding the vicar's lodger Joseph. He was still riddled with doubt.

But what if I'm wrong in accusing this man of deception. The village people might retaliate and especially the ladies who like Joseph.

He reached the Vicarage just in time to see Joseph, now dressed in his German pilot suit being escorted, by military policemen, into an army vehicle. William stood rooted to the ground, trying to comprehend what he was seeing.

I was right after all. I should have come to see the vicar earlier.

The Reverend Kelly noticed William approaching and beckoned to him.

'Come in William, I could do with someone to talk to.'

'I could hardly believe what I saw – I was just coming to see you about my worries.'

'What worries would they be William?'

'About Joseph. But I can see you've enough on your plate to listen to me at this moment.

'It won't take long before the whole village finds out. But I'd be grateful if you would keep the news to yourself, until I've made it known to the family.'

'Of course vicar...... He was the pilot after all?'

'Yes. His name is Wolfgang Rumfler. I'll make it public knowledge at the church service tomorrow morning.

'I was on my way to see you, because I had suspicions that he was not all he made out to be. But I'll give you my word that I'll say nothing.'

'Thank you William. Come have a cup of tea, a mug if you prefer and I think I can find you a bun that my wife has baked. Tell me why you suspected Joseph?'

After William had revealed all his doubts and suspicions to the Vicar, William agreed, that his observations, could be passed on to the police if they were going to be helpful.

'Come William, I'll walk down into the village with you.'

Christopher decided to speak to the family all

together, so he left a note on the family's notice board. It had become a routine long ago for them to check the family board throughout the day, enabling them to keep up with the comings and goings in the busy day of a Vicar's family. On this occasion he simply stated IMPORTANT WE ALL MEET TOGETHER THIS AFTERNOON 3 O'CLOCK. -FATHER.

Rose and Ruth were the first to read the notice.

'It must be important, 'Rose said.' We haven't had a family meeting since we skipped school in April.'

'Perhaps they have cut the toffee ration again,' suggested Ruth.

'I was supposed to be helping with the delivery of the Parish Magazine, Can't do that now.'

Elizabeth read the notice when she came in to start the preparation for the evening meal. She called up stairs 'Joseph are you in? Any chance of some help? Come on lazy bones, have you dozed off?' Since Joseph joined the household he had made it one of his duties to help Elizabeth prepare the evening meal. She enjoyed his company and he made her laugh. It was their quiet time together before the family rolled in for their meal. There was no response to her call and feeling a little disappointed she got on with the job in hand.

He'll be in any minute now. I wonder what Father wants; it's unusual for him to write a message like that. I hope nothing is wrong. Ah here comes Joseph.

But, as she turned, it was her Father.

'Hello Elizabeth, have you read the message?'

'Yes, what's it all about?'

'Best if I speak to all the family at the same time.' As he spoke Margaret and the girls entered the kitchen.

'It sounds serious, can't you give me a clue?'

'You must be brave, all of you. It's about Joseph.'

Elizabeth sat down not knowing what to think; anxiously she looked at her Father.

'Where is Joseph? I was hoping he was going to be here, to help me with preparing dinner. Is he all right?'

'This is going to be so hard for me to tell you, Sit down. It is about Joseph I'm afraid he's not who he said he was my darling. He's the pilot from the crashed plane, his real name is Wolfgang Rumfler.'

'He's a German!' Elizabeth called out in disbelief. She sat down on a chair, tears spilling down her cheeks.

'Don't say anything.' Her Father placed his arms around his daughter, trying to shield her from the hurt. 'He has been taken to the Prisoner of War camp at Fellside. He did apologise and I know he sincerely thought a great deal about you.'

Margaret put her arm around her daughter's shoulders, 'Don't cry. I hate you crying. It'll start me off.' She rummaged in her overall pocket and pulled out a white linen handkerchief and gave it to Elizabeth, to dry her eyes.

'I can't believe it Father. How is it possible?'

'We had a telephone call to check his credentials. He never had any. So he confessed and I had no choice but to inform the authorities.'

'But what will happen to him now?'

'I expect he'll be assessed and will either be sent to Canada, or to a Prisoner of War camp here in England.'

'When will we know?'

'I should think it will take a few days.'

'Why did he do it?' Ruth wanted to know.

'It's all because of the war. It's like an octopus, the long tentacles, reaching out. War is like that, it affects everyone in different ways.'

'He could have told me.'

'Maybe, but I doubt it.'

'Won't we see him any more?' Rose asked.

'Don't, I can't bear it. It's all so cruel. Just when we were getting to know each other.' Elizabeth buried her face in her hands sobbing.

'No darling you won't see him. We have no way of knowing how long the war will last.'

Margaret's face was crestfallen, she felt a deep sadness, confused, bitter, angry.

'Why can't we see him,' insisted Rose.

'Because it wouldn't be permitted. I'll ring around and see what I can find out,' Christopher walked out of the kitchen into his study.

After several telephone calls, he was still no further ahead and reported back to his wife and daughters.

'No news I'm afraid.'

'But father I've got to know what's happening. I love him.'

The twins stood open mouthed at the news, while her parents glanced at one another, confused as to what to say to relieve her suffering.

'We guessed you loved him,' Margaret confessed. 'We'll find out some way as to his whereabouts, try not to worry too much.'

But, Elizabeth's thoughts remained with Joseph and

what was happening to him.

Is he all right? Why didn't he say something to me, I would have understood. What's going to happen to him now? How can I keep in contact with him?

'Don't cry Elizabeth.' The twins were cuddling her; she gathered them to her.

'We love him too,' said Ruth, her tears falling over her cheeks.

'It's not fair father. Why can't he stay with us? Asked Rose.

'Because he's German and we are at war with Germany.'

'But he's nice. Not like those nasty men stomping all over the place.'

'He was kind. He loved us too.'

'I know girls, but it's the law and he must join other German captives in a 'Prison of War Camp'. He can't stay here now.

'But father.'

'No buts, it's the law of the land and that's all there is to it.'

'Father can we find out which Camp he is in?' asked Elizabeth.

'Leave it to me I'll see what I can do.' Christopher looked at his pretty daughter's face, her eyes red from tears. He knew he just had to find where Joseph (Rudolf Wolfgang) had been taken.

THIS IS THE BBC HOME SERVICE
AND HERE IS THE 9'OCLOCK NEWS
LONDON TRANSPORT STARTS CALLING
IN COUNTRY BUSES
FOR USE IN THE CAPITAL.
SINCE SO MANY OF LONDON'S
RED DOUBLE-DECKERS
HAVE BEEN DESTROYED
IN THE BOMBINGS

THIS IS THE END OF THE NEWS.

Operation Bullseye

John-Paul, an experienced operator, received the coded message from the BBC – *Jack meets Jill over the hill.* He nodded. The next parachute drop would be at the full moon. He quickly relayed the message to his compatriots. There was sweat on his brow. He sensed that a German detector vehicle was not far away. This was his constant worry, but risks had to be taken. The task was to inflict heavy losses on the Wehrmacht. Success of this mission would help towards this main objective. John-Paul quickly disconnected his radio and returned it to its hiding place.

The full moon brilliantly lit up the surrounding countryside. In the shadows members of the French Resistance group lay in waiting. The ground was damp and cold. Only a few kilometres away the streets of Lyons were quiet too – it was curfew time.

John-Paul shielded the light from his torch and directed it at his watch.

'They're late,' whispered a voice from the shadows.
'Any minute now.'
Minutes ticked away.
'Where are they? The wind's picking up'
'Quiet, they will be here.'
The hum of an aeroplane's engines could be heard.
'At last. Lights on,' whispered John-Paul.

The dark figures of three men, crouching low, moved quickly through the ploughed field. They fanned out forming a wide triangle, only then did they switch on their red flashlights. John-Paul signalled the message 'Bullseye', his flashing white beams directed at the aircraft.

Led by John-Paul, the French freedom fighters moved silently towards the floating paratroopers, their parachutes blending in with landscape. They searched the ground for any men blown off course. He stepped on a twig snapping it in half.

'Sacre-bleu'.
'John-Paul is that you?'
'David it's good to see you again.'

The friends vigorously shook hands. David quickly introduced the other S.O.E. agents John and Colin. Both were dressed in dark polo-necked pullovers.

'We need to move quickly. Our truck is close by.'

It was a bumpy ride to the farmhouse. There was little conversation. The men held tightly on to their seats as the truck bounced along the rough track. There were twists and turns in the road and a few expletives were exchanged.

'I'll introduce you all to the farmer and his wife,' said John-Paul, as the truck came to a sudden stop. John-Paul entered the farmhouse, the rest followed. The crackling flames from a log fire were most welcoming.

'Meet Joseph and Marie.'

Joseph shook hands with his guests and kissed them on both cheeks and with outstretched arms encouraged them to get warm near the fire.

'Fire..warm,' he said in his limited English.

There was food on the table and they ate heartily

on slices of home cooked ham, spicy smelling sausages, strong tasting cheeses. The aroma of freshly homemade bread permeated through the kitchen. Joseph made sure they had enough red wine to drink. Whilst they were eating, Jean-Paul gave them details of the layout of the farmhouse and its outbuildings.

'You will see that your sleeping quarters and centre of operations can only be entered this way.' John-Paul opened a cupboard door. It was more like a walk-in wardrobe.

'You can see the shelving in the corner – follow me.'

'Shelves – yes, but a ladder too. Clever, n'est pas?

John-Paul climbed inside the cupboard and opened a trapdoor into the roof and using the short ladder, he climbed up into the attic. He switched on a dim light and stepped on to the rafters carefully making his way to the furthest corner. At this point, the attic had been boarded over. On the floor stood an antique desk and a chair. John-Paul pulled the dusty seat towards him and immediately sat down. He pushed open the roll top to the desk to reveal a transmitter. Cautiously he raised the telescopic aerial through the slates in the roof. He lent over and switched on the power and picked up a set of headphones. He adjusted the Bakelite dial, twisting it backwards and forwards – the set crackled into life.

I won't be able to keep this up for much longer. The Germans are always vigilant, listening in for coded messages. We wireless operators are only expected to last for about six weeks. Mon dieu, my time is practically up.

'Having trouble?' David called out.

'Non mon ami. The set, she is very old and takes a long while to warm up.'

Finally, Jean-Paul sent the coded message that everything was set for the mission ahead. He replaced the headset, turned off the transmitter and pulled down the roll top to its closed position and carefully stepped towards the trapdoor, switched off the light and pulled down the ladder.

'There that's done. Let's hope that we can soon send the message 'mission successful."

The group assembled in its new headquarters and home for the duration of operation 'Bullseye'.

'Everything set for tomorrow?' asked David.

'It is,' confirmed Jean-Paul.

All the agents sat quietly around the table eager to hear the details of their mission. They were dressed in dark brown working clothes and black laced up boots, ideal for cover during the darkness of the night ahead.

'It's to be the bridge at Sochaux.' David explained.

They all studied the map spread out on the table.

'You will see the bridge, into the Peugeot Plant Works, is on the artery road.'

'Mon dieu, you know they're producing gun-carriers and tank turrets for the German Panzer?'

'Exactly, that's why it must be blown.'

'It's going to be difficult. The works are guarded day and night.'

'This is a directive from Colonel Buckmaster.'

'Say no more, mon ami, it will be done.'

'It's to be a two pronged attack. John and Colin will go for the plant itself, they are experts in this field and then it is up to us. We're to blow the bridge.'

'Oui, oui, d'accord.'

'The explosives, they're safe?'

'They're well hidden in the barn – they're safe, don't worry mon ami!'

'I'm bushed. I'm sure the rest of you are tired too. More details tomorrow after a good night's sleep.'

The S.O.E. agents wriggled their way into sleeping bags.

'I've a good feeling about this job.' Colin said, pushing back his dark hair.

'I'm pleased about that. But nobody's told the bloody Germans,' John replied.

'A pessimist, that's what you are,' David joined in on the banter. 'A pessimist.'

'I remember on another mission.'

'Not now Colin, we don't want to be reminded.' John yawned.

'Let's get some shuteye. It will soon be time to get up. Good night.' David turned his back towards his comrades. He was asleep as soon as his head touched his pillow. The next minute loud snores vibrated around the small room.

'I don't think I'm going to be able to drop off.' John complained.

'Try counting sheep.' Colin advised.

'I'd rather count money.'

It was dawn, the start of the working day on the farm. The cows were gathering near the farm gate. It was milking time and livestock had to be fed.

'Bon jour.' David wandered into the heated kitchen. The smells of newly baked bread and freshly made coffee filled the kitchen. Several men were seated at the pine table, busily tucking into a cooked breakfast of bacon, eggs and fried bread. They dunked crusts into their bowls of coffee.

'This smells wonderful, just like home.' He gave Marie a nod as he sat down.

When the breakfast was over the conversation turned to the operation ahead and the preparation of explosives. The French agents insisted on calling them 'bombs' so David followed their lead.

'In preparing the 'bombs' you slice the explosives into cubes. Colin and John, you can push the primer into its centre. Don't forget both ends of the detonator must come out through one side of the cube.'

'David, do you still think I'm a novice at this?' John grinned.

'I keep forgetting how time flies.'

'Here's the black cloth to wrap it in… and the insulating tapes.' David threw them over to Colin and John.

'Well caught both of you – no doubt you both played rugby.'

'I can never get over the smell.'

'What the rugby ball?'

'No the explosives. It always reminds me of marzipan

on the Christmas cake.'

John chuckled as he secured the explosives with the black tape. Joseph stared at the scene before him in his kitchen.

Never in all my years have I seen such behaviour. Mon dieu they must be so determined and their steely resolve to succeed is amazing.

'Thanks to the Maquis,' said Jean-Paul, 'we have details of an old barge moored up-stream with an interesting name '*The Grande Duchesse*'

'Here's how we will proceed.' David indicated on the map its exact position.

'We will board at nightfall and allow the barge to float under the bridge. Once in position we will work undisturbed.'

'Tres bien, Jean-Paul.' David slapped him on his shoulder.

'We'll wait for dusk. Do you think there's a real chance we will accomplish the mission?'

'The success of it rests with you and your men. Without you all, this would be impossible.

Although the men rested, nervous tension showed in their clipped chatter, the drumming of fingers on an empty cigarette packet, and their willingness to help Joseph empty his bottle of Calvados. John- Paul came to their rescue with a few lively tunes on his mouth organ. But, nothing could disguise the tenseness of the waiting moment. The time seemed to be passing extremely slowly.

John-Paul opened up his transmitter and signalled a message to London – "Bullseye is sweet".

I hope it will be sweet. It's going to be a rough mission.

The men were ready, their faces blackened. They climbed into the covered truck. A final check was made to see that a short ladder was in place with the explosives. They checked their pistols and belts of bullets. The engine spluttered into life and ticked over sweetly as it slowly moved off into the night. They approached the canal. The water flowed silently, its surface reflecting the stars in the still night air. The truck pulled to a stand still a few yards from the towpath. John and Colin made their own way towards the Peugeot Plant, while David, John-Paul and the other members of the group, nimbly jumped on to the road and passed through a gap in the hedge to the towpath, and headed towards the moored boat. They moved quickly and silently.

I'll be glad when this mission's over. I don't think about the family. It's the only way I can get through these episodes. Cutting my self off from them and solely divert my thoughts to the job.

David carried the ladder over his shoulder. He glanced at the slow moving water and smiled at his own silhouette. A few more minutes and they would be on board the barge. As they climbed on to the *Grande Duchesse*, she creaked with the extra weight. The towpath team undid the mooring line and at a steady walking pace followed the barge toward the target not allowing the rope to drop into the water.

David took command of the Grande Duchesse trying to keep in mid stream. At first the Duchesse wanted to drift to the opposite bank. David pulled the brass tiller over and she righted herself into mid stream.

'I see you can handle the old girl,' whispered Colin.

Thank god we went on the Grand Union Canal trip for a few days. I didn't think I'd need those skills again. We're going to be lucky if we pull this off. All I hope is that the Germans don't spot us.

All eyes were focused on the bridge ahead as they drifted nearer. The stone built arch loomed like the mouth of a giant whale. On each of its flanks, the agents spotted two guards armed with rifles. The Grande Duchesse continued silently on her journey, the quiet ripples of the water, sleepily carrying her into the darkness, transporting her deadly cargo.

John-Paul signalled to the group on the towpath with one white flash from his torch. The Grande Duchesse seemed determined to continue on her way. It was like a tug-of-war and the towpath group was losing, but the French agents knew their canal bank and already the rope had been looped round a mooring post. Then with some difficulty, the Duchesse was brought to a halt, at the planned spot under the bridge.

'Halt Machen.'

Everyone went rigid, listening intently to the guttural voices of the guards as they questioned a cyclist.

'Forsezen'.

The cyclist rattled away, disappearing into the cold night. The group waited whilst the guards continued their patrol to the centre of the bridge, just above their heads, and then marched back to their appointed positions.

David got to work. He placed the ladder against one of the bridge's supports.

The towpath team, straining on the rope, made sure the Grande Duchesse was holding steady.

Precariously David climbed up into the breastwork of the bridge. His sack of explosives was swinging from his belt like the pendulum of an old grandfather clock. He moved carefully and methodically. He could hear the blood pounding in his ears as he placed each of the explosives with unhurried skill. He secured them to the stonework with black tape and set the charges for twenty minutes.

His heart hammered in his chest as he placed the final 'bomb'. His fingers were now numb with the cold when the explosives slipped from his palm and with the quickness of a cat striking out, he managed to catch it with his other hand. With trembling fingers he managed to attach the tape.

Keep going you fool. My fingers I can hardly feel them.

He took a deep breath and made sure that everything was in place. The final charge was set for ten minutes.

Bloody hell that was a near thing. Lady luck was riding on my shoulder.

Carefully he lowered himself back on to the deck of the barge, his legs hardly supporting him. The men on board climbed down into the hold. David signalled to the waiting agents on the bank to pull the narrow boat up to its moorings. Slowly the boat progressed back up stream, inch by inch, without warning the frayed rope snapped in half. There was nothing anyone could do. The boat shuddered and swung around changing direction and started to float back towards the bridge.

Bugger it. I knew it was too good to bloody last. I won't be able to say goodbye to Margaret. Oh shit, here it comes.

He instinctively crouched down shielding his face with his hands.

The explosions were instantaneous, six eruptions cracked out into the night. The brilliant glare from the ignited explosives illuminated the surrounding countryside, revealing the devastation. The force of the detonation peppered the old barge with masonry and concrete destroying its wooden planks as easy as snapping a match in half. A piece of concrete struck David on the back of his head. He dropped on to the deck, unconscious. The boat started to sink. Cries came from the entombed men below the decks.

'Au secour, au secour.'

David slowly regained consciousness, drifting back into reality when the men's shouts for help cleared his foggy mind.

'Au secour'

God I'm lucky to still be alive. Who's that calling for help? Jesus Christ.

Frantically, with his bare hands, he grabbed at the splintered wood. He dragged the hot stove away from the broken door and heaved it over board.

John-Paul called out 'Never mind us David, go, save your self'. He took no notice of his friend's advice. With frenzied movements he carried on, his hands and head bleeding profusely. He heard a loud explosion.

'Could that be from the Peugeot Plant?' With a feeling that the second prong of the mission had been successful gave David the extra strength he needed to carry on. Somehow, one by one he managed to pull out the four-trapped men. Coughing and spluttering, they climbed back on to the canal bank

'Is everyone here? Have we lost anyone?' David shouted.

'No, we are all safe.'

Heading for the Peugeot Plant, John and Colin stealthily made their way along the canal bank, turned off to the right towards their target. The factory was in darkness.

'That doesn't seem right. Where are the guards? John whispered.

'Maybe they thought the guards on the bridge were enough,' replied Colin.

'Could be,'

'Any way let's go, but keep your eyes open.'

'There's a lock on the door.'

'That's no problem.' Colin took out a piece of wire from his jacket pocket and proceeded to pick the lock.

'I can see you've done this before.'

'Always wise to be prepared.'

'Were you in the Boy Scouts?'

'Yes, how did you guess?'

'The 'be prepared' bit.'

'Ah.'

They pulled open the double wooden doors and entered the large building. Colin flashed his torch into the darkness revealing machinery in the half gloom.

'Come on, let's get back to work.' John urged.

The two men tucked the plastic explosives amongst the mechanisms of the iron structures setting the timers as they went along.

'Let's go. It must be nearly time for the others to have finished their mission.'

'You're right.'

'We won't close the doors.'

'You silly sod. There'll be nothing left of them.'

'Quite so.'

Several explosions sliced into the night air.

'Sounds as though David has been successful.'

'Thank God,' John looked at his watch. 'Hit the deck.'

The force, of the detonation of the explosives, threw the two men into the nearby bushes.

'Shit, that was close.'

They picked themselves up and made their way back to the others.

'What the hell's happened to you all?' Asked Colin.

'The bloody rope broke on the barge and we floated back to the bridge when the explosives went off.' said David.

'We heard them. We didn't think you were in trouble though.'

The group made its way back to the waiting lorry, they were all thankful to have survived. John-Paul turned to David.

'What can we say mon ami. We owe you. You saved our lives.' He studied his tired blooded face.

'Come on, let's finish the job.'

They climbed into the lorry and the driver drove off making his way back to the farmhouse.

Back at their base John-Paul grabbed a box and using it as a step pulled himself up into the loft. He made his way over the rafters to the desk and grabbed the radio. One switch and it crackled into life. John-Paul sent the message - 'Bullseye'.

He sat back in his chair, closed his eyes, and scratched the stubble on his chin.

Thank God that is over.

'You dropped off up there? David called out.

'Non mon ami.' He switched off the power and carefully made his way back to the hatch in the loft and dropped through into the room below.

'Everything all right?'

'It is now.'

THIS IS ALVA LYDDELL
FOR THE BBC LONDON.
HERE IS THE 9'O'CLOCK NEWS
ON THE 24TH MAY 1941

BREAKING OUT INTO THE ATLANTIC
THROUGH THE DENMARK STRAIT,
THE GERMAN BATTLESHIP 'BISMARK'
SINKS THE BRITISH BATTLE CRUISER
'HOOD'
AND DAMAGES THE BRITAIN'S MOST
MODERN
BATTLESHIP THE 'PRINCE OF WALES'.

THAT IS THE END OF THE NEWS.

Wolfgang was driven into Camp no 177 through heavily barbed wired gates. His escorts accompanied him into the Commandant's office. The room was sparsely furnished with only a desk and a chair.

'Attention.' Shouted one of the guards in his ear.

The chief prison officer walked in. He walked around the desk and sat down on the chair and proceeded to read the contents of his 'in-tray' drumming his fingers with rhythmic timing.

'I see you were picked up in Stylecroft village.' He looked up at the young man and waited for his answer.

'Yes sir.'

'And you've been given a white rating, hence your appearance here and as you pose no threat to our country, you will live out the rest of the war at camp 177.' He snapped shut the folder and proceeded to make a telephone call.

'Yes.' He spoke into the mouthpiece. 'Number 210 has arrived.' He replaced the receiver.

'Let me give you a word of advice. This POW camp is situated in a deserted spot. There are wide expanses of scree-slopes and slag-heaps, surrounded by fells and woodlands. I'm giving you this information to discourage any thoughts of escape. All escapees have returned because of the difficult terrain, so it's useless to try.'

Wolfgang was dismissed with a wave of his hand.

'About turn.'

He was escorted along a concrete path, which led into the centre of the prefabricated buildings. There were seven Nissan huts all in alignment and four huts deep. All had curved asbestos roofing, each with green painted windows.

Wolfgang was escorted through the door of Hut 'C'. *So this is going to be my home for the duration of the war.* There were two rows of beds and cupboards along each side of the hut. A smell of fumes came from the stovepipe in the centre of the hut where a fellow prisoner was poking the stove. The only other odour, Wolfgang recognised, was that of floor polish.

Not like my attic room at the Vicarage.

Each prisoner was dressed in a grey uniform.
'Smart you think?' A hand was held out in friendship as Wolfgang approached.
'Different,' answered Wolfgang, shaking hands.
'My name is Wolfgang.'
'Mine – Kurt. Nice square yellow patch on my trouser leg you think? And to match yellow circle you find on the back of a mackintosh in your cupboard.' They walked down the line of beds.
'This one is yours.'

Wolfgang examined the mattress on his bed it looked like old sacking. Thick course blankets were neatly folded at the head of the bed with a single pillow on top. A chair was placed between every other bunk bed and a rope washing line strung between the beds. Dolly pegs danced up and down on the line as other prisoners pushed past eager to meet the new arrival.

Introductions over, Wolfgang took the opportunity to test the comfort of his bed.
Looking up to the ceiling Wolfgang watched a solitary

light bulb swinging gently from side to side. The heat of the stovepipe created distorted shadows across the hut.

What's going to happen now?
Would he see Elizabeth again?
Would there be any future for them?

The yearning inside unsettled him and he rose up and walked over to the opposite side of the hut and looked behind the sacking that served as curtains. He rubbed away the condensation on the window with his fist to reveal an imposing stone built building surrounded by barbed wired fencing. The outlook was depressing.

'Looks grim, doesn't it? Kurt Fuhrmann.' He held out his hand.

What another Kurt.

'Wolfgang Rumfler.' The two men shook hands.
'I suppose we must think ourselves lucky?'
'Ja.'
'Wie wohnen sie?'
They swung around as they heard the bolt of a 303 rifle being driven home. Silhouetted in the doorway stood a guard with his rifle up against his shoulder pointing directly at them.
'Speak in English, only English.'
'Ja, ja. Yes, yes.' Kurt raised his hands in a defensive gesture.
'Dumm,' he muttered under his breath.' Let me introduce you to Martin Dieter and Jutta Piper.' The two

men nodded, still busy with their game of cards.
'Want to join in?'
'Thanks.'
'We're playing for money.'
Wolfgang walked between the beds and under the string washing line, sat down at the table and picked up his cards. They played until 'lights out' was called.

Time to dream of escape, dream of his homeland, or just to sleep.

The early morning call made for a long day. Wolfgang pulled back the sacking from the window to reveal the virgin snow, reminding him of winter in his fatherland.
'Come with me,' said Jutta. 'I'll introduce you to your fellow countrymen.'
'I hope I will soon get to know you all. I'll try to remember all your names, but you must help me.'
'Come and see, how industrious we are when were unable to get outside.'
Wolfgang was amazed to see all the items the prisoners had made. Whittling, draughts pocket chess sets, dolls, clowns with moveable arms and legs, model boats, dominoes and wooden toys of all description.
'Where do you get all the wood? Wolfgang asked.
'There's no shortage of material, as the woods close by supply all our needs,' Kurt replied.
'Last year when we were snowed in and our supply of wood was difficult to find. One of the inmates decided to cut off the legs of a chair and use it for whittling.
'What happened?'
'He landed up in solitary confinement for a week.'
'Poor devil.'

Wolfgang noticed the wall art, landscapes, cartoons and women.

'It's fantastic. You could hold an exhibition here. Where do you get your materials from?'

'We beg and borrow from the guards.'

'How big is the camp?'

'It's quite large. There's a cookhouse, a church, grocery and produce store, two dining huts, two recreation huts, two ablutions and latrines blocks. A camp reception station, plus twenty-three living huts. Then there's the Red Cross building. Oh and a water tower and of course the living quarters for the guards.'

'It's like a village. What about electricity?'

'That's generated by the water wheel.'

'Self sufficient then?'

'It has to be as there is only a single spine road for access here. It's very isolated.'

Martin joined in the conversation. ' Best sit out the war, you're better off.'

'You might be satisfied with that, but I'm not.'

'You'll learn. The odds of escaping are practically nil. Men have tried of course, but they always come back. You'll meet only fellow prisoners and the camp-guards. We're occasionally let outside the camp, but that is to work on the local farm. Come and visit our recreation hall.'

Wolfgang, Martin and Jutter pulled on their topcoats and went out into the cold.

'If it carries on snowing, we'll be on snow-clearing duties.'

'Here we are.' Jutter announced and the men pushed

their way through the wooden doors.

'This is it.' Martin said.

Before them was a stage at one end and rows upon rows of wooden benches.

'Look at the artwork on the walls.' Wolfgang was amazed at the beautiful landscapes, which adorned the walls.

'You've even got the red velvet curtains. How on earth did you manage to acquire them?'

'The villagers around here are quite friendly and we do a show from time to time for them. One of the villagers donated the curtains. Before that we had painted curtains. Much better since we've had the material ones.'

'Take a look at this.' Martin dropped to the wooden floor and prised up one of the floorboards and reached inside.

'Is anyone coming?'

Wolfgang looked out of the door. 'No.'

'Good.' Martin lifted out a small Bakelite radio set.

'Where on earth did you get that from?'

'One of the locals had thrown it away. We managed to get a valve for it and it works perfectly. We can listen to the news, we think its mostly propaganda, but we wouldn't like it to be discovered.'

Martin replaced the wireless into the cavity and pushed down the floorboard with his heavy boot. 'We get regular mail from the Fatherland, so it's a fairly comfortable life here, if you're content with conditions, content to be incarcerated in this hell hole.'

'Rumfler 210'

The two men turned to see a guard standing in the

doorway.

'Yes.'

'Rumfler, you are wanted at the Commandant's office.'

The two men entered the office where the Commandant sat at his desk.

'Ah Rumfler.' He looked up from his paperwork. 'We have to confirm any skills you may have.' His pen was poised at the ready. 'Well!'

'I can use any farm machinery.'

'Yes, what else?'

'I can drive. I'm pretty good at carpentry.'

'Anything more?'

'I don't think so.'

'Sir.' The guard dug him in his ribs his ribs with the butt of his rifle.

'Sir.'

'Right. Your name will be added to the list of 'Work Parties'. Sergeant'

The sergeant came to attention and saluted his officer.

'Prisoner, about turn. Quick march, left right left right, left right.'

Wolfgang was all smiles when he entered his hut.

'Why the big grin Wolfgang?'

'I'm on the list for work-parties.'

'Good for you. Let's hope the weather improves. It never seems to stop raining here, and now we have snow.'

'Well, what are our plans for today?'

'I've worked out a 'Time-table,' announced

Kaufmann. 'It has been approved by Herzog.' He pinned the programme on to the camp notice board.

There was a good variety activities and the grunts of approval brought a smile to Kaufmann.

'Not bad, eh?'

'How to speak English,' 'Craft work,' 'Painting,' ' Choir,' 'Drama' 'Creative Writing' 'The Night Sky' 'Cooking' - had them all chatting.

'What about plans to escape?' Voiced one prisoner.

'Not an item that we would place on a Notice Board I think!'

One of the guards entered the hut. 'Letters from your homeland.' He handed them over to Kaufmann for distribution.

'Klaus Muller, Hans Koch,'

'Nothing for me?'

'Not this time Wolfgang.'

Wolfgang sat on his bed. All was quiet, so he picked up a book from the shelf 'How to speak English.' It was not long before Wolfgang was able to try out his improved conversational English.

'Wolfgang, you have been assigned to Beckside Farm – you start work there tomorrow.'

'Great, I can't wait.'

It didn't matter to Wolfgang that the winter months were spent clearing snow, rescuing lost sheep, and repairing jobs in and around the farm. His efforts were appreciated and the POW – Camp Commandant – placed Wolfgang Rumphler on his 'trusted' list.

With a cold winter and a not too pleasant Spring,

summer could not have come quick enough.

'At last the English weather has decided to kind to us' announced Kurt.
'Yes, look at the sky. Red sky at night, shepherd's delight.' Wolfgang pointed towards a red sun disappearing behind the mountains.
'This is a English saying is it not?'
'Yes, red sky in the morning is shepherd's warning.'
'Oh no, you mean that tomorrow when we all go out with our work parties it will be raining again?'
'No, not after this glorious red sky.'

The following morning covered lorries arrived in the compound. The sky was clear.
'Look blue sky.'
'Pay attention.' All conversation ceased.
'As your names are called move quickly. 'A' Party ......'
Names were rattled out through a hand-held speaker – all the work parties left in a convoy of three lorries heading for different farms in a pleasant area of the English Lakeland. The excitement of the prisoners was clearly recognised as they burst into song and even silenced the singing of the birds.
Wolfgang was the first to leap out of the lorry and met Tom Hargreaves the farmer.
'My name is Wolfgang, I am pleased to meet you sir.'
'Nay lad don't call me sir, I haven't been knighted yet.'
Wolfgang could not quite understand Mr Hargreaves' comment.

'May I introduce the rest of the work party?'

After the introductions were over, with Wolfgang speaking for his fellow countrymen, it was not long before he was able to tell them that they would be working in a field for the next two weeks – picking peas.

'Now lads,' said Mr Hargreaves 'You can eat as many peas as you like, but I would not recommend too many – you could make yourselves sick. Besides, I would like you to fill as many of those wicker baskets as you can,' he pointed to a pile of baskets, each basket looked enormous.

'And, if your work is satisfactory, there could be more work for you on this farm. It's up to you. Those not keen – may just as well stay in the camp. It's up to you lads. I'm asking Wolfgang here to act as your representative, so if you have any problems asked him and if I can I'll sort it out. I'll see you all later. But first, I'll demonstrate how to pick peas.'

Soon they were all at work. It was clear that on each plant there were several pods and each one had to be taken off and dropped into the basket. A farmhand came across the field from time to time to make sure the job was being done properly.

'It will take us ages to fill even one basket,' grumbled Hans.

'Don't forget – you're out in the fresh air, it might be boring work but surely its better than staying on the camp all day,' said Wolfgang.

They all agreed and set to work and once more burst into song. The baskets filled slowly, a few pods were prised open and the peas eaten – but not many. At the end of the day the average number of baskets filled by each man was four.

'Wolfgang, I've other jobs that need doing, can any of your men do carpentry, or is good at mechanics?'

'Well, you can put me on the list to start with and I think I'll find a few more with these skills. Leave it to me Mr Hargreaves. I see you have a few Land Girls working for you Mr Hargreaves. Is it all right if we speak to them?'

'Well, the girls know you're here, that's for certain. So if you get chance to have a chat, provided it doesn't interfere with you work, and your guards are happy about it, the best of luck to you.'

'The guards,' said Wolfgang, 'I'd forgotten about them. I'll check with them now.'

It took most of his break period to find where the guards were. There were only two of them and they were chatting with one of the Land Girls.

'Oh good,' said Wolfgang, 'I can kill two birds with one stone.'

'Very good Wolfgang – where did you get that one from?'

'From my book.' He pulled a 'How to speak English' book out of his pocket.

'Well, get stuffed then.'

'You can't say that,' interrupted the Land Girl' 'If he want to speak to me he's quite welcome. He's not bad looking.'

She pulled a cigarette packet out of her pocket.

'Would you like a Senior Service?'

'I was only joking.' The Guard intervened and took a cigarette himself.

'This is Daisy. Daisy, meet Wolfgang.'

Wolfgang accepted a cigarette.

'It's all right then if we talk to the Land Girls?'

'There's no harm in talking.'

It was not long before the Land Girls were passing English cigarettes to most of the German prisoners. There were lots of chatter and laughter.

'Where do you come from?'

'Have you been here for long?'

'What jobs are allocated to you?'

'What's your name?'

Wolfgang resigned himself from the possibility of ever hearing from home. The Camp Commandant had told him that all enquiries suggested his family were dead or missing. But, he still had hopes of renewing his relationship with the Kelly family and Elizabeth.

It came as a surprise when Wolfgang had taken his basket of peas for weigh-in that Farmer Hargreaves was there to greet him.

'Wolfgang, I've a message for you.'

'For me, who is it from?'

'Well, it came to me really, it was from a Rev. Kelly. He sends you his best wishes from himself and family and hopes you will meet up with them again in the near future.'

'That's great news Mr Hargreaves.' *I can hardly believe*

it, Christopher sending a message. There's still hope for me, for us. On my God there is still a future to look forward to Elizabeth my love.

The farmer looked on with great pleasure. 'Soon the picking will be completed', he said.

'But, there will be more work to do grubbing up the old plants and clearing the fields for other crops. There will be better days ahead. I'm sure.'

'We all hope for that Mr Hargreaves.'

'Of course you do. It's what we all want lad.'

This is the BBC Home Service

Here is the 9 o'clock news
on December 7th 1941

Japan bombs the US base at Pearl Harbour
on the Hawaiian Island of Oahu,
sinking five battleships, destroying 200 aircraft,
severely damaging a number of Destroyers
and cruisers and killing 2,500 personnel.

That is the end of the news.

It was Elizabeth's 18th birthday. There was great excitement in opening her presents. All the family was seated as usual around the kitchen table.

'Mother, Father. Thank you, the handbag is lovely. I can smell it's real leather and it will come in very useful when I go to college next week. Rose, Ruth, thank you too for the talc. It's just what I needed.'

Both of her sisters sat smiling at her.

'Do you really like it?' Ruth asked.

'Love it,' Elizabeth replied.

'There you are. I told you she'd like it.' Ruth directed her comment to Rose.

'Now you two, not today. There's to be no arguing on Elizabeth's birthday.' Father warned the quarrelling twosome.

'Oh, they'll be good, won't you girls?'

They only nodded their reply.

'Let's tackle these now,' Elizabeth picked up the pile of envelopes stacked at the side of her plate.

'Look at this.' Elizabeth held the twin's card up for all to see.' Now that's really special.' The smile on their faces was an extra gift. They both giggled and fled from the table.

Several villagers had also remembered her birthday. Elizabeth placed the cards on the shelf and returned to the table to open up her last card.

'Who's it from? Mother asked.

A gasp of excitement and pleasure escaped her lips.

'It's from Joseph, I mean Wolfgang.' She clasped the card to her breast.' I didn't think he would remember.'

'Well that's nice of him.' Her Father looked at Margaret's reaction.

'Yes very kind.'

Elizabeth ran up stairs to the privacy of the room, which had been Wolfgang's. She sat on the bed and carefully opened the envelope and pulled out the card. It had a simple design, a silhouette of a woman standing alone looking out at the sea. She turned to the greetings which read - *To Elizabeth. For someone who's so special to me, Happy Birthday, all my love Wolfgang.*

Tears stung the back of her eyes. She held the card close to her chest as though gaining strength from his treasured words.

Thank you my darling. You don't know just how much this means to me.

Elizabeth was full of excitement at the prospect of going to college. She would often pull out Wolfgang's greeting's card and read the message over and over again. Somehow the words comforted her in the knowledge that Wolfgang still thought about her. Her love for him remained steadfast.

How can I discuss this with my parents, especially after his deceit? I understand his reasons for doing so, but well, my parents that's another matter.

She desperately missed him. He was constantly in her thoughts. She dare not think about the Prisoner of War Camp. She had heard such awful stories and she refused to let her mind dwell on the subject too long. Somehow she knew that her feelings for him wouldn't change. No words had passed between them, only an occasional look of longing, and a look of promise. She sighed. Wolfgang had been forcibly marched out of the vicarage by the Military Police. Tears welled up and spilled down her cheeks, she brushed them away.

Elizabeth made sure she had packed everything that she would need at the college. Her excitement heightened nearer the day of departure.

I can't believe I'll be there in a couple of days.

The Kelly family stood on the platform waiting for the arrival of the Liverpool train. Elizabeth's trunk stood by her feet.

'It's coming,' her Mother said, wiping away a tear with her cotton handkerchief. The train entered the station with steam belching around its engine like a warm blanket. .

'Now don't worry Mother, I'll be quite all right. It's about a two-hour journey to St. Catherine's Training College. There's only the taxi to hail and I'll be there.' She gave her Mother a big hug and whispered 'Don't worry, I'm a big girl now.' She turned to her Father, 'I'll be careful and work hard.'

He nodded, realising that his little girl was now a grown woman. He gathered her into his arms.

'Take care, stay safe.' He lifted her trunk into the luggage van with the help of the guard.

'All aboard.' The guard looked up and down the line.

Hastily Elizabeth gave her sisters a quick peck on their cheeks.

'Be good.' Then she climbed on board, slamming the

door behind her.

'We will, we will.'

On board, Elizabeth pulled down the window and leant out.

'Ring when you've arrived.' Mother called out, raising her voice in a shrill cry. The guard waved his green flag and blew on his whistle, the train moved forward slowly and gradually picked up speed. Elizabeth sat back into her seat and peered out of the window, watching the countryside flash by.

'Liverpool, here I come.' She hugged herself in excitement and expectation. It would only be two years study and she would return to Stylecroft as a fully qualified teacher. It was then that her thoughts returned to Wolfgang.

How was he? Was he coping all right? Did he get on well with his fellow prisoners?

There were so many questions that could not be answered. She would have to wait. There would be a solution in the future, so she would have to be satisfied with that thought. She rubbed the condensation on the window, it ran down in tiny droplets until it reached the wooden frame and gathered there, in a miniature stream.

The clitterly-clack clitterly- clack of the wheels enticed her into a hypnotic sleep.

Wolfgang was with her and they were walking holding hands across a field of yellow buttercups. They sat down on a fallen log. His arms were around her shoulders, pulling her to him. Their lips met, with such sweetness and gentleness, she could feel the warmth of his body.

'Tickets please.'
Startled she stared at the man.
'Tickets please.'
'Oh, just a minute.' She delved into her leather handbag.' I know I put it in here somewhere.' The ticket collector stepped backwards, tutted and waited.
'Ah here we are.' She handed it to him.
'Thank you Miss,' clipped her ticket and returned it to her.
An hour later the train chugged into Liverpool station. Stepping down out of the carriage, she hailed a railway porter to help with her luggage. Her trunk safely stowed on a trolley Elizabeth followed the porter and walked out on to the street and waited for a taxicab to arrive.

The taxi driver was more than helpful. He lifted her heavy luggage, assured Elizabeth that he knew the College well. Not only did he arrive there in good time, but also he entered the college grounds and pulled up outside an impressive large old oak door.
'There we are Miss. Welcome to St Catherine's. You will find someone to show you where to go if you go though that door.'
'Thank you so much. I don't know what I would have done without your help.' She said and passed over the taxi fare.
'That's all right Miss…thanks' He doffed his cap and climbed back into this cab.

Elizabeth stood beside her trunk, drinking in the enormity of the majestic building covered in Virginia creeper.

How on earth am I going to find my way around? It's so different from home.

'Are you lost?' Elizabeth spun around.
'I beg your pardon.'
'Are you lost?' A cleaner stood at the side of her, a bucket in one hand, and a mop in the other. She wore a wrap-around-overall that was tied at the back. And on her head, a scarf tied at the top with a large knot.
'You'll be the third today,' she grinned, showing a row of chipped teeth.
'I beg your pardon?'
'Students. You'll be the third today'.
'Ah. Can you tell me where the porter is?'
'Bless you dearie. There are no porters 'ere.'
'But the trunk.'
'Come on I'll help you. Have you found out what house your in?'
'No'.
'Look on the board there,' she pointed behind her and Elizabeth walked over and traced her finger through the list.
'Found it?
'Yes. Would you believe it, it's on the third floor.'
'Oh I'd believe it all right. Come on, grab the other end.'
Both women lifted the heavy trunk. And started to climb the stone stairs to the first landing, here they lowered the trunk and rested.
'Ready?
'Off we go again.' The two of them struggled up the next flight and rested again.
'Last lap.'

There was a door at the top of the stairs. They shuffled through the doorway, dropped their heavy load on to the floor and stood there gasping for breath.

'Hello.'
'Good after noon.'
'I'm Beryl Stagg.'
'Elizabeth Kelly. And this kind lady helped me up with that,' she kicked the trunk and looked towards the door, but the cleaner had gone, ' I never thanked her for her help. I don't even know her name.'
'It's Madge Russell.'
'I'm bushed. I suppose I had better unpack. Have you all ready?'
'Yes, I've been here a couple of hours.'
'Where do we get our meals? Do you know?'
'In the refectory I believe.'
'Good, because I'm starving.'
'Then we'll have to find out where the college shop is. Come on, unpack later.'

The two girls, laughing, ran out of the room, then down the stairs and out on to the quadrangle. They were taking more steps to independence and discovery.

The young student teachers found the little shop at the back of the bicycle sheds. It was no bigger than a broom cupboard. One side of the room hung new blazers and skirts. On the opposite side was a sale of items left by old students. The cramped conditions encouraged them to have a quick rummage round then leave.

'Well that was an experience. I didn't know you could get so much stuff into a box room.' Beryl said.

Back out into the sunshine the two friends wandered

around the college. A hand bell rang out.

'I wonder what's that for?' Elizabeth quizzically asked.

'Dinner time girls,' Madge walked around the corner.

'Good. I'm starving! By the way Madge…..'

'Yes.'

'Thanks for the help this afternoon.'

'A pleasure dearie.'

They made their way into a large dining hall. Oak panelled walls surrounded the rows of tables and wooden benches. Soon many more students entered the refectory. Above their heads was a high ceiling. At on end of the room was a hatchway. It was pulled open by a lady in the kitchen. Two young ladies, from each table, collected dinners and returned several times until all the students were happily tucking into their evening meal of potatoes, vegetables and mincemeat. With the first course over, the servers returned the empty plates and collected the next course of pudding. On this their first meal at St Catherine's, it was the notorious 'spotted dick with thick custard.'

After their evening meal all the students were free to explore the college grounds and buildings. Beryl and Elizabeth made their way back to their room and changed into their jim-jams. They talked until well after lights out.

'My dad's an engineer in Sheffield. I've two brothers and a sister. My mother works as an assistant caretaker in a School for Infants. What do your parents do?'

'My father's a vicar in a small village called Stylecroft. Mother helps with the church. Then I have two sisters. I miss them all already. Oh no!' Elizabeth remembered with horror.

'What ever is the matter?' Beryl asked concerned.

'I promised to telephone my parents and I've forgotten.'

'So have I.'

'We'll have to ring them first thing tomorrow.'

'Won't your parents worry?'

'Yes, but it's far too late to call now.'

'What is the time?'

Elizabeth strained her eyes, in the semi-darkness, to look at her wristwatch.

'It's one thirty in the morning.'

'Oh my god, I'll not be able to get up early in the morning.'

'Yes you will. I'll wake you up. Night.'

'Night.'

Elizabeth settled into the narrow bed willing sleep to come. But, with her mind in torment she could not sleep. *What would they be thinking back home m when she had not phoned….. I wonder how Wolfgang is coping at the camp.*

Finally her eyelids became heavy and sleep followed……………

For almost three months time seemed to fly by. There was so much to learn so much to do. Each student had to choose two specialist subjects and attend lectures on

Education, Religious Knowledge, Basic Mathematics, English Language and Hygiene.

The specialist subjects had to selected from a list which included; English Literature, Advanced Mathematics, French, Latin, German, Chemistry, Physics, Biology, Scripture, Art, Physical Training, History, Geography, Domestic Science.

There were many Clubs and Societies to join. Then, on top of all these lectures and activities, there were educational visits to be made, and most important of all, Teaching Practice where all the students would be sent to a school in the Liverpool area and take charge of classes whilst under supervision from a qualified teacher.

End of term and Christmas vacation could not have come quick enough for most of the students.

THIS IS THE BBC HOME SERVICE.
HERE IS THE 9 O'CLOCK NEWS
ON MAY 2ND 1942.

THE JAPANESE TAKE MANDALAY;
BURMA IS NOW ENTIRELY UNDER
THEIR CONTROL.

THAT IS THE END OF THE NEWS.

Elizabeth had only just made it home from Liverpool for the Christmas vacation, when the first flakes of the snow began to fall.

Oh, great it going to be a white Christmas, how lovely.

Elizabeth, struggling with her suitcase and carrier bag full of presents, entered the vicarage. There were whoops of joy from her sisters. Mother came out of the kitchen wiping her hands on her apron and gave her a big hug.

'Put the kettle on girls, I'm sure Elizabeth would welcome a cup of tea.'

'Where's father?'

'He'll be home soon, he had a meeting with some of the Mothers' Union in the church.

'Sit yourself down, and tell us all about St. Catherine's and your friend from Sheffield – Beryl isn't it?'

'All in good time mother.'

There was the sound of someone kicking snow off his shoes at the back door entrance.

'Your Father's home already.'

'Father look who's back.'

The family, as usual, sat around the kitchen table. There were lots to talk about.

'Did you like your college Elizabeth?' Rose asked.

'Of course it's so different from school.'

'Why different?'

'Well, for a start, you are responsible for yourself. Choosing your subjects you wish to specialise in, buying the books you need and making new friends, joining different societies and clubs inside the College, making new friends. You also have your own tutor that you can talk to and seek advice.'

'Did you miss us?' Ruth asked.

'Of course I did, you silly goose. That's why I will always try to write to you both at least once a week.'

Their father came to sit with them.

'Had a busy day Father?'

'Well, I sorted out all the readings with the Mother's Union – then I saw the snow falling, I thought it best we should all head home. If it keeps falling like this the village will be cut off. I saw William coming back into the village. I think he will be lodging at Mrs Richard's until spring.'

'The snow is really settling, look father, you can't see any footprints on the garden path.'

'Better check to see if you can find your wellington boots.'

'Good, can we play out and make a snowman?'

'Wait till the snow stops falling, then I'll help you,' said mother.

The snow continued to fall through into the evening. The Kelly's stayed in front of a lovely log fire roasting chestnuts and playing card games.

The following day there was a strange silence over the whole village. Few people ventured out. It was usually quite busy in the village the week before Christmas, but with the deep snow now above the level of the stone walls along the roadside and the temperature so low only the postlady braved the elements.

'I'd like to check on some of the elderly parishioners

and see how they are coping with this severe weather,' said Reverend Kelly. He picked up his phone was and spoke to one of his Churchwardens who shared his concern for the old folk in the village. Then contacted some of the farmers They too had their problems with sheep still high on the fell.

'Elizabeth, would you like to come with me?'
'Just, wait Father, I'll get my Wellington boots on.'

It was not long before lots of the villagers were out with their spades digging a way through to the church and the pub then across the village shop. Although Donald Hodges, the shopkeeper, had stocked up on necessities, goods were running extremely low.

'I've only enough for two days. Three if I reduce the ration.'

'Now don't worry Donald, I'll see what I can do. It's not what you know, but whom you know. Leave it with me.'

The vicar and Elizabeth hurried along the path to the vicarage. He hastily wiped his feet on the doormat and entered his office.

'Make a pot of tea will you Elizabeth?'

Christopher sat down and lifted up the telephone.

'Hello, to whom am I speaking?' The telephone crackled.' Sorry the line isn't too good.'

'This is Blackpool 249 R.A.F. Station Wheaten –how may I help?'

'I'm Flight Lieutenant Kelly. Can you put me through to Air Commodore Hinton on your red line?'

'What is your pass word for the red line sir?'

'Isle of Man.'

'Thank you sir.'

Within seconds Christopher was through to the Commodore.

'Hello Kelly, how can I help you?'

Chris knew he could count on his old friend. They had both been involved with missions for the Special Operations Executive.

'Hello sir. I'm afraid the village of Stylecroft where I live, is in a bit of bother. We're snowed in and food is running out for us, as well as the animals. I know you're very busy. But do you think you might be able to help us?'

'Say no more dear chap, it's as good as done.'

The Commodore knew he had the resources to help and picked up the telephone on his desk and issued orders for a 'Supply Drop'. Within hours 'Operation Snowfall' was under way. The Lysander stood on the runway ready to receive the cargo. Three men walked towards the aircraft, chatting easily together. They climbed on board and revved up the engines. Slowly the aircraft moved forward

'Snowfall to tower, permission for take off.'

'Tower to Snowfall, runway two. I repeat runway two.'

'Acknowledged runway two.'

The aircraft gathered speed and it seemed to labour under the weight it was carrying.

'Come on old girl, up you come. There you are, she only needed coaxing.' Frank Darby the pilot pulled hard on the joystick.

Operation Snowfall was under way. The pilot reduced height, flying low over the frozen Lakeland valleys looking for landmarks to guide him to the village of Stylecroft. Snowy rooftops blended in with the frozen land making it extremely difficult. On the horizon the church spire appeared and the relieved pilot banked around, circling the village.

Smalley's Farm had received a telephone call giving instructions to mark out the dropping area with the letter 'C' in the frozen snow. The pilot was extremely grateful to whoever had organised the giant sized letter. Farmer Smalley and his wife and helpers had used their remaining bales of straw to make a giant sized letter 'C' in the snow.

'They're sure to see that,' said one of the helpers.'

'I hope so,' replied Mrs Smalley, as she wiped the sweat off her brow. They all returned to the warmth of the farmhouse for mugs of tea.

'Listen…is that a plane?'

Mrs Smalley and her helpers quickly wrestled into their outdoors clothing. They left the warm cottage and headed towards the dropping zone. It was hard going as they struggled through the deep snow.

There's our target – there's no mistaking that marker.

'Jack,' he called to his navigator, 'I'm going round again. When I give the word, push out everything.'

The snow had started to fall heavier and the visibility lessened dramatically. He banked around again, over the top of the church and on to the marker.

'All right Jack, this time. Then one more circle and

we'll head for home. **Now**,' he shouted. It took two drops before all the containers and bales of fodder had been dispatched.

'Mission accomplished,' he reported back to base. 'We'll take one more circle, then head for home. Make it double whiskeys Bill. Over and out'.

A disaster had been averted.

'I can see the villagers coming,' Farmer Smalley called to his wife. Mrs Smalley stopped her chores and looked to where her husband was pointing.

'Thank the Lord,' she called, her breath crystallising in the bitterly cold air.

'Look over there.'

'Yes I see them.'

A long line of helpers, led by the Reverend Christopher Kelly, battled against the elements. It made its way towards the farm. Everyone helped to pick up boxes and fodder and moved them nearer to the farmhouse. Sheep, goats, cows and two horses had come down from the hills. One hour later the job was done.

'Come inside and warm up before you set off back.' Farmer Smalley had all ready opened the door. They all gratefully accepted and gathered round the open fireplace, with its flames dancing up the chimney. The fire roared away when Mrs Smalley encouraged it with an iron poker.

'Thank God for the RAF, is all I can say,' Bob Whittam commented.

'How did you manage to get their help Vicar?'

'It's a case of who you know,' Reverend Kelly replied.

'That's a true saying, if ever there was one,' Bill Turner agreed.

Mrs Smalley produced a tray of mugs of steaming hot tea.

'No sugar I'm afraid.' She placed the mugs on to the kitchen table.

'Help yourselves.'

'We're all getting used to going without sugar,' Donald joined in the conversation.

'In fact now, I prefer unsweetened tea.'

A tray of scones appeared from the kitchen and were soon devoured.

'Well, thank you for your hospitality. We'd best be off and get on with the job.'

The Reverend Kelly headed outside and his party followed. Their arduous labours had produced results. They headed for the village. Donald's empty shelves in his shop would soon be filled.

'I can't thank you enough Reverend. I was getting worried about the stocks getting so low. It's taken a great weight off of my shoulders.'

The ribbon of meandering villagers finally filed into the shop, off loading their precious cargo. Reverend Kelly heaved a large parcel on to the counter.

'Goodness knows what's inside that.'

'Here I'll open it up and find out,' Donald offered.

He cut the restraining hessian sacking with a penknife and tins of condensed milk spilled out over the counter.

'You can't get a better sight than that Vicar.'
'You're right there.'
Mabel Whittam popped her head around the shop door.' You selling any of that?'
'Not until tomorrow Mabel. I have to make an inventory first. Then it will be on sale.'
'You and your inventories. Thanks Donald, I'll see you then.'
'I don't know how you managed it Vicar, but you have certainly saved this village and everyone of us should thank you.'
'I wouldn't want that. I'm only too pleased to have been able to help.'
'It was certainly our good fortune when you were sent here. Thank you Vicar.'

His job finished, he made his way slowly home exhausted, back to the vicarage through the pathways of compacted snow.

'Oh, look at you. Come and sit down. You look completely done in.' Margaret hastily made a cup of strong tea. 'No brandy I'm afraid.'
'Tea will be fine, God what a day.'
'Did the drop go off all right?'
'Yes, thank goodness. The villagers were fantastic. All the merchandise is in Donald's shop and apparently will be on sale in the morning. Any biscuits?'
'Sorry my love, they have all been eaten.'
'Ah well, I'll have a quick read of the Times and I think I'll get an early night.'
'I'm going upstairs now; don't be too long, '

Christopher thumbed through the newspaper. It was all bad news about the war.

This looks as though it's going to last longer than the Government had predicted.

He sighed and he folded the paper up and placed it on to his desk. Wearily he lifted himself out of his comfortable chair and made his way upstairs. He entered the bedroom, Margaret was sat up in bed reading.
'Interesting book?'
'It's one of the classics, Jane Eyre.'
'What a day!' Christopher climbed in the bed beside her.'
'Let's hope no one needs me during the night and I can get a full night's sleep.'
'The twins were pretty good to day and they were helpful too. I was wondering what it is they're wanting. They are as crafty as spiders catching a flies.'
There was silence and Margaret looked across to her husband, he was fast asleep.
With a sigh she closed her book and placed it on the side table and turned off the light. She lay her head on to a soft pillow, willing sleep to come. But, her brain refused to turn off.

Thank God the food supplies arrived in time. Marvellous how all the villagers came to help. Still it was in their interest I suppose. I wonder if Elizabeth will teach here in the village school when she finishes her training.

I hope Wolfgang is getting on at the Prisoner of War Camp. I have a feeling he and Elizabeth will re-kindle their friendship when the war is over. These two little angels of mine. I wonder whom they will meet when they grow up. Still there's plenty of time to think about that. I must remember to make the potato pie first thing in the morning...oh and the bread...and ....the ....

THIS IS THE BBC HOME SERVICE
AND HERE IS THE 9 OCLOCK NEWS
ON NOVEMBER 4TH 1942

MONTGOMERY LEADS THE BRITISH
TO VICTORY OVER ROMMEL AT EL
ALIMEIN,
FORCING AXIS TROOPS
TO RETREAT FROM NORTH AFRICA.

THAT IS THE END OF THE NEWS.

The POW's lived in close proximity and occasionally tempers were frayed. Most of the winter their main activity, which kept them moving was clearing pathways in the snow between the huts. They had their hobbies, there were letters to write, and thoughts often wandered to their fatherland and families back home. It was not unusual to talk about their chances of escaping from the camp.

'Gutten Morgen Rolf,' Kurt was trying to be cheerful

'Gutten Morgen.'

Wolfgang joined them.' Come on you two, try and keep to English, or the guards will think we're plotting an escape.'

'It's hard to remember.' Kurt replied slowly.

'You're doing well. You never know it may be an advantage if we're to escape.'

'Pigs might fly.'

'Let's go over to the reception area and get on with painting the woodwork.'

The three men pulled on their grey overcoats and made their way out into the adverse weather. They entered a large prefabricated building

'Welcome to our theatre.' Rolf gestured with a sweep of his hand.

'This is great'

'We're practising for a Christmas concert right now. Do you sing?'

'No not really.

'That's a pity. You could have joined the choir.'

'I'd empty the hall if I started to sing. I'm tone deaf.'

'How about being the back end of the donkey. We're still looking for one.'

'I bet you are. I don't fancy that much either. The front end may suffer with wind.'

'I know. I've just the job for you. Father Christmas.'

'Doesn't anyone want to do it?'

'No.'

'All right, I don't mind doing that.' Wolfgang said grudgingly.

'That's settled then.'

'Who comes to the show?'

'Mainly nearby farmers and their families. Here grab a paintbrush and help us finish off painting the door.'

Later in the day, disruption interrupted the daily running of the camp, when a convoy of lorries appeared at the gates. Prisoners filed out of their huts as the word spread, they were all inquisitive as to what they were doing there.

'What the devil do they want?'

'You don't think they're moving us.'

'I wouldn't be surprised at anything.'

'Nobody was expecting them that's for sure.'

Two guards slowly pulled open the heavy restraining gates and allowed the lorries into the compound. All the chatter ceased. The prisoners stood in silence, studying the goings on. The drivers jumped down out of their cabs and looked at the silent gathering. A Sergeant marched forward and directed them to the camp reception area.

Inside the building, Burt the lorry driver handed over the paper work to the Commander.

'Delivery from the Ministry of War Production sir.'

The lorry driver stepped forward and handed the

Commander the relevant paper work. He then read the information.

'Give the orders for the prisoners to help unload the buildings, Sergeant.'

'Very well sir.' He guided the workman back out into the square and gave the order.

'Gutten tag,' Rolf greeted the English men.

'Ere. Burt. What's this geezer on about?'

'Sorry mate, no idea. It's all-French to me.'

The men worked hard for most of the morning and the pre-cast buildings lay in separate piles within the compound

'Seems a funny time to be delivering sections of buildings when there's snow on the ground. We had difficulty getting through, most of the road are impassable.' One of the drivers spoke to the Sergeant.

'We have a big problem here. We don't have the room for all the extra prisoners. We've had a large influx lately, no where to put them.'

'Ah that will be the war.' He nodded and walked away.

Heavy tarpaulin lay over the backs of the lorries; Kurt and Wolfgang seized their opportunity. They vaulted up on to the lorry, behind the cab and under the cover, hoping that no prying eyes had seen them. They lay there, their hearts thumping, hardly daring to breathe.

'All right Burt, tell the others and let's get out of here. This place is giving me the willies.' Pete shouted and signalled with a wave of his arm. He climbed into his cab, slammed the door and started the engine.

'Nein sprechen,' whispered Wolfgang.

Slowly the lorries gathered speed as they trundled out of the compound and on to the spine road. They travelled for a time before the German prisoners carefully looked out from beneath the tarpaulin. The moors looked desolate, never more so than in mid winter. Low cloud had become a dense fog and the drivers had slowed down to suit the conditions

'Polizei?' Kurt asked.

'English Kurt. No, they've slowed down because the weather's closing in. When the lorry takes a bend in the road we'll jump. Ready, go.'

The two men rolled off of the lorry. They lay there breathing heavy, their hearts pumping like old steam engines, as the other lorries passed by.

'We're clear. Don't forget English from now on.'

Kurt nodded.' Which way do we go?'

'I've no idea. What I do know is they will be looking for us by now.'

'Which direction then.'

Wolfgang shrugged.' Your guess is as good as mine is.'

Kurt took a step forward and immediately fell down a large hole.

'Um himmelswillen.'

'English Kurt.'

'I nearly broke my ankle.'

'That's the least of our troubles. The fog is getting thicker, the snow is not helping and we don't know where we get our bearings. We're a right couple of escapees. I can't see if there are any landmarks, everything's white.'

'What are we going to do then?'

'Well as I see it, we have two choices. First we go off blindly-or we find a bit of shelter, until the fog lifts. What do you think?'

'No point in walking about aimlessly. Let's see if we can find somewhere to shelter.'

The two men walked on and they came upon a cluster of gorse bushes. It was here they decided to wait until the weather cleared enough for them to continue. They huddled together trying to keep warm. After dosing throughout the night, daylight brought no relief; the weather was still bad.

'See any landmarks?' Kurt asked.

'Nothing. It looks as though we had better make a move or we'll starve out here.'

'Which way then?'

'Look at the gorse bush, the way it's leaning. You can see which way is the prevailing wind and that usually comes from the seaward side. So an educated guess, I'd say that way would be south,' he pointed a nail bitten finger.

They made their way across the snow-laden moors, cold, hungry, and lost. No words were exchanged; each lost in their own private thoughts. In front of them was a slight incline, which they tackled very slowly.

'Halt, who goes there,' a voice shouted. A figure appeared out of the mist. A rifle pointed at them. They both raised their hands in a submissive gesture.

'You can't tell us where we are?'

'In the hands of the Home guard, matey.'

Their bid for freedom had come to an abrupt end. All they had to look forward to in the near future was a period of solitary confinement. Following a telephone call, the civilian police were the first to arrive.

'And how long have you been absent?'

'Two days.' Wolfgang replied.

'Ah, we have a German who speaks English. Wonders will never cease.'

They were housed in a small cell, until the camp soldiers arrived several hours later.

A patrol of guards arrived in the afternoon.

'Now what do we have here, a couple of prisoners who thought they knew better. You were warned when you first arrived. The moors are no place to be on, especially in the winter. Ah well, you'll be able to think about your errors when you're in solitary.' The guard helped the two prisoners into the waiting lorry.

'They never learn do they?'

'No, they think they know it all.'

'Ah well, it gave us an outing. Back to work.'

It was an uncomfortable ride back to the camp. They were wet, tired and hungry. Only the joshing of the guards kept them awake. The lorry slowed down as it travelled along the spine track leading to the camp.

'Open the gates, prisoners on board.' They came to a stop outside the Commandant's office.

'Right come on, let's have yer in line. Quick march; left, right, left right, left right.' They marched into the Commandant's office.

'Halt….Stand easy.'

'I see you decided to take no notice of my warning.' The prisoners stood in silence.

'Very well, solitary confinement for one week. Take them away sergeant.'

They were taken away to a special block. Each to separate cells. Doors slammed shut with a clunk-click as the bolts went into place.

All was quiet.

Why did we take a chance like that? Our minds must have been frozen - dumkoff, of course we knew better. The trouble is we never thought about it seriously. The moment just presented its self. And we were stupid enough to take it on. Now we'll have plenty of time to think – a whole week.

THIS IS THE BBC HOME SERVICE
AND HERE IS THE 9'OCLOCK NEWS
ON DECEMBER 1ST 1943

ECONOMIST WILLIAM BEVERIDGE
PRODUCES HIS REPORT ON
SOCIAL SECURITY.
THIS PROVIDES A BLUEPRINT
FOR THE WELFARE STATE

THAT IS THE END OF THE NEWS

The Red Lion, built in the mid seventeenth century, served as a meeting place for most of the villagers. Dark oak beams supported its low roof. There were two bars; the saloon was slightly smaller than the pubic bar. A door from the public bar opened to stairs leading to the living quarters and a large empty room, often used as a meeting place. A second door opened to a small cobbled yard where there was an outside toilet. A door at the rear of the bar opened into a kitchen. There was a trap door to the cellar.

Stylecroft buzzed with the news that there was going to be a Darts Match.

'Have you heard Margaret?'

'Heard what Mabel?'

'There's going to a competition for anyone who fancy theirs chances playing darts.'

'What ladies as well as men?'

'Yes, it's going to be 'Women versus Men.'

'How did you find about it?'

'Well, I heard in the shop yesterday.'

'Whose idea was it, do you know?

'I reckon it was Dick Robbins at the Red Lion.'

'I expect he's trying to drum up more trade.'

'I don't know about that. But all the men have decided to have a few practice nights to find the best players.'

'It should be fun. Let's find out if there are any other ladies that would be interested in entering a team.'

'Best, go to the Red Lion first and see what Dick Robbins has in mind.'

'I haven't been in a pub without Christopher, I'd better speak to him first.'

'I know one or two ladies in the village, who have husbands in the Forces, meet once a week for a get together.'

'Maybe we could join them. I'll mention that to Christopher when I speak to him. I'll do that today.'

'Good, if he thinks it's a good idea and I hope he will, perhaps we'll go this Friday, that's when the ladies meet.'

'We'll do that, leave it to me.'

Dick Robbins had pinned up a notice in the pub. 'DARTS MATCH, MEN v WOMEN'. Names on the list of all those interested. Six in a team. Handicaps to be decided by the organiser. Signed Dick Robbins.

The response to the notice was most encouraging and the match was arranged for the following Friday evening. It gave the team organisers six days to find their teams. Dick Robbins made sure that everyone had equal opportunities to practise.

The Match

The ladies entered the enemy's lair knowing that a good win on their first game would give much encouragement to the other lady players. With this in mind Margaret and Mabel were very focused and gave a great deal of encouragement to the Ladies Team.

Dick Robbins announced the match handicap.

'Ladies and Gentlemen, for this very special match 'Men versus Ladies'– I have decided that it will not be necessary for the ladies to start their games with a double.

So let play begin the first to the 'ockey' - Margaret and Eric.'

'Eric stop dancing about,' warned Dick.

'He's not troubling me,' said Margaret, 'does he need to go to the 'gents'?'

Margaret stood behind the white line on the floor, took careful aim and threw her first dart.

'Double top, 40 scored,' announced Dick.

Margaret's next two darts landed neatly into the twenties. There was a loud applause from all the spectators and players.

'I didn't know ladies could play darts, said Eric. 'Are you sure about the handicap Dick?'

'Stop whining,' said Dick. The play continued.

Double sixteen will give me the game.

Margaret's dart hit the double in the centre. 'I've done it.' She turned and shook hands with Eric.

The next game Bill Whittam was drawn to play Mabel Grimes. It took Bill some time to find his first double and Mabel only needed double one to win. The ladies called out 'Come on Mabel.' But Bill caught up with his opponent. He too required double one. There was a deathly hush. Followed by a big cheer from the men as Bill achieved the double first.

It was all square after the first two games. But, Jessie Lambert, the Postlady, excellent at getting envelopes through letterboxes, found darts a little more difficult and her opponent Bill Bentley showed no mercy.

Bill Turner had a close game with Mabel Whittam, but it was Bill who scored the final double to win his game.

Madge Cunningham, inspired by her team Captain and a glass of whisky from her husband surprising beat Donald Hodges noted for his skill with the darts.

The final score was 4 to the Men and 2 to the Ladies.

'Ladies and Gentlemen,' Dick Robbins called from behind the bar. 'The drinks are on the 'house'. Everyone cheered.

'One final announcement, said Dick Robbins 'The POW Camp are staging a Christmas Concert to which everyone, in the village, is invited – details will appear on various notice boards by the beginning of next week. So keep an eye out for them.'

THIS IS THE BBC HOME SERVICE

HERE IS THE NEWS ON THE 16TH MAY 1943

THE RAF 'DAMBUSTER' RAID
DESTROYS TWO DAMS IN THE RUHR.

THAT IS THE END OF THE NEWS

The Christmas concert began at 2.00. Low wooden forms lined up, row by row, filled the prefabricated building. Wolfgang, who was out of solitary confinement, had swapped his prisoner's uniform for Father Christmas's red costume. He nervously tugged at the bushy beard, which was tickling his nose and restricting his breathing.

I hope I can pull this off all right, I've not dealt with children before.

He looked around the decorated hall. A tall Christmas tree stood at one side of the stage covered in hand made coloured baubles and looped coloured paper-chains hung from the ceiling and looped around three walls.

The wooden doors were pushed open by a couple of the inmates to reveal a long line of waiting parents with their excited children – out in the cold winter weather.

Oh, I don't think I can do this.

The crowd surged forward and Santa Claus greeted the incoming visitors.

'Velcome, velcome.'

'Are you the real Father Christmas?'

Wolfgang looked down into a bespectacled pair of piercing eyes.

'Of course.'

'Where's your sleigh then?'

'Outside.'

'No.'

'No?'

'I already looked.'

Why did I volunteer for this?'

'Do you think it its stolen?' the boy asked.
'Oh no. Blitzen's probably gone for his tea!
'Reg, come along now. Sorry Santa, he's always asking questions.'
'Mum, what's going to happen?'
'Nothing yet pet. Sit still.'
'But mum, I need the lavvy.'

Wide-eyed children filled with expectancy of the young, sat on their coats beside their parents. Gradually the building filled to its capacity. People were standing at the back of the hall, crammed in like cattle in a holding-pen. The volume of chatter rose higher and higher.

The House Lights dimmed and conversations ceased. A figure dressed in black walked on to the middle of the stage and the audience cheered and clapped.

'Dank you ladies and gentlemen, dank you. Mine name is Kurt Fuhrmann and I'm your compere for this afternoon. I velcome you all to our Christmas Concert. To start off the proceedings, may I introduce you to our vonderful songsters The Fell Valkers. They did exactly that a few months ago, but the Home Guard soon brought them back.' He paused until the laughter and cheers had died away.

'So mine ladies and gentlemen – The Fell Walkers' Kurt walked backwards to the left of the stage.

Wolfgang chuckled to himself.

Good, Old Kurt's doing well, considering it's his first time on a stage.

The German male voices echoed around the hall. The harmonising singing then filled the building with carols in English and German. A single voice could be heard singing 'Oh Danny Boy' as he finish his rendering, the audience cheered, stomped their feet, whistled and clapped for several minutes. Kurt walked back on the stage.

'Dank you, dank you.' He held up his hands and all went quiet

'Now we have a real treat for you. Our recently formed band, who have been playing together for only a few months. Mine ladies and gentlemens our UMPA BAND.'

Vibrant, lively music echoed around the building, the audience and Father Christmas, clapping in time to the rhythm. As the music faded the applause from the audience continued for quite some time.

'You are too kind.' Kurt wandered back on stage.

'Now, I vant to introduce you to the serious side of our presentation this afternoon. At great expense, dancing the Swan Lake by Tychovski - the terrible two-some.'

Two of the POWs, dressed in tutus, twirled their way on to the stage. One wearing a black Hamburg hat and smoking a fat cigar, the other carrying a wand. Both were wearing heavy army boots.

The audience rocked with laughter at their antics as they tried to dance to the music. Gradually the music faded and the ballerinas rotated their way off stage to a thunderous applause. Kurt reappeared.

'Vee vill now have an interval.' There are refreshments at the back of the hall, dank you.'

The flap of the kitchen opened and the audience lined up; the sweet smell of confectionery filled the air.

'This is a treat. I don't think I have had any cakes since the war started.'

'What a surprise. I didn't expect this.'

'Can you pass me a cake before they all go.'

'Mum can I have another one?'

'Don't be greedy son.'

Once again the Hall lights dimmed. They made their way back to their seats. Kurt again moved to centre stage.

'Please give a varm velcome to our choir The Fell Valkers. He walked off stage as the choir broke into song. The deep voices of the choir harmonised to several well known carols. The compere walked on stage clapping along with the audience.

'Vonderful, vonderful, what do you think?' The audience cheered, whistled and clapped their appreciation.

'Next, vee have a group of dancers for you. They are accompanied by the mouth organs and yodelling.'

The dancers skipped on to the stage, formed a circle and twisted and turned to the sound of the harmonicas and yodelling. Father Christmas was watching too.

They must be fit to keep that up.

The audience, with a deafening applause once again, showed its support.

Kurt, back on stage, waited.

'Now for the last part of our Christmas Concert – 'Away in a Manger.'

Silence fell on the audience mesmerised by the male voice choir.

The voices of the 'Songsters' blended well. As they sung the last note they moved aside to reveal the stage set of the manger with Joseph and Mary in tattered clothes, looking down into the crib. The choir sung softly as Mary knelt beside basket tending to her baby. As the carol ended, the gap closed; the voices faded away. The audience was spell bound and Kurt once more walked back on stage to a thunderous applause.

'Thank you. It has been a pleasure for us too. Now we will finish with Stille Nacht'.

This time the choir sang in German. Their rich tones brought tears to many eyes as the music quietly faded into silence. There followed a standing ovation. Gradually the hall emptied. The villagers made their way home chatting about the wonderful concert.

'I thought that was just wonderful'

'That's what Christmas is all about.'

'The children enjoyed meeting Father Christmas.'

'Mum, can I have another cake?'

'No you can't. Go on with you or I'll box you ears for you!'

The doors, into the hall, were now closed and the inmates could relax. Some of the men sat on the stage their legs dangling and swinging them backwards forwards like children on a swing. Others sat on the forms at the front of the hall.

'How did you find dressing up as Father Christmas? Kurt asked.

'It was uncomfortable and hot.' Wolfgang replied.' The beard kept on itching my nose all the time.'

'That's all part of it. The children loved it.' Rolf joined in the conversation.

'I know. But I've not had any experience of children before this.'

'Vould you do it again then?

'Kurt I'm not really suited to it.'

'Ah, we didn't tell you but, if you've done it once, then you're expected to do it next year.'

'That's not fair, who made up that rule?'

'I just did.'

The whole group laughed at the banter.

'I've just been made a scapegoat.'

'Oh never mind. Let's just hope we wont still be here next year, said Rolf.

'You can say that again.'

'Oh never mind….' Raucous laughter was interrupted by the sound of the hooter for 'lights out'.

'That was my first Christmas in England.' Wolfgang said.

'Let's hope it will be your last.' Kurt answered.

'Amen to that.'

THIS IS THE BBC HOME SERVICE

HERE IS THE 9 O'CLOCK NEWS
ON JUNE 1ST 1943

BRITISH ACTOR LESLIE HOWARD DIES.
HIS PLANE WAS SHOT DOWN
BY THE GERMANS
OVER THE BAY OF BISCAY
ON ITS WAY TO BRISTOL FROM LISBON.
HE WILL BE REMEMBERED
FOR HIS PART AS ASHLEY WILKS
IN 'GONE WITH THE WIND'.

THAT IS THE END OF THE NEWS.

Gradually winter's icy fingers loosened her grip on the countryside. As the thaw took hold, lakes emerged from their frozen state, where the wild life returned and resumed their daily business of breeding and feeding.

Village life returned to normality. People catching up on any gossip they may have missed during the freezing weather. Mabel walked into the village shop.

'Morning Donald. Did you hear the radio this morning?' She didn't wait for his reply.

'Apparently, there's a housing shortage and that prefabricated houses are going into production

'I did.'

'And what about the Bevin Boys?'

'I didn't hear about that.'

'Some lads as young as fourteen, have gone down the mines. Labelled like parcels, as they wait to be collected on the stations.'

'I heard that and I think it's dreadful.' Mrs Smalley joined the group.

'Conscientious objectors were called Bevin Boys. Never heard they were young children though.'

'All our family crowded around the wireless of the up to date news. Nothing new though.' Margaret chipped in.

'Now what can I do for you ladies?'

'Oh I'd like the sugar ration please.' Mabel turned the leaves in her beige ration book and placed it open on to the counter. Donald cut the coupon out, weighed the meagre amount and tipped it into a brown paper bag.

'Anything else?'

'Not today thank you.' She placed the precious book into her shopping bag.

'Best not lose that. Or the fat would be in the fire.'
'It certainly would.'
'Mrs Smalley, what can I get you?'
'The 2oz butter ration please Mr. Hodges.' She passed her book to him and folded her arms under her breasts whilst she waited.
'There you are. Will there be anything else, dear lady?' He wrapped the small amount up in greaseproof paper, folding it neatly into a parcel before handing it over.
'No thank you.' She gathered up the paper bag and walked out of the shop.

'It's no use going to the shop for your newspaper,' Elizabeth called out to William who was trudging up Broad Street.
'They've sold out all ready, seems as though were soaking up the war news like blotting paper.'
'Thanks Elizabeth. You've saved me a journey.'
'You'll have to listen to the news on the wireless to hear how it's all progressing or you can pop into the pub.'
'I'll do that,' and with a wave William was off. Elizabeth pushed open the wooden gate and walked into the vicarage.
'Hello Mother, here's the shopping.' She placed the wicker basket on to the kitchen table and pulled out a bag of flour, small brown packet of sugar and a pat of butter.
'Good, I can get on now?'

Margaret proceeded with the job of baking for the family. She deftly mixed the flour with the butter. Then making a little well in the mixture, she poured a measured amount of water into it and brought the ingredients together to form a dough. Then with a floured wooden rolling pin, she started to roll the out the dough into a rough circle then which placed it on to a metal plate.

'Mother, I know you're a good cook. But how do you eke things out. I really don't know.' She was fascinated by her Mother's activities

'It just comes naturally. It will be the same for you when it's your turn.'

Margaret filled the well of the pastry with small pieces of streaky bacon and poured over two well-beaten eggs. She then cut another circle of pastry and placed it on top of the mixture, pressing firmly down on the edges. Next, she glazed the top of the pie with a little of the egg wash and placed it in the oven.

'There, that's for our dinner,' she brushed the flour from her hands. 'We're lucky to get fresh eggs from Mr Smalley.'

'How did you learn all about cooking Mother?'

'It was passed down from your grandma to me and I will give you all the hints and wrinkles.'

'Oh, I don't know if I could.'

'You'll see, I feel it in my old bones. You'll be able to cope.'

'You're not old Mother.'

'That's kind of you to say, but some times I feel really ancient.'

'You're not,' she gave her other a squeeze and they got on with the rest of the chores.

'Mother, can I ask you something?'

'Of course you can, what is it?'

'Well, did you have and qualms about marrying father?'

'No, never, I knew it was right.'

'That's how I feel about Wolfgang mother.'

'I 'm pleased you do. It makes me feel a lot better about the wedding.'

'I know we'll get a lot of animosity at first, but it should die down after a time, shouldn't it mother?'

'Don't fret darling. But there will be some who have lost husbands, sons and other loved ones, it will take years to accept any contact with the Germans.'

'I know. But our love is strong and will get us through these times I'm sure.'

'Both your father and I will give all the support we can..'

'I know, that's why I love you both very much.'

The Red Lion hadn't seen so many customers for a long time. The beer was getting low and Dick Robbins the proprietor decided to telephone the brewery.

'Hello, this is the Red Lion at Stylecroft. I'd like to put my regular order in please.'

'I'll put you on the waiting list sir.'

'Waiting List! But I'm running out.'

'Sir, we are all in the same position. It will be a few days.'

He had to accept the answer and wrote on a blackboard that from now on beer was to be rationed.

'It's not good enough Dick.' Bill Turner spoke to the proprietor. 'Cutting down on our beer.' Bill held up his half-supped mug.

'I've done the best I can. You'll just have to wait like every one else.'

'What with the war, now my beers to be rationed.'

'Oh, stop moaning Bill. You're getting on my nerves.'

Eric Denson wandered into the bar.

'See if you can cheer him up,' Dick indicated with his thumb.

'Now what's the trouble Bill?'

'My wireless has gone on the blink. I've not been able to hear any of my favourites, like 'Itma', 'Henry Hall's Guest Night', Worker's Playtime'. I'm right fed up.'

'It's probably one of the valves gone. I'll see what I can do.'

'Thanks Eric, I would appreciate that. Would you like another?'

Eric looked at his practically dead glass.

'Thanks. Two pints of beer please.' And placed the two jugs on to the counter.

'I'm restricting every customer to two pints only.' Dick declared.

'For how long?'

'Till the brewery delivers my order and not before.'

Bill walked back to the table, placed the two pints glasses of ale on to the wooden table and sat down.

'Want a fag?' Eric held out the green packet of Woodbines'

'Thanks.' Bill pulled out a cigarette from the silver-paper wrapping - pulled out his lighter from his pocket and struck the metal wheel with his thumb.

'Cor, I can do with that. I've had a stinker of a morning.' Eric took a deep drag of the cigarette, filling his lungs and made smoke rings as he expelled the air from his mouth.

'What's wrong then?'

'It's to do with the Home Guard.'

Eric dismissed the problem with a wave of his hand.

'Anyway you don't need to hear my troubles.' Bill took the hint and they mulled over the facts about the war and all its implications.

'What do you think about the war. Is it going to last?'

'I reckon it will Bill, a lot longer than they are estimating.'

'All our mates from the village; it makes you think if we'll ever see them again.'

'It makes my skin crawl when I hear about the camps and the all the gassings.'

'Come on, talk about something a little less morbid. I need cheering up, that's why I came here for a pint.' Eric said.

'Two more pints bartender.'

Dick filled the pint jugs with mild bitter and passed them over the counter.

'I'm going to have to restrict you all to two pints each until my delivery arrives.' Dick repeated the news about the restrictions.

'I dunno, food rationing, clothes rationing, sweet coupons, petrol coupons and now beer.' Complained Eric.

'If that's all you've to moan about, you can think yourself bloody lucky. What about the poor buggers in London. None stop bombing, homes destroyed, lives lost. You don't know you've been born.' Dick turned away.

'All right, you've made your point.' Eric picked up the drinks and walked back to his seat.

'Cor, Dick's a bit edgy today!'

'I think he's having a job with the Brewery order,' Bill said. 'I heard him earlier talking to someone.'

'He was talking sense though. We don't really know what this war is about here. If you think about it, we're hardly affected at all.'

'I was only saying that yesterday.' Agreed Bill.

'You take your garden space for instance. Here we've plenty of it to grow our vegetables to help out with the family food. The posters are right 'Dig for Victory'.

'In London, why most of them have only a yard, no garden. No where to dig.'

'You're right, we don't know how lucky we are.'

'I feel sorry for all those evacuee children, but I'm sure we could find them homes here in Stylecroft.'

'We've got the Germans in the P.O.W. camp a few miles away. I'd sooner have some poor kids staying here.

The wail of the Air Raid siren invaded the clear night air.

'Poor devils. Looks as though the docks at Barrow are in for another nights bombing.'

Bill stood outside the Red Lion and Eric joined him. The two of them stood watching the searchlights scanning the night sky. They could hear the aircraft, but could see nothing.

'Cut that light out!' Bill shouted.

'Sorry,' Eric rushed to close the door.

'You will if jerry sees it.'

By this time several villagers joined them all looking up towards the evening sky.

'Evening Reverend. I was just saying. It looks as though Barrow is being hit again. Makes your blood curdle.'

'God save them all.' Christopher stood watching along with the others.

'I wouldn't save the bastards who's dropping the bombs.' Eric's voice rose an octave higher.

'I know what you're saying Eric, but you must remember that most of the young pilots are indoctrinated by Hitler into all this mess.'

'All I know is my fellow workers are taking one hell of a hammering and for what? What have they done to deserve that?'

'All right Eric, we all know it isn't right. But there's nothing we can do to stop it.' Bill entered into the conversation.

'Calm down. There's enough grief going on now, without us having a go at each other.'

'Yes, come on, the pints are on me.' Christopher led them back into the pub.

'Drinks all round barman.' Christopher struck the bar with his fist.

'Bang goes all my resolve to limit you all to two pints.' Dick said.

The all clear siren sounded. You could feel the relief. It was back to their drinking and laughter.

Back at the vicarage, the Kelly's children were allowed out from their air-raid shelter underneath the stairs.

'Are we going to die Mother?' Rose whispered.

'Of course not. That's why we hide under the stairs to protect ourselves.'

'We think its fun.' Said the twins

Rose and Ruth read their comics until it was their bedtime. Christopher joined them.

'Sorry I'm late. I had to sort out a few things at the pub.'

'Of course you did darling,' a big grin spread over Margaret's face.

Once again the piercing sound of the air raid siren and Margaret called the girls downstairs to sleep under the stairs. She tucked them in and tried to comfort them as best she could. The drone of the oncoming aircraft stopped any conversation. They held their breath, listening intently.

'Are they Germans?'

'They're passing. They're going for the docks again poor devils. It's like London, where they are constantly targeted.' Christopher spoke quietly trying not to wake the girls.

'We can hear everything your saying.' Ruth called out.

'Yes, we're not asleep.'

'I might have known that. Go to sleep girls.'

'Can't. I keep dreaming the Germans are coming to get us.' Ruth chipped in.

'Don't fret we're all safe. Try and sleep good girls.'

'They won't sleep now. Come on girls let's play I spy,' Christopher suggested.

'Yes let's. I'll be first.' Rose offered. 'I spy with my little eye, something beginning with T.'

'Torch,' shouted Ruth excitedly; 'something beginning with B.'

The steady whine of the 'all clear' sounded and the children were ushered back under the stairs, just in case.

'Can we read?' Ruth shouted out.

'I don't think so young lady. It's way past your bedtime and you've school in the morning.' Christopher reminded them.

'But we're both wide awake.'

'Sleep.'

'It's not fair.'

'You don't want any pocket money this week?'

There was silence.

'I can see we're going to have trouble with them tonight.' Margaret said.

Christopher wandered out into the night and looked towards Barrow Docks. The trees were silhouetted against the red glow in the sky.

'No, they are the ones who have the trouble.' He nodded towards Barrow. Margaret joined him. They stood watching until the glow disappeared.

'Come on. It's depressing looking at their troubles.'

He turned to go in and grasped Margaret's hand and led her inside the house.

They settled down in the bed together, in each other's arms, talking over the day's events.

'How are you really feeling now Christopher? Any better?'

'Yes I'm all right,' he gave her a squeeze. 'You stop your worrying. It's in the hands of God, he'll look after us.'

'But I do worry. It's my nature, I can't alter it.'

'You'd take the whole world's worries. I think that's why I love you so much.'

They fell silent and they entered the world of sleep and dreams, where for once, all was peaceful.

THIS IS THE BBC HOME SERVICE
AND HERE IS THE 9 O'CLOCK NEWS
ON 17TH AUGUST 1943

THE U.S. AIR FORCE CONDUCTS
ITS FIRSTBOMBING MISSION
OVER EUROPE, MAKING AN ATTACK ON
RAIL COMMUNICATIONS AT ROUEN.

THAT IS THE END OF THE NEWS

'David' was to be secretly shipped out to France along with other agents, 'Peter' a gangling man, and 'Jack' who was short. At dusk, all three men climbed on board the 'Mutin' a sixty foot French Yawl.

'Bon jour Pierre.'

'Bon jour mon ami.'

'Peter, Jack.' David introduced the two agents.. They shook hands with the Skipper.

'We'll sail very shortly.'

'Isn't the tide too low?' asked Peter.

'No, she's wide on the beam and she'll draw nine foot six of water. That's why we use the moorings here in the Helford river.'

'Ah, I wondered why you used Devon for preference.'

As the men crept below decks, the boat silently slipped her moorings and glided towards the open sea making her way for southern France. Down below, a small hurricane lamp swung with the motion of the boat. Curtains were pulled across the narrow windows, cutting out any light. The diesel engine putt, putt, putt, putted its way towards the Brittany coast.

'It's a treacherous coastline,' Pierre said as he came below decks.

'It's not only the Germans, but the rugged rocks are a hazard too.'

'Do we pass St. Malo, Pierre? Jack asked.

'You make a joke, mon ami? Non, that's the Gestapo Headquarters. So we give them a wide berth. We're heading a little further south to Dinard. There's still the danger from the German patrol boats and sailing on a night with no moon light makes it even more dangerous, so everyone keep your fingers crossed, as you English say.'

He climbed back up the steep steps to the upper deck, then turned and looked back down through the hatchway.

'There's a beer in the ice-box.'

'Merci Pierre.'

To relax was impossible, nervous tension filled the cabin. The heat became almost unbearable. The men chatted about the dangerous mission ahead.

'Keep your voices low chaps, sound travels across the water.' Advised David

Peter was finding it difficult to get settled. His long legs hardly fitted under the table.

'Here, change seats with me, you'll be more comfortable. Those spindly legs of yours can stick out at the side,' said Jack. They stood up and shuffled round the table.

'Thanks mate.'

'I don't have any bother being only five foot eight inches. Did your mother put manure in your shoes when you were young?'

'She must have done. None of my parents are tall.'

Time passed slowly as the 'Mutin' drew closer to the French coast. Pierre looked through the hatchway.

'Nearly there, he whispered.'

'Synchronise your watches,' David instructed. They moved in unison.

'Three o'clock, five, four three, two, one.' The time was set.

'What are we waiting for? Jack whispered.

'A signal from the mainland.' Pierre answered.

Skilfully, skipper Pierre steered the Mutin as close to the land as he dared. On shore a white torchlight flashed.

'We're here, quietly does it.'

They climbed the rickety steps to the upper deck, taking in deep breaths of fresh air.

'Lower the dinghy, ' Pierre said quietly.

There was hardly any sound as it entered the water.

'Pete, Jack you get in first and I'll follow.'

'Bon voyage, David.'

'Merci beaucoup, mon ami.'

The three men pushed off away from the boat and paddled towards the shoreline. David looked back. The Mutin was all ready making her way back across the black English Channel. A white light flashed again, guiding them to the shore.

Thank God we've got some help

They lowered themselves into the cold sea, pulling the dinghy behind them as they came ashore.

'The potatoes are sweet,' a voice whispered from the darkness.

'Georges.'

The two men quickly shook hands.

'Best be quick, it's dangerous to be here too long. You can hide the boat in the pine trees.'

The three agents lifted up the dinghy and hurried towards the protection of the trees.

'Hop on board,' Georges held up the canvas cover at the rear of the truck.

The men piled in and sat amongst sacks of potatoes. The truck moved forward. It was only when they were away from the beach that Georges switched on the lorry's lights. They travelled over rough terrain for almost half an hour.

'Not much further,' Georges peered through the windscreen into the dark night.

'Madame Louise runs the safe house. You'll not see too much of her, as you will be housed in the cellar.'

The truck turned off of the road on to a dirt track and pulled up outside a stone farmhouse.

'Follow me.'

There were no lights anywhere. The saboteurs, carrying their equipment, filed after Georges. He stopped, bent down and pulled open two wooden doors set low against the wall.

'In you go,' Georges shone his torch down a steep flight of wooden steps. Then closed the doors behind him, then switched on the light of the cellar. The soft glow, of a low wattage bulb, lit the area. Three camp beds were placed side by side There was also a table and four chairs, a sink, and a gas ring and a single storm-lamp. In the far corner a flight of stairs led up to the farmhouse.

'I'll signal London that 'Dragonfly' is hovering. Then I'll see if I can find some food.' He picked up the storm-lamp, climbed the steps and disappeared into the farmhouse. He made his way to the barn and stables. He held out the lamp in front. Dark shadows were thrown across the stables. The horses became restless. Georges moved across towards a stacked pile of hay bales. He carefully pulled out the lower bale. It came away easily. There, hidden behind, was a wireless transmitter. Georges quickly attached the aerial, then the power lead to the battery. He turned the controls searching for the correct frequency on 353 Kc/s. The wireless-transmitter sprung to life. He signalled London, 'Dragonfly is hovering.'

'Now to find something for the lads to eat.'

'Not quite the Ritz,' Jack stated, looking around the cellar.

'Oh of course, you're used to that,' Peter grinned, showing a row of white teeth.

'And you would know what I'm used to?'

'Let's not go over the top fellahs,' David sensed an argument developing.

God that's all I need right now is for them to have a go at each other.

The cellar door creaked open and Georges elbowed his way through, carrying food supplies of fresh bread, chunks of mild cheese, home cured ham and several carafes of red wine. He kicked the door shut, negotiated the steps and placed the food on to the table. Then he pulled out four wineglasses from his pocket.

'Well done George. How can we help?'

'Let's fill the glasses first and then we'll talk business.'

'Right,' David opened up the map on the table and smoothed out the creases.

'We must disrupt the German troop movements in this area. Our mission is to blow up the railway line, here.'

'What about all the equipment you'll need?'

'We've brought that with us,' David patted a 'Helford' metal container in a bag behind him.

'We're going to blow the section of track between Dinan and Rennes.'

'When?'

'Tomorrow night.'

'I can take you to Dinan. But, then you'll have to find your own route. It's the best I can do. My permit does not allow me in the town. I'm sorry.'

'That's fine Georges.' David folded up the map.

'Who fancies a game of cards?'

'Come on then, anyone like to play nine card brag?'

The game carried on until late. Peter yawned.

'The red wine is having an effect. I'm off to bed.'

'Good idea, we all need the rest, hit the sacks lads.' David was the first to move.

'Bon nuit,' said Georges. He climbed the steps.

'See you in the morning.'

'Hey Georges, where do we pee?'

'Outside, but, don't forget the light.'

The men finally made themselves comfortable on the camp beds and turned out the light.

The following morning, Georges quietly came down the flight of steps carrying a large tray. He placed a large plate, filled with sweet smelling croissants, on to the table, followed by jam and cheese and a large coffee-pot, and four bowls. It could have been the smell of the coffee that roused Jack.

'Now I call this service,' he looked over his thick blanket and called out, 'Breakfast is served'.
'Speak softly. This is a working farm. We don't want to advertise you're all here.'
There were grunts of satisfaction from all of them.
'We'll be careful, Georges.'

The rest of the day they checked and re-checked their equipment in readiness for their assignment. Dusk fell. The SOE saboteurs, each carrying a bulky sack containing their charges and plastic explosives, climbed into the truck.
'Are you all right in the back?' Georges nervously glanced over his shoulder.
'We've all got our bucket and spades,' Jack said with a wide grin.

How can they joke when they're carrying explosives?

'Yer, we'll soon be building sand castles,' Peter joined in.

Les Anglais!

Stars twinkled in the night sky as they reached the outskirts of Dinan.
'It's up to you. Bon chance. I'll be waiting!'

The agents jumped down carrying their sacks as the truck rolled to a stop. They silently slipped down an embankment into a ditch. David signalled for Peter and Jack to follow him. They walked easily in the moonlight. After several minutes they approached the railway line.

'Jack take your position here.'

'Peter, that's your post. I'll go further back along the track.'

David reached the spot he considered suitable. He squatted alongside the rail. He slid the sack off of his shoulder and placed it on to the ground. He delved inside it, pulled out the charges and attached the thin wire to the explosives. He then fixed the devices to the railway line. Working with the deftness of a surgeon, he checked and re-checked. Satisfied his work was finished he started to re-trace his steps back up the line.

A huge explosion rocked the area. David felt pain in his back and fell unconscious to the ground. Peter and Jack came running to find out what had happened.

'What the bloody hell do we do now?'

'We'll get him back to the truck. Georges will know what to do,' Peter said.

They carried David, stopping occasionally to take breath. David groaned as he drifted in and out of consciousness. At last, the truck could be seen in the gloom ahead.

'What's happened?' Georges asked.

'Timing delay fault maybe- who knows.'

'Put him in the back,' Georges held the canvas aside

for them and then he climbed in after them to take a look at David.

'Don't worry we'll sort him out.'

He started the truck and they moved off.

'Was it a success?' Peter and Jack looked at one another.

'Those bastards won't be moving any more troops along that line,' Peter confirmed. It was a silent journey back to base nobody spoke. There was only an occasional groan from David.

'Sans histoire,' Georges said, with some relief showing in his tired face, as the truck entered the farmhouse. Peter and Jack carried David into the cellar, while Georges made contact with a vet he knew. After the telephone call he walked out to the barn and pulled out the hidden transmitter and signalled

'One of dragonfly's wing is broken'. London would understand, the short and to the point message. Georges was well aware that the Germans would be listening out for coded messages, but it couldn't be helped, this was an emergency.

A car drew up outside and voices could be heard. Peter and Jack waited with some apprehension. The door of the cellar swung open, Georges and another man stood at the top of the stairs.

'You had us worried there,' Jack said.

'This is a friend of mine; no names. He's come to look at our wounded colleague.'

David lay face down on the camp bed, groaned with pain, his breathing shallow. The man lent over him and cut his shirt away to reveal the bloody mess.

'You've not been too careful,' the man observed.

'He's the most careful person I know,' Jack jumped to his friends defence.

The medic cleaned up the wounded area of David's back peppered with metal and stones with great care he removed the debris. He made a fuller examination, checking from head to toe, making sure David was comfortable, then packed away his instruments.

'In a few days, he should be on his feet.'

'Merci mon ami.'

'Yes, thank you very much,' Peter said.

A few handshakes later, his friend left as the sun was rising.

There was a crackle from the transmitter and a coded message was received. Georges acknowledged the communication, pushed the transmitter back into its hiding place and headed towards the cellar.

'The boat will arrive tonight.'

'But what about David? He can't travel yet.'

'It'll be all right Jack. Don't worry. David will follow in a couple of day's time. Congratulations come from London.' Peter and Jack spent the day with David. When evening's twilight came they were taken back to the truck.

'Safe journey.' David said.

'See you in London and don't get into any more trouble.'

'I won't. Don't worry.' David winced as he moved.

They retrieved their hidden boat and waited. Out of the darkness flashed a single beam of a red torchlight.

'Ah, they're here,' Georges signalled back with a white beam.

'Thank you Georges. Without you we couldn't have done it.'

A quick shake of their hands, Peter and Jack lifted up the rubber dinghy into the waves and silently paddled their way towards the waiting boat.

'Bon chance.'

David drifted back into consciousness and was aware of a female form beside him.

'Merci beaucoup Mademoiselle,' he murmured.

She turned and the bluest of blue eyes stared back at him. She closed the door quietly. David drifted back into a drugged sleep.

'Bon jour mon ami.' Georges appeared with a hearty breakfast for the invalid.

'Bon jour Georges. Did they make it back all right?'

'They did. I had confirmation earlier.'

'That's a relief.'

'Now, you've to concentrate on getting better.'

'I'm starving.'

'That's a good sign. Here's your breakfast.' He placed a tray on his lap.

'What is this, Milk?'

'Oui. You're convalescing now, remember mon ami, no more wine for a while.'

'But, that's sacrilege.'

'You are going to be a good patient aren't you?'

'Of course I'll behave. What are the plans for my return?'

'In three days, Pierre will return with the 'Mutin' to pick you up. So now you comply with my instructions and rest. There's a pile of books there for you beside your bed. Now I must be off and go to work.'

'Merci Georges.'

Three days later they were waiting on the beach for the signal. It soon came.

'There you are, you're on your way.'

'Thank you my dear friend.' After two bear hugs they shook hands. The red light signal stopped and a rowing boat came towards them.

'Quick as you can.' Advised the rower.

Georges helped David into boat.

'Au revoir.'

'Bon voyage mon ami.'

George waded back to the shore, turned and watched the two men blend into the darkness of the night.

'Bon chance,' he whispered.

Gradually the dingy made its way to the Mutin. On board, Captain Pierre waited for the boat to draw along side.

'Give me your hand ami.' David was helped on board.

'Rest down below decks.' Pierre advised. David carefully negotiated the steep steps and then gratefully sank onto the bed.

'You look all in David. Sleep till we reach the Helford river.'

David gratefully accepted the advice and let his eyelids close and sleep came easily.

THIS IS THE BBC HOME SERVICE
AND HERE IS THE 9 0'CLOCK NEWS

ON DECEMBER 2ND 1943

THE FIRST BEVAN BOYS
DRAWN FROM YOUNG MEN
CALLED UP FOR THE ARMED FORCES
GO DOWN BRITISH MINES

THAT IS THE END OF THE NEWS

The Reverend Kelly held his sermon at arm's length, he was finding it hard to read lately.

Mnn. I'll have to get myself some glasses soon.

He re-placed the papers on to his desk, gingerly pulled himself out of his comfortable chair, picked up the papers, tucked them under his arm and made his way to the vestry. He looked around the door into the body of the church. Parishioners were sitting in the pews, quietly talking to one another. He pulled his cassock closer to him, then took a deep breath and strode towards his place next to the choirmen and boys.

'Hymn number 264.'

Every one stood up in unison. The organ began to play the introduction then the congregation raised their voices in adoration. After the prayers and a reading from the bible a second hymn was sung. The vicar kneeled in prayer, then made his way to the pulpit. When the hymn finished the vicar gave his blessing and the congregation sat down, some shuffled and coughed. When all was quiet, the Reverend Kelly gave his sermon on forgiveness.

He then read out the names of all his parishioners who had been killed during the war; those who were injured and in hospitals and those who were still serving in the different theatres of war.

There were a few members of the congregation reaching for their handkerchiefs. The vicar announced the number of the final hymn. When the last notes of the organ vibrated around the church. The Reverend Kelly made his way along the aisle to the great oak doors. Here he stood to shake hands with his congregation.

'Thank you so much for coming,' his words were said with feeling.

'Reverend.'

'Yes Mrs Walton.'

'I can't say that I agree with all of this forgiveness lark. It's all bunkum if you ask me. Look at what the Germans have done. All the heart ache, all the deaths.' She stood looking at him, staring.

'I know that Mrs Walton, but we have to find it in our hearts to forgive. There's goodness in all of us. Don't you agree?'

'I don't see it as you do Vicar. Look at that German you had at the vicarage. Ugh, it makes me shudder.'

'But he is a good man, Mrs Walton; look how he did jobs around the village. Even for you. I understand he came to fix your fence for you and received no payment for his work,' he reminded her.

'Only because he had to hide his identity,' she snapped back.

'Well Mrs Walton I must say my goodbyes to the rest of the congregation.' He passed by her and continued shaking hands and making a few comments to those remaining.

'Not everyone looks at the situation in the same way, you know.'

Mabel stood talking to him, trying to raise his spirits.

'I know, but when you have to fight that attitude as well as the war, it's not easy you know.'

'There now, that went fairly well, don't you think?' Margaret joined them and put her arm through his.

'I'm not sure about Mrs Walton's views. She was quite adamant, especially about Wolfgang and the way we were all deceived.'

'But surely that's what it's all about. People behave differently because of their circumstances. We would have reacted in the same way, had it been us. There's good and bad in all of us. You know that.'

'Yes you're right,' he patted her hand and they strolled towards the vicarage.

'You know, you're my rock and I really don't know what I would do without you.'

She smiled and squeezed his arm. 'Come on silly. Let's put the kettle on for a cup of tea.' Christopher sat down heavily at the kitchen table, while Margaret was busy making their drinks.

'How could Elizabeth and Wolfgang make any sort of life together, when there's so much animosity around?'

'Not everyone's the same Christopher. It will get easier after the war. Who knows, we have to be there for them and give support when needed.'

'But how would they cope? That's what worries me.'

'They have each other. If their love is strong enough they will survive anything. Remember when we first got together.

'I know what your saying is true. But I still worry for them.'

'Of course you do. You're a loving parent.' She put her arm around his shoulders and kissed the top of his head. 'Is that a bald spot I can see?'

'Don't be cheeky.'

The slam of the front door called a halt to their conversation, as the twins burst into the kitchen.

'What's for lunch, we're starving.'

'See what I mean. You'd miss all that,' Margaret smiled at her husband.

'What would you miss?' Ruth asked.

'You my darling, you.'

'What about me?' Rose said.

'And you too my love.'

'Can I have some money?'

'Ruth, you had some last week.'

'I've spent that Father.'

'On what?'

'Comics.'

'Can't you pool your monies, it would go further.'

'But, Rose reads different ones from me.'

'Ah! All right. What jobs have you done?'

'Well, I took old Mrs Watson across the road.'

'But, she didn't want to cross.' Rose chipped in.

'Have they been helpful to you mother?'

'They helped me make fairy cakes the other day.'

'And, we tidied up.' Ruth reminded her.

Christopher put his hand into his pocket. 'There we are 2d for you, and 2d for you.' He placed the coins into their eager hands.

'And what are your going to buy young lady?'

'*Rainbow*, Father.'

'And what about Ruth?'

'*Radio Fun*, Father.'

'So Rose you'll have one penny change to go into your piggy-bank.'

'Yes, Father.'

'Good, you're a lot luckier than many children.'

'Yes father we know. Thank you.'

'You spoil them too much.' Margaret said.

'Maybe, but they're only young once.'

'They should be saving part of their pocket money.'

'But Margaret they're so young to worry about that sort of thing.'

'They're not that young to learn about money matters. I always had to save half and could spend the rest when I was a child.'

'Ah yes that was back in the year dot.'

'You cheeky thing, just because I'm a few years older.'

'Ah well, there you go, a wiser head on your shoulders I'm sure.'

'Are you trying to wriggle out of a situation?'

'Yes. I would like my dinner cooked for me.'

'You're very shrewd.'

'I love the smell of the kitchen when you're cooking.'

'You're changing the subject Christopher.'

'Of course I am. Have you ever known me to win an argument with you?'

'We never argue, I'm always right.'

'Well, there you are then. Women always come out on top.'

'I agree.'

THIS IS THE BBC HOME SERVICE
AND HERE IS THE 9 O'CLOCKNEWS
ON JUNE 6TH 1944

START OF OPERATION OVERLORD
SEVEN ALLIED DIVISIONS
TWO AIRBOURNE
LAND ON NORMANDY COAST

.

THAT IS THE END OF THE NEWS

The next morning the Kelly family had a letter delivered by Jessie Lambert, the post lady.

'Morning all,' She delved into her satchel. 'You're popular today.'

'Thanks. How are you?' Margaret asked.

'Oh fair to middling.'

'Let's hope the weather holds until you finish your round.'

'I hope so.' And with a cheery wave went on her way.

Margaret gave the post to Christopher.

'Oh that's sick.'

'What's the matter?'

'Read that.'

The piece of paper was folded into four. Margaret read. *We want no Nazi's here!* there was no signature.

'That's awful. What a horrid thing to do. Why has some one written that?'

'It's prejudice. They're bigots. Tear it up.'

'But it must be someone in the village.'

'Pay no mind to it.'

'I don't like it at all.'

'Give it to me. I'll tear it up.'

'Who in the village would write that.' She waved the letter in the air.

'Don't get upset about it my love. Sit down and we'll talk about it.'

'But who would feel that passionate about it to send us this?'

'I haven't got the answers, Margaret. No one will own up to it.'

'Oh my God, Elizabeth.'

'What about her?'

'We mustn't tell her about this.'

'Do you think it wise to keep it a secret?'

'Christopher, I don't want her to know that someone in the village thinks that way.'

'She knows there's animosity here. Parishioners have relatives in the war. Stylecroft isn't affected by it as much as London. In places it's reduced to rubble, people killed in their own houses. Here, we have ridden out the war in relative calm, with only an occasional air raid when they are going for the docks. Then there's the separation of the children from their parents. Ours haven't had to endure that.'

'I know we've been so lucky here. That's why I find it so hard to understand why there's such feeling's here in the village.'

'Perhaps they have family who are suffering, or have a family member who has been killed. There's many reasons Margaret.'

'I know, but I still feel sick that there's that level of emotion here, to warrant that.'

'Tear it up Margaret. Forget it ever came. It's for the best, you know it is.'

She nodded and slowly ripped the letter into tiny fragmented pieces.

I wonder who it was? It makes me feel so insecure. It could be anyone. I do wish they would face us and tell us about their feelings. I suppose you don't know who it is. They don't have the courage to come forward and face us. Margaret threw the torn letter into the Aga its flames greedily engulfed the paper.

Christopher was right, evil-minded people.

She wiped her fingers down her apron several times as though the paper had contaminated her hands.

I'll have a word with Mabel. May be she'd have a suggestion as to who it is

Margaret's opportunity came when she visited the corner-shop for a few supplies.

'Hello Mabel, Donald. Everything all right?' She joined the queue.

'Good morning dear lady.'

'Are you in a hurry Mabel; only I'd like to talk something over with you.'

'Yes, All right, I've not got anything planned.'

'Now dear lady, what can I get you today?'

'I've run out of matches, Donald.'

'There you are, can't have you going without a box of matches can we?'

Margaret took the box

'Sorry I've nothing smaller.'

'Not to worry I've plenty of small change.'

'Thank you Donald.'

The two friends walked out of the shop.

'Now Margaret, what's the problem?'

'Well,' she looked around her making sure that no one was within hearing distance. 'This morning, with the post, we had an anonymous letter.'

'What did it say?'

'Well it simply said – '*We want no Nazis here.*' Who on Earth could have sent it?'

'Oh how awful. Especially with Elizabeth's relationship with Wolfgang.'

'I know. David said destroy the letter forget it.'

'But who do you think would send a letter like that?'

'Well, I said to David, we'll have to keep it quiet and not tell Elizabeth. Can you imagine how it would upset her, I wondered if you might have an idea.'

Mabel thought carefully. 'I'm sorry I don't know what to say. Best do what Christopher suggests, tear it up. Burn it.'

'I all ready have. But, I can't stop thinking about it.

''Just forget it. Put it out of your mind. Busy yourself with other things. We'll laugh at it all – later on.' Mabel tucked her arm into Margaret's.

'Come on, let it go. Don't waste your time on bigots.'

'Yes, you're right. I won't let them spoil my day.'

THIS IS THE BBC HOME SERVICE
AND HERE IS THE 9 O' CLOCK NEWS
ON THE 16TH JUNE 1944
THE FIRST V1 FLYING BOMB HITS BRITAIN

THAT IS THE END OF THE NEWS

Colonel Buckmaster head of the Southern S.O.E. was at their headquarters in Baker Street London. He pressed the button on his desk to summons his secretary. She walked in carrying her pencil and pad.

'Vera. I want you to contact our agent 'David'. I've a special mission for him. As soon as he arrives, I'll see him.'

'Yes sir. All being well, he should be here within the hour.'

David arrived. Colonel Buckmaster wasted no time. 'I've a tricky assignment for you. I think that you're the one to do it.'

'Sounds ominous. What is it?'

'Several radio operators have been captured and are now being held in the Chateau Blois, on the outskirts of Lyons. We need to get them out before the Gestapo get their hands on them. Your contact there will be Marcel. Vera will give you all the documents you'll need. Good luck.'

David walked to the outer office where Vera was sat at her desk typing.

'I believe you have some documents for me?'

Vera reached into the lower drawer of her desk and pulled out a brown envelope.

'There you are David. I hope it's a complete success'.

'Thanks Vera.' He pocketed the papers. He left the office and trundled down the wide staircase, out into the brilliant afternoon sunshine.

The Lysander stood waiting with it's propellers slowly

turning over. David, kitted out in a leather flying suit walked calmly towards it.

'Ready sir?'

'Let's go.'

The operations room gave permission for the take off. It was a clear night and visibility was good.

'It will only take around two hours sir,' said the flight engineer.

'Thank you.'

'Have you flown in a Lysander before sir?'

'Oh yes. But I never get used to it.'

'I don't think any of us do if we're honest. My guts are always twisted in a knot.'

David sat back closed his eyes and tried to relax, by breathing in deeply.

The fields were a vibrant green as they wandered along the towpath, hand in hand. Mayflies danced on the calm water while silver winged dragonflies dipped their way along the bank of the river. Other people had taken advantage of the warm spring weather. People sat with picnic hampers and children were chasing one another, screaming as they passed by.

'Margaret, let's hire a rowing boat,' Christopher suggested.

'Oh that'll be fun.'

They paid for the boat hire and walked on to the pontoon. Christopher untied the mooring rope and clambered in, holding on to the jetty.

'Climb in it's safe.'

'But it's bobbing about.'

'Come on trust me.'

Margaret gingerly put one foot into the boat. As she did so, a motor launch passed by, creating a large wake, it snatched the pontoon from Christopher grasp, causing the rowing boat to separate from its moorings, with Margaret astride the two.

'Help! Christopher.'

As if in slow motion she fell backwards into the Thames.

Christopher rowed with only one oar, going round and around in a circle, laughing so much, that tears ran down his cheeks.

'You pig, wait till I get out of this.' *She was furious her best clothes were ruined.*

People on the bank gave her a hand to climb out and she sat down on the grass drenched.

Laughing, Christopher came alongside of the pontoon, climbed out of the boat and secured it to a pole. He turned as Margaret ran into his arms.

'You stinker.' She beat his chest with her fists.

'Don't set me off laughing again.'

'Sir we're over France.' The engineer shook David's shoulder. 'Beat's me how you can sleep.'

'Practice laddy, practice.'

The pilot consulted his map and banked his aircraft to the right, searching for the coded letter. Far below a white beam sliced through the darkness signalling the correct code letter. He banked around again, losing height rapidly, guiding the plane down safely between red flashlights

'Tell the Captain, I'll be here in three night's time. Thanks for a safe journey.' He grinned, showing a row of white teeth, lent over and picked up his rucksack and jumped down on to the hard ground.

'Good luck,' the engineer's voice was lost in the noise of the accelerating engine.

'David you've heard then.' Marcel greeted him with a handshake.

'What happened exactly?'

'I can't pin anything down. It all went wrong two days ago. There must be a mole within the group. They were captured all at the same time. It was as though the Germans had specific information.'

'Any idea who this mole might be?'

'No.'

'How did you find out?'

'I had signalled each of them. But there were no replies from any of them. It was a messenger from the Free French who came to see me and told me of the arrests. How he found out I've no idea.'

'One arrest could be viewed as normal, but all four? No. That's too much of a coincidence. You'll have to investigate further.'

'It's all ready under way, mon ami.'

'Good man. I knew we could rely on you. You'll signal London with your findings, yes?'

'Of course. That goes without saying David.' They went into the barn and Marcel pulled away a few boxes on the shelf to reveal the transmitter. He switched on the power and the set burst into life. He sent a coded signal to London. *Can find no connection this end. Message ends.*

The 'safe house' was in darkness. Marcel unlocked the door and cautiously entered.

'The owners are away, but they know we will be using the premises.'

'It's very generous of them, considering the probable trouble they could be in, if we're caught.' Marcel pulled the heavy curtains together, before he lit the kerosene lamp.

'We have to be on our guard more than usual mon ami. We don't know what the Germans have learned from our operators. All I have discovered, from certain quarters, is that they are being held in the Chateau Blois.'

'Right, this evening we will reconnoitre the area. We need to know how many guards, and their routine tour of duties. Also where the prisoners are housed.'

'Do you think we can do that David?'

'We'll do our damdest Marcel. Buckmaster's orders are 'get them out.' Do you know the Chateau at all?'

'I've been there once, many years ago.'

'Right, jot it all down on paper, anything you can remember.'

Later, the two men sat down and enjoyed a meal. Then Marcel packed chicken, cheese, bread and a flagon of red wine for their journey. After making sure that the farmhouse was securely locked, they climbed onboard the lorry and headed towards the Chateau. Their journey had lasted for just over an hour, when Marcel pulled off the road on to a rough track hidden by trees.

'The Mansion is about a mile away. My men will be here tomorrow night.'

'Good. But how many?'
' Four. That's all I could muster.'
'That's fine. The Germans won't know what hit them. I will find out the exact drill movements of the guards.'

They settled down and tried to get a few hours sleep. It was scarcely daylight when they made their way to where the prisoners were being held. They came to a stop at the edge of the wood and surveyed the area.

Chateau Blois stood in its own grounds. Its grey square stone building with high turrets and drawbridge made it look impregnable.

'Is there a way out at the back?' David whispered.
'Yes.'

Marcel pulled a piece of paper from his pocket and smoothed out the creases. 'Here, to the left, there are two floors, with three separate windows on each floor; to the right of the building the same layout.'

'Where exactly are the stairs to the upper floor?' David poured over the map.

'Opposite the front entrance.'
'Right. The Kitchen?'
'To the back of the Chateau.'
'Look! The guards are changing,' David pointed out.
'That makes a change every four hours.'
'Looks like it. I reckon they'll keep the prisoners upstairs; easier to guard them.'
'I agree mon ami. I think there must be six guards to give round the clock protection.'

It was about 10 o'clock when a white bread van pulled up out side Chateau. The driver jumped out of the vehicle, went around the back, opened the doors and stretched out his arms inside the van and pulled out an armful of baguettes. He took them into the castle. Then he returned to the van and drove off.

'What time are your men arriving?' David asked.

'Tomorrow, first light.'

They kept their vigil for the rest of the day, carefully monitoring the change in personnel on guard duty. When evening came they withdrew and opened a bottle of red wine and shared a cooked chicken.

'Who said only the rich eat well?' Marcel asked.

'I don't know, but I've got to go for a pee.' David elbowed his way deeper into the wood.

The first rays of dawn filtered through into the morning sky. David was already awake. Marcel stirred.

'You're up early,' he spoke leaning up on one elbow.

'Nerves I think.'

'You! You have none.'

Marcel struggled out of his sleeping bag and produced a bag of bread rolls.

'Quiet! I thought I heard something.'

'That will be our men.' As he spoke four men appeared from the trees.

'Bon Jour.'

'Bon jour mes amis.'

They all squatted down and David smoothed Marcel's sketch map on the ground.

'Now we go at 10 o'clock.'

'Why 10 o'clock?' Marcel asked, mystified.

'La boulangerie – the breadman delivers then. We use the van for cover when he's just going in. It's the only time the guards will be distracted. We think there are six guards in all. I want one person sat at the wheel of the van, with the engine running. The others make your way in, find the prisoners and bring them out to the van. Any questions?'

There was silence.

'Right, all we do now is to wait for the bread to be delivered.'

The men lay dozing as they waited. As the rising sun rose announcing the dawn long shadows were thrown across the lawn.

'It must be nearly time,' Marcel said.

'Almost ten,' David confirmed.

'Good all this waiting about, is doing me in.'

There was no sign of the bread van.

'What's the time now?'

'Nearly ten past, he's late damn it.'

'I can hear an engine,' a voice whispered behind them.

The Maquis agents stood ready.

'Are you sure it will work?' Marcel asked.

'Not a good question to ask now,' David replied.

The baker's van came into view. The guards on duty made a perfunctory check on the vehicle. It drew up slowly, then proceeded to reverse. After finishing the manoeuvre, the driver climbed out of the van.

'That's a piece of luck, saves us doing it,' Marcel whispered.

The driver disappeared inside vehicle and brought out an armful of baguettes and walked into the building.

'Now!' David said with urgency. The agents charged

at the van and quickly climbed the steps into the castle. The guards were dealt with silently. Once in the hallway, two other German soldiers, watching the driver delivering his bread, turned too late, the Maquis overpowered and despatched them.

David crept up the broad stairway and along the balustrade opening each door as he made his way along. The third door was locked. He signalled to his companion to stand at the other side of the door. With his size 13 boot he forced the door open and charged into the room.

Three soldiers were sitting at table playing cards. They reached for their guns but too late. They were shot. Their bodies fell on to their cards soaking the red stains up like blotting paper.

The four prisoners in the bedroom were tied securely to iron bedsteads David stepped forward putting his finger to his lips. They were untied and he signalled for them to follow. They moved, as silently as they could, towards the stairs.

In the hall-way, the Marquis held the baker at gunpoint.

'Now what are we to do with you?' David asked thoughtfully.

'I'll come with you.'

'No. It's safer to leave you here, for your own sake. Sorry old chap.'

The baker never saw the butt of the gun striking the back of his skull.

'Into the van,' David directed.

One after the other they piled into the vehicle.

'Let's go.'

The van's clutch was let out too quickly and the vehicle stalled.

'Have you driven one of these before?' Marcel's head appeared between David and the driver.

'No.'

' Let the clutch out slowly this time.' Marcel advised.

Gradually the kangaroo petrol ceased, as the driver handled the van with a gentler foot. They turned left out of the drive and on to the road, heading for Lyons. Only a kilometre into their journey they could see, ahead of them, the staff car of the Gestapo followed by a lorry. As they drew nearer, the driver waved them down.

Of all the bloody luck, thought David.

'Quiet. Gestapo.'

The driver walked across the road to them.

'Das brot bitter. Das brot bitter,' pointing at the baguette painted on the side of the van. The substitute baker held up one finger.

'Nein.'

Two fingers.

'Nein.'

Three fingers. A smile spread over the German's face. Marcel placed three baguettes into the hands of his companion, who turned and handed them through the lowered window. The soldier turned and walked away and the German staff car slowly moved away.

'Halt.'

What now! David's heart lurched.

'Funf, Funf,' He held up five fingers.

Marcel placed the two extra baguettes into the driver's

hands. The van edged forwards and left the Gestapo with what could have been their breakfast.

'We'll have to get off the road quickly. They'll be on our trail in no time.'

The rough terrain made the journey longer than they had anticipated.

'Let's dump the van and separate. We'll go back to the safe-house by foot.' There were hand shakes all round. The freed prisoners headed north, the four free Frenchmen to the south, David and Marcel – west.

'I'll signal London the good news.' Marcel pulled open the cupboard door and tapped his message out in Morse code. 'Four pigeons fly free.'

The party that night was one of celebration, four Frenchman had been snatched from the under the Gestapo's noses.

'I wonder what excuses the Gestapo made to their Commandant,' ventured David.

'Mon dieu. The poor men were outwitted by higher intelligence.'

'I don't think they would say exactly that Marcel.'

'Probably not. Are your plans all ready set for your trip back to Engaland?'

'Yes, the Lysander will be here tomorrow, just two hours before the pick up. I have arranged for three of the French agents to be at the field to guide in the Lysander.'

'Come David, its time.' Advised Marcel.

They went out into the night, clambered on to the footplate of the waiting lorry and scrambled along to the side of the driver.

'It won't take long mon ami and we'll soon have you homeward bound.'

'Thanks to you and your men it has been a successful mission.'

The lorry came to a halt. Marcel and David jumped out of the vehicle.

'We wait now until we hear the aircraft.' Marcel said.

'What about the others?'

'They're there. They will show themselves at the right time. Don't worry.'

The two men sat on their haunches, waiting. The engines of an aircraft could be heard.

'Here we go.'

Marcel stood up and flashed out a white signal. Three red lights beamed up the points of a triangle. The throbbing engines grew much louder as the rescue plane came out of the night sky and flew into land. Then, without warning shots were heard and the guttural voices of Germans shouting.

David felt a push in the middle of his back – 'Go, run, run'. David took one glance at his friend.

'Go!'

David weaving, ducking rapidly made his way to the Lysander. Two pairs of hands grabbed and pulled him into the moving plane. The Lysander within seconds was airborne. David fought to regain his breath.

'What's happened to the others?'

'Sorry old boy. Following orders.'

David peered out of the window, but could see only darkness.

I guess I'll find out later what happened to them all.
He sat back and tried to relax.

Only a few short hours and I'll be back with Margaret and the family. Goodness only knows what they would say if they ever they find out what I've been involved in.

Snores filled the fuselage. 'Thank the Lord I don't have to sleep with him.' The navigator said to the pilot. 'It would drive me bloody mad.'

David awoke with a start. It didn't make sense.

The Germans were waiting for us. They were there, waiting. The truth filtered through his tired mind. *Has Marcel escaped capture? I hope so. The poor devil. If he has been taken, he wouldn't stand a chance.*

'Can you signal London from here?'
'I can try,' the engineer answered.
'For the attention of Buckmaster. The mole must be in London.'
'That's fine. He should have received the message by now.'
'Good. That's a weight off my mind.'

Buckmaster was furious. He thumped his desk with a clenched fist.

'*To think that the leak has come from my Department.*

'Vera!' he barked.

Vera made a dive for her notebook and pencil and hurriedly entered his office.

'Yes Sir?'

'It's believed that there's been a leak of information from this office.'

'But how is that possible? There must be a mistake.'

'The agents out in the field don't think so. The question is what to do about it?'

'Lay a false trail?'

'Good suggestion Vera. Let me think a moment.'

'Perhaps.'

'I have it. Take a memo Vera.'

'Yes Sir.' Vera sat down on a leather armchair, crossed her slim legs, turned over her writing pad to a clean page and waited.

'Message received from France. Two informers picked up, will send names later. Message ends. Got that Vera?'

'Yes Sir.'

'Leave it on your desk before you go home.'

'But, I always clear my desk Sir.'

'Not today Vera, leave it where it can be seen easily.'

'Yes Sir.'

'That will be all Vera. Thank you.'

It was dusk, the building was in darkness. All was quiet. The telephones were silent, the type-writers were under wraps. There were footsteps along the hallway, they stopped outside Vera's office door. Slowly the handle turned and in stepped a woman carrying a pail and mop. She turned to switch on one light, placed her bucket down on the floor, dipped the mop into the warm water then proceeded to wash the floor.

Finishing her first task, she pulled out a yellow duster from her overall pocket and started to polish the desk. The smell of lavender permeated the air as she continued with her cleaning. She stopped when she saw the notebook pad. She picked it up and read the message. Then she looked about her, tore a page from the pad, picked up a stub of pencil from the desk and copied down the message.

The click of the master switch and several spotlights flooded the room. Colonel Buckmaster stood erect like an officer on parade.

'What are you doing?' He bellowed.

The woman stood silent. Buckmaster walked over to the desk and pressed the red button. There was the sound of heavy footsteps approaching the office Two Military Policemen marched into the office.

'Take her away for interrogation,' bellowed the Colonel.

Buckmaster added his own message for his secretary. 'Vera, ripped trousers now mended. He then put the notepad into the drawer of the desk, closed and lock it, the calmly walked out.

Hopefully that's put paid to the leak from this office. We'll have to be more alert.

This is the BBC Home Service.

Here is the 9 o'clock news on August 3rd 1944

The British Parliament passes an Education Act
which provides all children
with free Secondary Education.

That is the end of the news.

Elizabeth packed away her books and clothing into the travelling trunk and pulled the lid down for the last time.

There, thank goodness that's done.

Her taxi was coming in five minutes time. She had said her goodbyes previously to friends she had made whilst at College. All that was left to do was to check she hadn't left anything behind.

'All right dearie? Madge asked.

'Yes thanks. All packed.'

'Well, have a safe journey home.'

'Thank you Madge for all your help. It was appreciated.'

'Bye dearie,' she walked away with her mop in one hand and her bucket swinging on the other.

'Ready. The taxi's here,' Beryl burst into the room. 'I'll give you a hand down with your trunk.'

'Thanks you're a real friend. You will keep in touch?'

'Of course. As soon as the war ends, I'll be up to see you.'

She struggled down the stairs with the heavy trunk.

'It feels a lot heavier,' Elizabeth groaned. The trunk was loaded into the taxi and the two women said their goodbyes.

'Where to missy?' the driver asked.

'Liverpool station please.'

The thought of home brought a smile to her face.

How I have missed all the banter, the meals around the table, the arguing, family squabbles, the love and Wolfgang being so far away. Would there be a reunion? Would there be a time when the village accepted him again? So many questions that had no answers.

She boarded the train and sat at the off side window. The countryside flashed past as a movie scope at the end of the pier. Nearly nodding off with the motion of the train, she pictured herself and Wolfgang together, walking the upland hills of the Lake District. The blast of the train whistle entering the station brought her back to the present. She was home.

She alighted from the steam train looking for her parents. She now looked the part of a teacher. A yellow ribbon, tied at the nape of her neck drew her long brown hair back. She wore a close fitting white blouse nipped in at the waist by her panelled brown skirt. A grey coat hung from her arm.

'Elizabeth! I'm so sorry I was late. A parishioner waylaid me.' She smiled at her Father's excuse, back as far as she could remember, he always did things on the run.

With her luggage stowed away in the Ford 8 they drew away from the station.

'Where's Mother?'

'She's helping Mabel.'

'With what?'

'To do with food I think.'

'Ah.'

They arrived at the vicarage and Elizabeth jumped out of the vehicle.

'Come on Father let's find Mother.'

She ran up the garden path and through the open door.

'Mother! Coo…ee, I'm home. Where are you?'

'In the front room.' She burst into the sitting room.

'Surprise, surprise.' Voices vibrated around the room.

Friends from the village had gathered in a surprise party. A home made banner on the wall 'Welcome home'.

'How lovely. Father you didn't let on.' Kisses all round, hugs, embraces and cuddles from the twins. She was home again, in the midst of her family, emotion bubbled up and a few tears fell.

'There's a letter for you.' Father waved an envelope.

'Who's it from?'

'We don't know for certain, but we've a good idea.' Elizabeth blushed.

Is it from Wolfgang? Yes it must be. Who else would it be?

Eagerly she ripped open the neatly addressed envelope.

'My dear Elizabeth,

It's been a few months since I last wrote. But you have been constantly in my mind. There is a rumour that we are to be repatriated as soon as this war has ended. But you're not to worry. I would dearly love to come back to England to see you. I still feel bad about all the deceit in which I found myself having to inflict on you and your family.

This is not my true nature and I would like a second

chance to prove myself to you my darling. Also there is a very important question I have to ask you.

Please invite me, let me know I'd be welcome in your home.

All my love.

Wolfgang. Xxxxxxx'

It seemed strange to think of him as Wolfgang. I'll write to him. No. That would take too long to get there. A telegram, yes that would be quicker.

'What's the time?'
'Just before five.'
'I won't be long.'
She ran as fast as a frightened rabbit along the cobbled street. Pushed open the shop doorway and stood there gasping for breath.

'You're only just in time. Another minute and you'd be too late. Donald stood with his back to the door, turned and saw who it was.

'Oh, it's you Elizabeth. Welcome back home. What can I do for you?'

'I'd like to send a telegram please, to this address.'
'And the message is?'
'Come. Love Elizabeth.'
'Is that all?'
'That's all,' she confirmed.
She paid the charges and made her way back out on to the street.

I've got away with that lightly. Donald is usually very inquisitive. I suppose he was anxious to close up for the night. To think that Wolfgang will be coming after the war had ended. Now I can plan ahead. Had he changed? He must have, after all his experiences. Look how father came back from the conflict suffering so. It was an awful thing, war. What was the question he wanted to ask me? I think I know really. I know I don't know too much about him, but that can be remedied with time.

'Well?' Her mother questioned.

'You had guessed right. It was from Wolfgang.'

'I knew it.' Mother sat back in her chair and folded her arms under her breasts.

'He wants to come and visit us after the war.'

'And?'

'Well, I've sent a wire.'

'Yes.' Her Mother sat forward, eager to hear her news.

'I've asked him to come.'

Mother sat back in her chair and digested the recent news.

'That's good news Elizabeth,' Christopher joined them at the table. 'To think he'll be with us again, that's wonderful.'

'You've no objections then?'

'None at all. Put the kettle on Mother and we'll celebrate with a cup of tea

Oh thank God. My problems would have doubled if they had disapproved.

'And he's coming to ask me a certain question.'
Her parents looked at one another.
'It was only a matter of time,' her Christopher said.

'Now tell us about collage,' Mother insisted.
'It was such an exciting time. Meeting with new people, doing things I had never done before. Standing on my own two feet. I've done a lot of growing up in that time. Now you two. What's been happening here?'
'Nothing much. We still have the Monthly jumble sales, to help the war effort. Of course Father has his parishioners to look after. We still have to queue for our groceries and if they sell out we go without.
'Still the same then.'
'Yes, no change. The girls are growing fast, as you can see.'
'They've certainly put on a growth spurt since Christmas. Any other news I should know about? Heard anything from Wolfgang?' Margaret looked at Christopher.
'It sounds as though there is something mother.'
'Well we did hear that he'd escaped with another prisoner.'
'Oh my God, is he all right?'
'Yes, they recaptured them soon after.'
'Why didn't you let me know?'
'There wasn't anything you could do and you would have only worried.'
'He wasn't injured was he?'
'No I don't think so. Shall I help you unpack?' Margaret changed the subject.
'No that's all right, I'll do it later. Tell me about the village.'

'There's not too much to tell you. We had a hard time during the winter and Father had to pull a few strings to get more provisions, for us as well as the live stock. Old William Williams came back to live in the village, because of the inclement weather. Of course the air raid sirens are pretty frequent.'

'I'm looking forwards to a long hot bath. I know we're still only allowed six inches of water. But it will be marvellous to what I've been used to.'

'What do you mean Elizabeth?'

'At St. Catherine's we only had a jug and a bowl. No warm water there.'

'Christopher, surely that's not right?'

'I'm afraid so my dear. They were lucky to get that. In my Mother's day they all washed in the same water.'

'But that's terrible.'

'You'd get used to it Mother. It was all right.'

'I'm speechless.'

I wish I had a camera. The expression on Mother's face, it's priceless.

'We had the ARP come around in the school the other day.'

'Yes we did.' The twin's chipped in. 'To inspect our gas masks.'

'It's time for bed girls.' Father spoke softly

'Oh, can't we stay up a little longer. We haven't heard all the news yet.'

'Please, please.'

'Very well. Only half an hour.'

'We've been busy too Elizabeth.'

'And what have you been doing?'

'We've collected newspapers in our dolly's pram.' Ruth said.

'Yes. It's to help with the war you know.' Rose added

'It's very important work.' Ruth insisted.

'I know. And I bet you collected the most,' Elizabeth grinned.

'We did,' they spoke in unison.

'And we saw a Spitfire doing a victory roll.' Elizabeth cuddled the pair of them.

How she had missed them.

'Bed time.' Father called out.

'Oh no. Just another five minutes, please,' begged Ruth.

'We'll be extra good. Won't we? Rose pleaded.

'We still haven't heard everything yet,' Ruth complained

'Please Father, Elizabeth has only just come home, please.' Rose looked up into his face.

'Please.' He knew he had lost the battle. The girls could wrap him around their little fingers.

'Five more minutes then and that's all.' There were screams of delight from the twins and they ran over to Elizabeth begging for more news of her travels. Nothing had changed.

Rose and Ruth chased one another down the stairs. In the kitchen their breakfast was laid out on the table for them.

'Sit down and don't make too much noise and wake Elizabeth up.'

'Why is she still sleeping?' Rose asked.

'Because she needs to catch up on her sleep.'

'Hasn't she been sleeping Mother?' Ruth frowned.

'You know she's only came home yesterday. All the studying she's had to do, it's been very tiring for her. All the exams she's had to study for. You know when you sit for your exams, you get nervous.'

'Yes, but she's older.'

'I know. But it still makes her tense.'

'I wouldn't like to be away from home,' Rose said.

'Oh I would, it would be super,' Ruth chipped in.

'Your only saying that. You'd be crying all day if you were on your own.'

'I wouldn't, it would be lovely to be away from you.'

'Now you two. Get ready for school. Don't forget to take your cardigans with you and don't forget to take your gas masks.'

'And don't forget to take your gas masks,' Ruth mimicked her Mother.

Margaret stood on the step and waved the girls, still arguing, off to school.

The girls passed by the village shop, calling out their helloes to Mr Hodges, who was up a ladder, busy cleaning the outside windows of his premises. Then they passed by the Red Lion and headed towards the end of Broad Street, where the Church of England School was situated. They joined friends as they made their way into the playground A large brass bell was rung by Mrs Winters and every child stood still, not daring to move.

'File in quietly,' she instructed.

'Why do we always have to be quiet?' Ruth asked.

'Because I said so,' Mrs Winter had bent down and whispered into Ruth's ear.

They filed into the small school through a black glossy door, down the hallway and into the tiny classroom.

'Hurry up and get settled,' Mrs Winters called out, thumping her flat hand on to her desk. 'Open up your desks and bring out your exercise books and no talking.'

Rose and Ruth sat together, lifted up their desks as they were told and shuffled inside for their books.

'I hate English,' whispered Ruth.

'So do I.'

'No talking.'

'No talking,' Ruth mimicked.

'So, we have little miss trouble maker,' Mrs Winters slammed Ruth's desk lid down, narrowly missing her fingers. Rose and Ruth looked at her with startled eyes.

'I'm in no mood this morning madam for your antics. Head for the punishment cupboard Missy.'

'But.'

'I said the punishment cupboard!' Mrs Winters, tight lipped pointed a bony finger to the back of the class

Ruth looked at Rose tears spilling down over her cheeks. She slowly walked to the back of the class, to the dreaded cupboard. Mrs Winters stood there, holding the wooden door open.

'In you go.' As Ruth took a step forward, Rose sprung up from her seat.

'Please Mrs Winters. Ruth had nightmares after last time. Please.'

'Sit down girl or you'll be spending time in there too.'

Everyone turned to look at Rose. She sat down with a resigned sigh. Ruth stood looking inside the black void. She wrinkled her nose, she hated the damp smell of the closet.

'In you go madam,' her teacher pushed her back. The door was slammed shut and the key turned in the lock. Ruth slid to the ground, trying to stop the panic within her from rising to the surface. She wouldn't give Mrs Winters the satisfaction of knowing that she was petrified. She would do as she had done before, in her mind, take herself out of the cupboard, across the green fields, over the hills to the sea, where she could run free and feel the wind in her hair. Rose kept looking at the cupboard, there was no noise from within.

'Concentrate on your lessons girl,' Mrs Winters voice made her jump

At the end of the lesson, Mrs Winters called out 'Let her out.' Rose dashed to the door and unlocked it and opened it up. Ruth stood there smiled at her to assure her she fine.

'Dinner hour. Back here in an hour.'

'Come on lets go home,' Rose put her arm around Ruth's shoulders.

'Are you sure you're all right?' Ruth nodded and they made their way home for lunch.

They arrived at the vicarage, just in time for home made tomato soup, bread and margarine.

'And how has your morning been?' Mother filled two glasses of milk for the girls.

'Ruth was shut.'

'And Rose came top in our English test. Isn't she clever?' Interrupted Ruth.

'Well done my love. I'll have to remember to tell , when I see him later. Eat up or you'll be late.'

On their way back to school Rose asked 'Why didn't you let me tell Mother?'
'Because I didn't want you to. It will only make things more difficult.'
'How will that be?'
'Mrs Winters will make it harder for me, that's how.'
'I didn't think of that.'
'That's the trouble you never do.'
'Do you think we could tell Elizabeth?'
'No. We tell nobody. It's the best way Rose.'
'All right, if you're sure.'

They pushed open the gate and into the playground, where Mrs Winters was standing waiting for them, her lips pressed into a tight line, her arms folded under her breasts.

'And what time do we call this?' she asked. The two girls didn't answer, but continued to walk into the school, holding their breath in fear of another reprimand.

'Move yourselves girls.' They quickly walked along the corridor and into their classroom.

'Our next lesson will be English. Exercise books out.' Mrs. Winter's voice boomed out, against the clatter of desktops, opening and closing.

For the next half an hour everyone was busy writing their essays, letting their imagination run free, far away from the confining classroom and their cruel bullying from their teacher.

THIS IS THE BBC HOME SERVICE
AND HERE IS THE 9 O'CLOCK NEWS

ON SEPTEMBER 8TH 1944

THE FIRST LIQUID FUELLED
V2 ROCKETS FALL ON LONDON.
KILLING AND INJURING MANY PEOPLE

THAT IS THE END OF THE NEWS

The operations room was hot and airless as the men sat waiting. The door was suddenly pushed open and Col. Gubbins, SOE Director of Operations, burst into the room. The operatives fell silent as their attention centred on the man who stood before them.

'Right men,' he slapped his desk with his baton. The sound of it rattled around the room. He pointed up to the map hanging on the wall.

'This mission will take place on the south bank of the Loire.' He swept the point of baton along the course of the river and stopped at one area on the map.

'The Germans have giant cranes that are lifting back the locomotives on to the tracks that have been derailed, they are attempting to repair all the damage we've previously achieved.'

He raised his voice. 'Information has filtered through, that they will achieve their objective unless we put these giant cranes out of action.' There were grunts of approval.

'The Germans have added new defences along the railway. They have a locomotive at each end with wagons front and rear, equipped with machine guns. It's well defended.' He moved his pointer to the English Channel.

'You will cross the channel to Carantec. Here the Free French assist. You'll be taken through the countryside and on to Vannes, and on to Nantes.' He traced the route on the large wall map with his baton.

'You'll be picked up from here.' He pointed at the town of Pornichet.

'Now for the weapons you will be carrying, we've decided to use the Piat. As you know, it's a spring loaded gun and the timing of its use is imperative.' There followed more grunts of approval.

'Right, any questions?'

'Sir.' David stood up. 'Who will be running the operation?'

'You will Captain. Your details will be issued an hour before you leave. Security reasons – you understand.' There was a moment of silence.

'Anything else? No? Very well gentlemen, carry on.'

Colonel Gubbins turned and marched out of the room with his usual purposeful stride, his baton securely tucked under his armpit and his moustache twitching.

My God he's like a whirlwind.

An hour before they were due to leave, their orders were delivered by a Military Police Despatch-rider.

'David' ripped open the communication and read out aloud their instructions for the group to hear.

Your three extra operatives will be - Claude, Henri and Martin. Your objective is to **damage**, not destroy the crane. You will be picked up at Pornichet after the mission.

The 'Maid Honor' rode at her moorings in Poole harbour, only the slap of the rigging on the mast disturbed the tranquil afternoon.

The seventy-footer had been converted to a yacht some years before the SOE had taken possession of her as a go between France and England.

Being ever mindful of the threat of the German patrol boats, the 'Maid Honor' slipped out of the harbour at dusk, on a cloudy night. Luck was with them. There was only a slight swell, allowing the boat to make good time. The men below decks passed the time by playing cards, reading or discussing the mission ahead.

The door to the lower deck opened. Alex Gregory the Captain leant through the hatch and put his finger to his lips then signalled for them to follow.

'Carantec's ahead,' he whispered.

The men clambered up the steep steps and into the freshness of the early hour. In the half-light of morning, they could see the French coast was only a mile away.

'We're waiting for the signal,' Alex whispered.

'How long?'

'As long as it takes. Not long I hope, as we're sitting ducks just waiting here.'

'There they are,' the voice of the mate carried on the cold morning air.

A white beam flashed. They returned the signal with a red reply. The four men stood around the dinghy.

'Lift, lower gently, one, two, three.' Alex gave the orders.

There was a slight splash as the dinghy slid into the sea. One by one they climbed on board. Each one picked up a paddle dipped them into the water and pulled strongly towards the foreshore. As they arrived on shore, a patriot of the Free French Army greeted them.

'David?

'Bon soir mon ami, Robert.' A small man dressed in a brown mac, belted at the waist greeted them.

'My men will hide your dinghy. Get into the truck and we'll be off. We'll be stopping at Vannes.'

The long drive there was tedious for the men in the back of the vehicle. They mostly dozed on and off as they travelled kilometre after kilometre. Finally they arrived at dusk, turning off the main road on to a dirt track. They pulled up at a detached house, which stood in its own grounds. They were ushered through the heavy oak door into a hallway. A flight of stairs was off to the right.

'Wait here,' Robert instructed. He walked away and disappeared through an open doorway. He then returned with a well-dressed woman at his side.

'Madame Beauchamp.'

'Bon soir, Madame Beauchamp,' David stepped forward to shake her hand.

She smiled and said, 'You must be quiet at all times. My girls entertain the Germans here.'

'You mean we're in a b b……,' Henri gulped.

'Quite so, a brothel.'

'Good grief. I don't know what my family would make of this,' David grinned at his mates.

'It's the last place the Germans would look for you mon ami, follow me,' Robert said. They quietly climbed the red carpeted stairs, then walked along a corridor to the back of the house. Madame Beauchamp opened a door and walked into the room

'Don't forget what I said about being quiet. Your meals will be brought to you. How long will you be here?'

'We should be here for two nights,' David answered

'I'll leave you now. Bon soir.'

'Bon soir Madame.'

'Now let's get down to facts. The RAF will be flying in tonight to drop the Piat. We will be there to pick it up for you. You'll make your move to Nantes tomorrow. Are these arrangements all right with you?'

'Robert you know we will fit into any plans.'

'Bon.'

'I will be back tomorrow morning early.'

'We'll be ready.'

Robert slipped out of the room, closing the door quietly behind him.

Time dragged on. The men sprawled out on their beds chatting about the mission.

'Have you used the Piat before David?' Martin leant forwards, placing his arms on his knees anxious to hear his answer.

'Only once. It's a difficult piece of machinery. You have to judge the firing accurately or you'll miss the object intended. It's rather like firing a naval cannon. It tends to kick very violently when fired, so be on your guard.'

'Commandant! You're going into the wrong room, you silly boy,' Madame Beauchamp closed the door to the room. The men held their breath.

'Jesus, that was too close,' Claude drew in a deep breath and looked at the others.

Early the next morning there was a knock at the door and Robert's head appeared.

'Ready?'

The men made their final checks and followed Robert along the carpeted hallways. Outside a truck was waiting for them.

'Climb on board and we'll be off.'

David joined Robert inside the cab and the others piled into the back.

'Did the Piat arrive?'

'It did David, no problems.'

'Have your men timed the convoy's movements?'

'Everything is under control.'

'Good. We can't afford any mistakes on this one. It's imperative that the mission is successful.'

The countryside flashed by as the group made its way to Nantes. They ate their lunch of homemade bread, cheese and coffee, whilst on the move. It was late afternoon as they drove through Nantes arriving at their destination on the south side of the River Loire.

Robert's team had found a great view of the railway, half hidden by bracken. The Piat gun had already been assembled and was ready to use.

'Our agents tell us that they will be moving the crane in on hour from now.' All watches were checked.

'Just in time to get the feeling of the surroundings.'

Four of the operatives manoeuvred the Piat into position facing the on coming crane. Satisfied that they were now ready they sat down and in the damp bracken, listened and waited.

'What's that?

'What? I can't hear anything,' David answered.

'I can hear movement of some kind.'

'You're right I can hear something. This is it lads. We only get one chance to knock it out. Here it comes.'

The locomotive slowly came into view, pulling the

enormous steel monster with a second engine pushing from behind. Slowly the convoy crept along the railway line.

'Steady, wait.' David whispered. Everyone held his breath.

The locomotive provided a degree of protection for the crane and the side carriages were added insurance against attack. But, as the carriages approached, the curve in the line left an opportunity to open fire.

'Steady…..steady'

'Steady.'

'Fire!' David carefully squeezed the trigger and the rocket flew straight into the front wheel of the wagon carrying the crane. The metal wheel disintegrated into millions of fragments. The gigantic machine tottered to one side.

'She's going!' Claude's voice was laced with tension.

The crane collapsed like a dying Dinosaur Rex floundering into its prime evil dust. Mayhem reined. It keeled over crashing on to the ground its twisted metal represented a piece of Modern Art. The Germans leapt out of their carriages firing in all directions, shouts and counter orders added to their confusion. It was a futile response; the operatives had all ready left and were making their way to Pornichet.

The journey back to the brothel was uneventful, but the men filled with excitement and elation at the mission being such a success.

'Couldn't have done it sweeter myself,' Robert grinned.

'They never knew what hit them,' Henri said.

'What about the chaos after?' Claude chuckled.

'It will be along time before they raise that baby again,' Martin joined in the celebrations. They drew up at the back of the establishment and jumped out of the truck.

'Quietly does it lads,' David advised. They crept up the stairs and along the corridors to the room they had been given.

'I'll get us some food and maybe a couple of carafe's of wine?' Robert suggested.

'Now you're talking.'

Everyone nodded in agreement. 'Not too much celebrating lads.' David advised.

'That's not like you,' Henri whispered. Silence reigned.

THIS IS THE BBC HOME SERVICE.

HERE IS THE 9 O'CLOCK NEWS

ON 12TH NOVEMBER 1944

BRITISH LANCASTER BOMBERS
SINK THE TIRPITZ

THAT IS THE END OF THE NEWS

It was late and Christopher was putting the final words to his sermon. He stood up from his desk and walked over to the bureau, shuffled his papers into a neat pile and turned the lamp off. He lent over to turn off the wireless and as he did so the classical music, he had been listening to, stopped. An announcer broke into the programme.

'We have an announcement to make, just one moment please.'

God what now?

'Aren't you coming up yet Christopher?'
'In a minute, there's to be a news bulletin. Ah here it is,' he leant forward and twisted the volume control.
'We now have the Prime Minister Winston Churchill.'
'Margaret, come down quickly, its our Prime Minister.' Her light footsteps sounded on the stairs.
'Listen Margaret.' She sat next to Christopher and took his hand.

The Prime Minister's voice, instantly recognisable, announced to the world that the war in Europe was over. Both Margaret and Christopher leapt for joy.
'Did you hear that? It's over. Christopher, it's all over, the war is over.' Margaret grabbed hold of Christopher and they did a jig round the room. Christopher opened a bottle of wine.
'Isn't that the Communion wine?'
'Not now it isn't.' He pulled out the cork and filled two large wineglasses.

'We can't drink a whole glass full!'
'Watch me.' Said Christopher.
The pair off them were not just dancing now, but singing as well.

Screams of delight, relief and exuberance woke up the rest of the family. Everyone piled downstairs to see their parents hugging one another.
'What's happened?
'What's wrong?'
'What's all the noise about?'
'The war it's over. It's over,' Margaret burst into tears. Christopher put his arm around her shoulder.
'Does that mean we don't have to wear these pesky things Father?' Rose held up the gas mask's case.
'That's right, you've no need to carry them around with you any more.'
The twins squealed with delight, twisting each other round and round.
'Come on, we'll have to let the villagers know, if they don't know already.' Christopher was charging out of the front door.

Now what's the best way to let them know? I know, the church bells.

He rushed along the pathway to the church, opened the door and turned on the light.

This will instantly alert the villagers.

He made his way to the bell tower, grasped the rope

with his hands and pulled and pulled with all his might, his whole body rejoicing in the wonderful news.

Villagers looked out of bedroom windows and street doors, questioning why the church bells were ringing.

'What on earth is all this? Waking everyone up.'

'Do you know why the bells are ringing?'

'Goodness knows. Unless it's a practical joke.'

'We had better go up to the church to find out what's it all about.'

'Surely we haven't been invaded.'

The news spread quickly, from mouth to mouth, volunteers taking hold of the ropes from the Reverend Kelly.

Christopher walked to the centre of the village where people were singing, some crying, all making as much noise as possible, in celebrating the end of the war. It wasn't until later in the day that there was a pause in the excitement caused by the Prime Minister's announcement. But there was still excitement and a general buzz following the good news. Groups stood around, discussing the effects the war had. No more blackout, no more scrimping, mending and making do. Tomorrow would be a better world for all of them.

Celebrations were spontaneous. Stylecroft was not going to miss out it was a time for everyone to let their hair down. Impromptu parties began. Buntings, flags decorated every house. There was dancing in the streets. Women formed a band, playing kitchen utensils, saucepan lids and paper wrapped around combs, in fact anything that would make a noise

As the good news spread throughout the country, there was great rejoicing. Bonfires and fireworks were lit in celebration. Beacons flared up on the tops of the surrounding hills. Railway engines hooted 'V' for Victory using the Morse code; three dots and a dash. Public Houses had their hours of opening extended. The sense of relief was everywhere; it was almost a tangible emotion that people could touch.

Bleary eyed the next morning Christopher re-read his sermon, he screwed it up and tossed it, as accurately as a basket ball player, into the woven waste paper basket.

This was time for rejoicing. His sermon took on an uplifting theme and the words just flowed. Magnificent, he held up the masterpiece and reread it.

Just the ticket. He placed the paper inside the Bible for safekeeping.

'And that dear friends is the end of our service for today. I have something else to tell you before you all go. It has been almost a spontaneous idea that has came from many of the villages to have a weeklong celebration of Victory in Europe. Mrs Pye is going to organise the whole thing. Posters will be made by our schoolchildren. Let's show them how Stylecroft do it!'

The whole village buzzed with the news, small groups stood around discussing the coming event.

'I heard it is taking place on one of the farms.'

' No, it's to be on the green.'

'All this speculation, we'd best wait for the posters the vicar spoke about.'

'I tell you it's on the farm.'

Grace Pye told the children of her plans for the posters and they all eagerly helped with the big job ahead even though school was closed.

V.E. Celebrations
Something for everybody. Join in the fun on the green, starting 2 o'clock. …………………..

<u>Monday</u>
Puppet Show
Horse shoe throwing

<u>Tuesday</u>
Dog Racing
Tossing hay over the goal posts.

<u>Wednesday</u>
Throwing the Wellington boot.
Treasure Hunt

<u>Thursday</u>
Hill Racing
Dog Show

<u>Friday</u>
Agricultural Show
Marching Bands

<u>Saturday</u>
Sheepdog trials
Marble Championship
Prizes awarded by Sir Harold and Lady Parkinson

Ending with a firework display.

<u>Sunday</u>
The children's street party.

The Boy Scouts were given the job of pushing the invitations through every letterbox and handing out posters to anyone who had space to put them on display. Buntings and flags were hung on every house down Broad Street leading to the green.

Several marquees had been erected. They were decorated with red, white and blue buntings and balloons. Excited children dashed in between the guide ropes playing chase.

'Mind you don't fall over,' Grace Pye called out a warning, but she might as well have been talking to herself for all the notice they took of her. Most of the preparations were finished by the weekend before the celebration. All of Great Britain joined in their merrymaking. Railway engines signalled in Morse code, street parties were held and there was dancing in the streets. At the Red Lion drinking hours were extended without fear of prosecution

'Did you hear on the news about women forming bands using kitchen utensils, saucepan lids, tissue paper wrapped round combs, anything that makes a noise.' Bob lent on the wooden bar.

Dick finished polishing the glass with a tea towel before answering.

'Yes I heard, everyone's so relieved it's all over.'

Christopher slapped Bob's shoulder.

'Hello vicar. We were just saying how the whole

country's celebrating the end of the war.'

' It's a normal reaction, the relief from the worrying, all the anxious times. The return of loved ones.'

'You can say that again vicar' Dick nodded. 'My brother's been in Colditz for the past two years.

'I didn't know that.' Bob said, finishing his beer.

'I haven't spoken about it, because I suppose, I'd given up hoping he'd come home like a lot of people in the village.'

'Well, I'm sure it won't be too long now for you to wait for his homecoming.' Christopher drained the last dregs of his pint and placed the jug back on the bar.

'Well I'm off. See you soon.'

As the vicar disappeared through the doorway Bill said 'I hope the vicar is all right.'

'Why wouldn't he be?'

'Well, I saw him coming out of old Doc Woods surgery.'

'Perhaps he was just visiting,' suggested Dick.

'Let's hope so. I'll se you.'

'Yeah so long.'

<u>Monday</u>

As the sun rose to a clear day Jessie Lambert started her round of delivering the morning post.

'Morning Jessie.'

'Morning Donald.'

'You're up early this morning.'

'I think everyone is. I started early to finish in time to join in the celebration.'

'I had the same idea.'

'See you on the green later.' Jessie pushed off on

her bicycle and disappeared down the road carrying her heavy load.

'Morning Milky.' She waved at the milkman on his morning delivery. She applied her brakes and stepped off her bicycle and lent it up against the dry stone wall. Then delved into her pouch and pulled out a handful of letters.

Reverend Kelly, Mr & Mrs Kelly, Miss E. Kelly, mnnn they know a lot of people.

She made her way along Broad Street delivering the letters.

I have to be careful here; the Alsation is far from friendly.

With some trepidation she walked down the path treading lightly. As she reached the door, the dog's face, snarling and growling appeared at the window.

'*I'm glad there's a window between us*

Jessie walked smartly away down the path, back to the wooden gate and breathed a little easier, as she pushed off on to her next stop.

'*I'll be glad when my John gets back from the war and he can have his old job back. I've had enough.*'

Pushing her bicycle up to the top of the hill, she stopped to look at the distant hills.

We're so lucky to live in this part of the country. The views are stunning. We've hardly been affected here by the war. Thank the Lord it's all over now.

She breathed in deeply, taking in the fresh fragrant morning air. Her round finished, Jessie hurried into her house, dashed upstairs and changed out of her uniform, into a skirt and blouse. She then brushed her brown hair and changed her stout shoes into sandals. She quickly came down the stairs and out into the sunshine anxious to join in the fun.

Mrs Pye, dressed in her Sunday best, stood on the rostrum and addressed the group of villagers
'Let's begin our week of V.E celebrations. This afternoon we start with a puppet show for the children.' There were screams of delight from the waiting youngsters, their faces lighting up with expectancy. The Boy Scouts band burst into life. Drums and trumpets were played with great enthusiasm, as the little ones sat in front of the tiny stage.
'Have you seen Judy?'
'No,' came the passionate replies.
'Is she shopping?' Punch asked
'Yes,' screamed the children in unison.
For nearly an hour the little ones interacted with the puppets, laughing, shouting, screaming.
'Take that,' Punch shouts.
'Go on,' the children goaded. 'Hit him.'
'And that.'
A cheer went up as the baddy received his fate. After the Punch and Judy Show everyone moved into the

Refreshment Tent where tea and lemonade were served with cakes made by the Mothers' Union.

Grace Pye had returned to the rostrum and was announcing the 'Horseshoe Throwing' competition. Mr Smalley was in the middle of the green using a mallet, hamming a sturdy post into the ground. A white washed start line on the grass gave them the ten yards distance needed.

The Boy Scout band, realising what an important job they were doing, played with verve and passion as they marched around the green. The men chatted in a group waiting for their names to be called.

'Donald Hodges'

Donald shook hands with his fellow competitors and strolled forward to the marked line. He gathered up four horseshoes in his right hand.

'Throw when you're ready,' the instruction from the Starter. Donald lifted up his right arm to eye level. He lowered his arm and raised it again, then tossed the shoe. CLANG the shoe hit the post and bounced off to one side.

'Oh shame,' a voice called from one of the spectators.

Donald took a second shoe. He took aim and let the shoe fly.

'Oh what hard luck.'

This time, steady, deep breath and …..   CHEERS.

'Well done, well done,' the voices of encouragement came from the spectators.

Donald grinned.

Mnn, I haven't lost my touch. Now the last one.

He expelled his breath in a controlled effort as the horseshoe left his hand.

'Now I call that skill.'

The Controller shouted out 'DONALD HODGES, TWO'. The cheers filled the air.

Donald stepped back and shook hands with the next contestant.

Bob Whittam moved towards the white line. He wiped the sweat off his hands on the side of his trousers, aimed and threw. However, just like Donald's first one, it bounced off the iron post.

'Come on Bob. Next time. You can do it.'

He lined up the shoe and the post and threw again. The clang of the shoe on the post and the spin as it dropped to the foot of the post, brought loud cheers from the crowd and Bob stood there beaming with a big grin on his face.

That was the only scoring shoe for Bob.

The Controller shouted our 'BOB WHITTAM...... ONE.'

'Let the Reverend have a throw next.' A call came from the crowd.

'Go on Christopher,' Margaret urged.

Rising to the challenge, Christopher picked up the four horseshoes and took position on the white line.

'Come on Father,' the twins shouted.

He took one horseshoe, lined it up as the others had done and heaved the metal object into the air. Unfortunately a little too hard, the shoe whizzed past the post and into the long grass. The crowd howled encouragement and Christopher threw another.

'What hard luck'

'Try again.'

'Better luck next time.'

'Come on, you can do it.'

The next shoe fell far too short of the pole.

'I took off too much weight, that time.'

'Never mind, at least you tried and that's the point,' Bill Turner said.

Several others tried their luck, but never got close to the winning shoes.

Mrs Pye climbed onto the rostrum.

'Ladies and Gentlemen. The winner of our competition is Donald Hodges. Whistles and clapping interrupted her speech.

'You've won yourself a free pint at the Red Lion.'

Again cheers sounded and Donald walked away wearing a large grin.

Tuesday.

Like the day before, people rushed around doing their daily chores, so as they were able to attend the Victory in Europe celebrations. The members of the Mothers' Union were busy in their kitchen cooking another batch of cakes.

'I'm pleased we've got a good supply of eggs Mabel, or we wouldn't have been able to make any more cakes,' said Margaret.

'Well everyone's given a little bit; sugar from Mrs Walton, butter from Mrs Smalley.' Margaret hooked out the hot cakes from the tray and put them to cool on a large plate.

'Can we have one mother?' Rose asked as walked into the kitchen.

'The smell is making my mouth water.' Ruth added.

'Go on then. Only one mind.'

The girls ran out into the garden giggling, pleased that their mother had given in so easily.

'Ladies and Gentlemen,' Grace Pye raised her hands for silence. Gradually the hum died down.

'Today with our VE Celebrations we now have another event for those of you who brought their dogs – it's a Dog Race.'

The children were held back by a string barrier, while the dog owners walked forward to the start line.

Earlier that morning Tom Hargreaves had soaked an old jumper in Linseed Oil. He had tied a length of string around the jumper. He arrived at the Green, out came the jumper from his canvas bag and he proceeded to drag it along the ground. His plan was to leave a trail of ever decreasing circles, which would end up eventually in the centre of the Green.

'All collars to be slipped after the count of three.' Shouted the controller.

The dogs strained on their leads, pulling hard, almost out of control.

ONE.....TWO...THREE – his voice raised an octave higher. The growling and barking of the excited of the dogs reached a peak as they leapt forward.

'Greyhounds have nothing on these,' shouted Tom.

The dogs lurched away from their restrictive collars, sniffing at the grass, to pick up the scent.

'Go on my son,' a voice called out from the crowd of spectators.

Four dogs dashed off as they caught the scent of the Linseed oil. Rory the Labrador stopped and sniffed around a bush and lifted his leg to pee.

'Oh no, trust him to stop,' his owner said.

'Come on,' the crowd was chanting.

Round and around the dogs raced past the bystanders

'Come on, come on,' the crowd chanted.

The dogs crossed the finish line, paw by paw, with nothing separating them. So the winner's owners all received a free pint of beer at the Red Lion.

The onlookers cheered and clapped their appreciation of the race.

The tea tent was packed.

'Two teas, sugar?' Margaret asked.

'Yes please.'

'Only half a spoon. We're still rationed.'

'We're lucky to get that,' Mabel chipped in.

The tune of 'Pack up your troubles in your old kit bag' drifted through the marquee.

'Who's playing today?' Mabel asked.

'I think it must be the Salvation Army.' Margaret replied.

'It think it sounds more like the Boy Scouts playing, they have two boys who play the tin whistles, I don't think the Salvation Army has.'

'You could be right.'

Mabel was taken by surprise as Margaret seldom agreed with her.

'Ladies and Gentlemen,' the familiar voice of Mrs Pye sounded above the noise of the crowd. 'We have come to one of the events you've all been waiting for - *Tossing the hay.* Each contestant will have six sheaves to throw over the goal posts.'

'WOOPEE.' Shouted the crowd.

'I'll pass you over to the Controller.'

Two goal posts had been placed side by side. Three stooks of wheat were placed for each competitor. 'On the count of three' called the Controller.

The men picked up their pitchforks. The Controller raised his hand and the crowd joined him with the count 'ONE ... TWO ... THREE'

The men jabbed their two pronged forks into their first stook and stepped towards their goal posts. They were level on the lift. One stook seemed to be slipping but up both stooks went over the goal posts one perhaps a fraction ahead of the other.

'ONE' shouted the spectators.

Then men turned and brutally attacked their second sheaf. 'DON'T KILL IT' some wit shouted.

With sweat pouring down their faces the combatants turned together and for a second time they were neck and neck. They were both in the swing of the competition now. It wasn't necessary the strongest man that was going to win, but the one with strength and technique. The crowd urged them on.

'COME ON FRED' from one section of the crowd.
'SAM'S THE MAN' from others.

'TWO' shouted the spectators as the stooks of wheat flew over the cross bar of goal posts. For the third time they turned and thrust their forks into the wheat turned and threw the sheaves over. 'THREE'

With no indication who was going to win, the Sam and Fred finally raced for the sixth and last stook. Sam stumbled on his pick up.

The last stook sailed over the bar. It was Sam's. He turned to meet Fred who held his hands in recognition of his win. Fred triumphant shook hands with Sam. It had been a close contest.

'Free beer for you both, Fred you can have two pints!'

As the cheers and applause died down the two men walked together to the Beer Tent and the Salvation Army struck up a cheerful tune.

Slowly the crowds drifted home. Another day of celebrations had come to an end.

Bill Turner poked his head around the open door of the Red Lion.

'Morning Dick. I reckon you'll be a few pounds out of pocket after this week is out.'

'Oh I don't mind. I can carry a few free beers, free

publicity,' he looked up from the tabletop he was wiping down.

'I reckon it's all going well, don't you?'

'Mrs Pye is doing a grand job. Not many people could carry it off.'

'I couldn't agree with you more. See you over the green later.'

'Yeah, see you later.'

'Delivery mate.'

Bill looked up from his chores at the unexpected voice.

'You couldn't have come at a more convenient time. The village is holding their VE celebrations this week.'

'So I heard,' replied the Drayman.

'I'll pop down and open up the cellar,' Bill threw the wet cloth into the sink and climbed down into the depths of the pub. He reached up and undid the steel straps, holding the iron flaps. They creaked on their hinges as they were opened.

'I'll have to oil them.' Bill placed long lengths of wood, through the opening.

'All right, it's ready.'

The grey headed man lent through the space.' All right mate.'

'Ready? Lower away.'

For the next fifteen minutes, barrels of beer were lowered down the planks and into the cellar.'

'Do you want a drink?'
' Thanks, that would be nice.'

Back up in the bar, Bill poured a pint of his best bitter for the thirsty man.

'Are things getting back to normal?' asked Dick.

'We've caught up on the back-log thank goodness,' replied the Drayman.

'We are using up more with the VE Celebrations.'

'I think everyone is doing the same. Celebrations are taking place all over the place.'

'Well, I'll be off. Thanks.'

'No its thanks to you. You were a lifesaver.'

The afternoon appeared quicker than anyone liked. The Mothers Union had only just finished setting up their stall, when the public trickled in. The Girl Guides took charge of the jumble stall; the Boy Scouts looked after the tombola stall.

Wednesday

'Ladies and Gentlemen.' Mrs Pye stood in her usual place on the rostrum this time dressed in a smart navy blue suit. 'We now have the Wellington Boot throwing contest. Good luck to you all.'

The contestants lined up and the first stood up to the white line, lifted the Wellington Boot by the leg and began to swing his arm round and around like a windmill sail and let it go. The crowd cheered.

'The furthest wins,' shouted the controller.

One after another, they stepped up to the line and took their turn of throwing the Wellington boot as far as they could throw it. There were resounding cheers as each boot hit the ground. The controller rushing around to measure the length and writing it down on his clip board.

After two throws each, the winner was announced.

'Ladies and Gentlemen, our winner for the tossing of the Wellington is, Farmer Smalley.'

Clapping and cheering filled the air as he joined Mrs Pye on to the rostrum.

'Your prise is of course a free pint of best bitter.'

Again a loud burst of applause greeted the winner.

'Thank you Mr Smalley. Now, for our next entertainment we have the church choir. They will sing a few songs for you.' Mrs Pye stepped down from her advantage point and joined in with the spectators, allowing the choir's conductor to use the rostrum.

They gave their rendition of 'skip to my loo my darling.' The harmonising captured the spectator's interest and gave them resounding applause as they finished. The next piece they sung was' The Autumn leaves.' Their voices carried far beyond the village and the bystanders were captivated with their power of voice. Thunderous applause filled the air almost deafening the youngsters.

Standing, on the rostrum, Mrs Pye announced it was the turn of the children.

'A treasure hunt.' There were screams of excitement from the little ones as they lined up.

'Ready steady go!'

They ran this way and that, searching for the sweets that had been hidden earlier. This gave the grown ups time for a chat to the parent stood next to them.

The afternoon's celebrations finished with the

Scout's Band, blasting out one tune after another, their enthusiasm knowing no bounds.

Words of congratulations were uttered as they finished their rendition of 'Abide with me.'

Thursday.

Donald Hodges changed his window display in his shop.

Might as well cash in on all this trade, he thought. *I've ordered in extra stock to carry me over this busy week.*

'Morning Donald,' Margaret pushed open the shop door and walked in.' I need some more self-raising flour. With all of this baking, I've run out.'

Donald turned and dragged a sack of flour from underneath the counter.

'Anything else Margaret?'

'Umm, I don't think so. I'll let you get on with your window dressing.'

'See you this afternoon?'

'I wouldn't miss it for all the tea in China.'

'It's all going extremely well, don't you think?'

'I certainly do. Mrs Pye is a miracle worker.'

'Bye then Donald. See you later.'

'You can be sure of that.' His voice was muffled as he lent again into the display.

People came from the surrounding area, all making their way to the village green, as the news had spread of their V.E. celebrations.

'Now Ladies and Gentlemen,' Mrs Pye opened the proceedings. 'It's so nice to see such a large gathering and we've reached the stage in our festival, where the athletes come into their own. It's the fell race. Now if there are any latecomers please let the controller know.'

The runners were lined up, their foot placed against the painted white line.

'Ready, steady,' the starter's gun echoed around the green.

The runners jostled for position as they made their way to the distance hills.

The course of five and a half miles twisted and turned past gurgling brooks. At the top of the steep hills volunteers manned the 'water tables'. On their return journey another water table was waiting for the thirsty, exhausted men. There was clapping that signalled the fastest of the runners and several minutes later the slower of the contestants staggered past the finish line.

'And the winner is number 8, Edward Smith.' There were cheers, the loudest from the Smith family.

'Well done. Get yourself a free pint of best bitter at the Red Lon.' Mrs Pye pumped the young man's hand up and down. 'Well done.'

'I could have done that run a few years ago,' William Williams spoke to Mrs Walton

'Nobody in their right mind would indulge.'

'Why ever not. It keeps you fit.'

The Boy Scouts drummed their way into the arena

and their buglers blasting as they marched around the green. The Drum Major signalled 'Mark Time' followed by a smart 'Halt'.

'Band! Band, Dismiss.'

The members of the band gave a smart half turn and saluted. The crowd applauded then moved over towards the 'Dog Show Arena'.

'Will everyone who's entering his or her dog please go to the area taped off for the Dog Show. Thank you.' The sound of Mrs Pye's voice echoed across the field.

Large and small dogs filed into the arena. Each animal peed on the same spot, as every one moved over to see the dog show. Children elbowed their way to the front of the crowd, enabling them to get a better view.

Rose and Ruth were no exemption. They pushed past trousers and skirts as they made their way to the roped off area. The dogs trotted around with their proud owners beside them, occasionally snapping at the dog in front of them.

'Look at that lovely Labrador, Isn't it cute? Do you think we'll be allowed to have a dog?' Rose asked.

'I don't expect so. Mother and Father would have some excuse why we couldn't.'

'We could ask, couldn't we? Oh, look at that puppy isn't he gorgeous,' Rose lent through the ropes and stroked the young Alsation. It nuzzled into her hand and lent into her as though it was starved of affection.

'I'm going to ask Father right away.'

'I'm going to ask if we can have an ice cream,' Ruth said. 'I love ice cream.'

The girls pushed their way out of the crowed and ran over to their parents who were talking to Mrs Pye.

'Can we have an ice cream Father, please?'

Christopher reached into his pocket. 'There you are, there's a shilling. I want the change mind.' The two girls squealed with excitement and rushed over to the ice cream man pushing his ice-cream bicycle.

'Two cornets please,' Ruth asked politely. The man dressed in a white jacket and a peaked cap, lent over and lifted up the flap to the ice container. He reached inside and pulled out the oblong ice bars, undid their wrapper and pushed it into the rectangular cornet.

'Mnn, these are lovely,' said Rose.

'Come on let's get back to the Show.'

The two girls returned just in time to see the winner trotting around the arena.

'I like the Alsation puppy the best, not the Collie,' Rose ventured. As the crowd moved away light rain came from the darkening clouds.

'Let's get home quickly or we'll get a soaking.'

'I hope it doesn't rain tomorrow.'

'I'm still coming even it is.'

Friday the sun came out again and the villagers were up early getting ready for the Agricultural Show. Several farmhands helped the villagers set up long tables for the farm produce. Then the farmers brought in the pick of their animals. The village ladies helped to arranged the farm produce on the stalls. The green was gradually filling up.

Toot –toot – toot- toot. The shrill whistle came from the steamroller making its way slowly down Broad Street. People quickly moved to one side to allow the eleven- ton roller to pass by. The driver, wearing a flat cap wiped his hands on his dark blue overalls, waved to the onlookers then adjusted the driving wheel to adjust the length of the chain of the front roller. He gave another toot on the whistle. The pungent smell of the burning coals filled the air as the driver stoked the boiler fire now raging in its belly. The driver wiped his oily hands on an old vest, gave the wheel a turn to the left and the roller moved on to the village green. With his steamroller sited and still, he jumped down, wiping his sweaty face on the oily cloth. Mrs Pye joined him.

'Thank you very much for coming Mr Sutherland. I thought you might not come following the heavy rain last night.'

'Oh a drop of rain wouldn't stop us Mrs Pye. Thank you for asking us.'

Lots of children gathered round, asking all sorts of questions 'Where do you keep it?'

'Does it have brakes?'

'Do you have to polish it?'

'Where do you get the coal from?'

The Salvation Army band gave its rendition of 'She's a Lassie from Lancashire' which held the spectators' interest. Everyone cheered and the conductor led the band into its full repertoire. The musicians looked weary as they departed from the green. As they departed, amid cheers and clapping, the Boy Scouts took centre stage. Their drumming was enthusiastic as the boys marched around with the trumpets blasting out echoing around the playing field.

'They're really putting on a good show,' said a delighted parent.

'I'm very proud of all of them'. Mrs Pye said.

'Halt! The Drum Major shouted at the group.

The applause was deafening and as the boys left the green spectators called out 'Well done.' Gradually the crowd dispersed and the green was left to the people tidying up.

'Mrs Pye.'

'Yes Mrs Hardy.'

'I'd like to say what a wonderful job, your doing.'

'It's not just me Mrs Hardy. There's a lot going on behind the scenes. But it's very kind of you to say so.'

'I heard we have Royalty coming to the proceedings, tomorrow.'

'Now where did you get that bit of information from.'

'Just a rumour going round.'

'I don't know, one can't keep a secret here in Stylecroft.'

'But that's what we villagers do gossip.'

Saturday.

The village buzzed with the news the Sir Harold and Lady Parkinson of Hornby Castle were expected at the celebrations that afternoon.

Mrs Pye had written, inviting them to the proceedings and for them to oversee the Marbles Championships. With such distinguished guests Mrs Pye took extra care with her appearance. After spending some time in a hot bath making lots of bubbles with her sweet smelling apple blossom soap, she wrapped her bath towel around her and made her way to her bedroom. From out of wardrobe she selected her dark blue worsted suit. She chose a white high collared blouse and a stout pair of sturdy shoes.

She sat in front of the dressing table mirror, pulled her hair into a tight bun and secured it with long hairpins. She noticed a wisp of black hair had escaped the fasteners.

Now that won't *do*. It was pushed back into place.

The telephone rang.
'Hello'
'Ah Mrs Pye. This is lord and Lady Parkinson's Secretary calling. Are there are changes we need to be concerned about?'
'Oh! No…everything is going well.'
'And they are expected at three o'clock, yes?'
'That's right, three o'clock.'
'Very good, we'll see you then.'
The phone went dead.

That was short and to the point.

Mrs Pye thumbed through her paperwork, checking that everything was set for the afternoon's entertainment. Now she had confirmation that Lord and Lady Parkinson were coming, she could breathe a little easier.

She had thought she'd hear before this. But that's the gentry for you.

Three sides of fencing had been hammered into the green and a five bar gate made up the pen. A rope barrier would keep the general public at bay.

People had arrived early to get a good view of the sheep dog trials. The small children were allowed to sit at under the rope, but only with their promise of not going any further.

Five sheep were led out on to the green followed by a farmer and his collie.

A loud whistle echoed around the green started the proceedings. The black and white collie spurted across the field to the grazing sheep.

'Come by lad, come by my beauty,' the farmer called out.

A shrill whistle signalled to the dog and he immediately dropped to the ground.

'Good boy, steady, steady.'

The sheep looked nervously at the dog, but one stood his ground, eyeing him defiantly.

'There's always one isn't there,' someone in the crowd spoke. The collie crawled along on his belly, inching slowly forward.

'Steady lad.' Still the defiant sheep held his ground. Again the farmer called out, 'Steady lad.' Four of the animals stood in a cluster and bleated.

The obstinate animal glanced back at them. The Collie pounced forward, resulting in all five sheep being securely locked in the pen. Cheers and applause were heard and the tall farmer raised his cloth cap in acknowledgement. The adjudicator noted the time.

The trails were still going on when the Rolls Royce silently moved down Broad Street and came to a stop at the entrance to the field. The chauffeur scampered around the vehicle to open the door. Standing smartly to attention, he waited. An elegantly dressed woman carefully climbed out of the car. She wore a light blue suit with a hat to match and round her shoulder she wore a red, white and blue striped silk scarf. A Lancashire Rose brooch on her lapel sparkled in the bright sunlight of the afternoon.

Sir Harold, a tall gentleman stepped out of the car, smartly dressed in a navy blue suit.

'Sir Harold and Lady Parkinson I'm so pleased you were able to come.' Mrs Pye curtsied and step forward offering her hand of friendship.

'A pleasure dear lady, one must do ones bit.' She adjusted her wide brimmed hat that matched the blue of her suit. 'Come along Harold. Let's get the show on the road She strode ahead in her high-heeled shoes.

'This way.' Mrs Pye led the way to the rostrum. The padded chairs were placed next to the public address system and Lord and Lady Parkinson made themselves comfortable whilst Mrs Pye stepped forward to speak in the microphone.

'Ladies and Gentlemen, we have with us today Lord and Lady Parkinson, who have kindly agreed to give out the prizes later in the afternoon.'

The crowd clapped and cheered and the distinguished guests waved back to them.

'Sir Harold and Lady Parkinson, Ladies and Gentlemen. We now come to the Marble Championship. Any late comers are still welcome to take part, just give your names to the controller and we'll get started.'

A large circle had been roped off and in it's centre sat numerous marbles.

'The object of the game is, that each contestant will be armed with three marbles each and to remove as many marbles from the circle, with each throw.' Mrs Pye explained as each competitor took their turn a huge cheer vibrated around the green.

'Well done, who's next?' The controller called out. Gradually they worked through the list, until the last player.
'Anyone else wanting to have a go? The controller said.
'Over here, put my name down.' Sir Harold pushed his chair back and stood up.
'Cor blimey, I never thought I'd see his nibs playing marbles,' Bill Turner said.
Sir Harold walked over to the centre of the green and took hold of the three glass spheres. He took aim and threw the first one. The crowd applauded. Then he threw the second, again the crowd applauded. Then he threw the third one. The crowd's approval was extremely loud.
'Five marbles,' shouted the overseer above the noise. Sir Harold made his way back to the rostrum where he joined Lady Parkinson.
'Well who's a clever boy then,' Lady Parkinson lent over and whispered in his ear.
'Sir Harold, Lady Parkinson, Ladies and Gentlemen.' Mrs Pye had to wait for the noise to taper off.' I'd just like to thank everyone for all their help in making this a really a fantastic week of celebrations. Now I have the

pleasure in introducing Sir Harold and Lady Parkinson, who are going to present our prizes for us.' Mrs Pye took a step backwards as the couple moved towards the microphone.

'It's with great pleasure,' Lady Parkinson said. 'We can congratulate Mr. Smalley for winning the Sheep Dog trials with his dog Megan.' She handed him a small silver plate trophy. The crowd went mad, the thunderous cheering echoed around the empty village.

'And now for the Marble Championship. It gives me very great pleasure to announce the winner and it's Sir Harold. Many congratulation darling,' Lady Parkinson kissed him on both cheeks. Clutching his trophy he raised it in the air as the public showed their appreciation.

'After all our events throughout the week, we now come to the last. I'm talking about our firework display of course,' A lively applause rippled around the spectators.

'Mummy what's fireworks?'

'Cor! Is it going to happen now?'

'Can we stay up to see it, please?'

'I've seen fireworks before.'

'Are they going to reach the top of the world?'

'It looks as though they are crying.'

A profusion of colour filled the evening sky, Roman candles, spilling out their sparkling hues. The jumping jacks, cracking into the night air frightening the young ones. Catherine wheels, shooting bright stars in all directions. The hand held sparklers and finally the loud rockets, shooting their up and nearly touching the stars. The exclamations from the crowds watching with their 'oohs' and 'ahs' were more then enough to know they were enjoying the display. Tired, fractious children were slowly making their way back home and to their bed. They made way for the Rolls Royce making its way back up the Broad Street.

Mrs Pye walked into her tiny cottage. Inside the first thing she did was to kick off her shoes and padded into her kitchen. She put the kettle on and lit another gas ring and made herself an omelette. Pouring the boiling water over the tealeaves she sat down to a well-earned meal.

'I'm really pleased the way this week has gone. I don't think we could have done better. We've done Stylecroft proud. Now all we have to think about is the children's street party tomorrow.

Slowly she climbed up the steep stairs and undressed, visited the bathroom, then snuggled into her bed. She fell asleep as soon as her head rested on her pillows.

THIS IS THE BBC HOME SERVICE

HERE IS THE 9 O'CLOCK NEWS ON APRIL 12TH 1945

PRESIDENT ROOSEVELT DIES AT WARM SPRINGS GEORGIA

AND IS SUCCEEDED BY VICE PRESIDENT HARRY TRUMAN.

THAT IS THE END OF THE NEWS

Stylecroft planned a party of all parties just for the children. For days the villagers collected anything that could be used cups, plates, flags, buntings and balloons.

The morning finally arrived and the children could no longer contain their excitement.

The adults had placed benches and trestles along the centre of Broad Street to form a very long table. Every household supplied tablecloths. Chairs were provided from each home for the children. Parents, grandparents all used their food coupons for buying cakes jellies, blancmange. Sandwiches made with potted meat, jam, fish-paste, eggs and Spam. There was home made lemonade by the gallons.

The school had been opened especially for the children to come in to make party hats for the festivities.

'Do your best children,' Mrs Pye had said. The children did exactly that. Now at their tea party they proudly wore their party-hats. They had never seen so much food.

Mrs Pye, the Headmistress stepped up on to a podium and raised her hands for silence.

'I'd like to say thank you to all concerned for this extraordinary party for our young people.'

The children shouted and clapped. Again the Headmistress lifted her hands for silence.

'We have to remember, all our brothers and sisters who have lost loved ones, or who have been bombed out of their homes, our thought's are with you all. Now at last our celebrations can begin. Enjoy our tea party.' Screams and shouts of approval came from the children, bursting like a big balloon. Unable to keep them in check any longer the children ran forwards and the parents stood behind making sure they behaved themselves.

'Ohhhh!'
'Ahhhh!'
'Cor smashing.'
'I haven't got a spoon.'
'What's this Mum?'
'Can I have a drink please?'
'What's this yellow thing?'
'That's called a banana, silly.'
'How do I eat it then?'
'Just strip the skin off like this.'
'Thanks Mum.'

Screams of delight and general noise assured the adults that all their efforts were definitely appreciated. The children gorged themselves on the goodies they had never seen before. Gingerly placing the food into their mouths and with looks of satisfaction on their faces, it was clear they liked what they had tasted.

'Mum I feel sick.'

'You've eaten too much you silly girl.'

A few young children became fractious, overtired and weepy. Parents gathered them up in their arms and they fell asleep before they reached their beds. An army of adults worked together to dismantle the long table and clear up the mess left by their young children.

'What an evening to remember,' Mrs Pye commented.

'I've taken a few photographs. I hope they will turn out all right,' Donald said.

'Well, if there is nothing else to do, I'll be off to my bed.'

The rest of the children made their way to the green

at the end of Broad Street to where a large bonfire had been built.

'Bring out Hitler,' Mrs Pye shouted.

Several of the older children appeared steering a wheelbarrow. Placed in the barrow was an effigy, of Adolf Hitler, which the youngsters had made. Cheers, hoots, screams all vibrated together as Hitler was hoisted to the top of the pyre. The pile was lit and the flames greedily clawed their way up the stack of wood enveloping Hitler Several men stood watching, shaking their fists at the scene before them.

'Just what he deserves.'

'That's his just deserts.'

'Serves him right.'

'That's what we think of him.'

The flames greedily clawed their way up and greedily devoured Hitler.' There was a loud explosion when Adolf's head was blown into smithereens. There was jubilation as the blaze reached its height. The crowd had to step back from the burning inferno. Bill Turner stood by with his fire-bucket full of water. A burning log shot out of the blaze and Bill was ready.

'Well done Bill,' said Rev.Kelly.

'That's all right Vicar, can't be too careful.'

Mr. Smalley took his wife's arm and they said their goodnights and started to walk home. Broad Street was quiet. A few loose balloons, blown by the wind, chased along the road. Bunting joined in, waving the balloons goodbye. Even the leaves on the trees seemed to be celebrating. It was the end to an era; the promise of a free world, where war would be no more.

THIS IS THE BBC HOME SERVICE

HERE IS THE 9 O'CLOCK NEWS
ON MARCH 18TH 1945

JAPANESE SCHOOLS AND UNIVERSITIES
ARE SHUT DOWN
AS EVERYONE OVER THE AGE OF SIX
IS MOBILISED FOR THE WAR EFFORT

THAT IS THE END OF THE NEWS

Family life in Stylecroft soon returned to normality. A few weeks later a telegram boy cycled to the vicarage, placed his bicycle up against the stone wall and walked along the path to the front door and knocked. Footsteps echoed on the tiled floor and the heavy door swung open.

'Hello Mrs Kelly,' and handed her the envelope.

'Oh dear I don't like receiving telegrams. It's always bad news.'

Margaret apprehensively opened up the communication.

'Elizabeth! Elizabeth! It's from Wolfgang.'

'It's not bad news then?'

'No. Definitely not.'

'No reply needed? I'll be off then. Bye.'

'Thank you young man.'

Elizabeth read the message. 'Mother he's coming here,' emotion sounded in her voice.

'When?'

'Saturday. Oh that only leaves two days. I'm so excited, there's so much to do.' She rushed upstairs and immediately came back down.

'We'll have to tell Father. Where is he?'

'Tell Father what?' The twins walked into the middle of the turmoil

'It's Wolfgang. He's coming on Saturday.'

'Where?'

'Here.'

The girls screamed with excitement and twisted each other round and round in a tight circle.

'Calm down the pair of you. Stop it.'

'What's all the noise for,' Christopher walked into the

room.

Everyone started to talk at the same time.

'One at a time please,' he said covering his ears.

'It's Wolfgang Father, he's coming back home, Saturday.'

Elizabeth, the twins and Mother were grinning.

'Well it certainly looks as though everyone's pleased.'

The village buzzed with excitement at the latest news that Wolfgang was returning and the word was he was coming on Saturday. The corner shop was the centre of gossip.

'Did you here Wolfgang's coming back to the village?'

'We did. But I don't know if it's a good thing.'

'I think it's far too soon.'

'Well we'll see then won't we?'

Elizabeth made sure the bedroom in the attic was made up for Wolfgang's arrival. The window was thrown wide open to air the place. The tape had been removed from the window and she put a small vase of wild flowers as her gesture of welcome home. The blackout curtains had been replaced with flowery material to brighten up the room. She tried to keep herself busy, but her thoughts constantly harped back to his return.

'Something smells good,' Christopher poked his head around the kitchen door.

Margaret was busy, rolling out the rough puff pastry into a circle, which she placed on to a metal plate and filled it with succulent apples. Christopher dipped his finger into the mixture.

'Don't do that.' She smacked his arm with her wooden spoon.

'Too late,' he laughed sucking his finger.

'I'll not have any left for the pie, if you keep doing that.'

'Any left for us?' Rose and Ruth chipped in.

'No there's not. You can have some tomorrow. Off you go to school and don't dawdle on the way, or you'll be late.'

'It's not fair.'

'School! Scat or there'll be trouble.' Christopher put on his stern voice. The girls looked at one another.

'Where's your satchel?' Ruth asked

'On the hook behind the door.'

'And don't forget your books, young ladies.'

'I'm glad we don't have to worry about taking our gas masks now.'

'So am I.'

'See you at lunch time,' Margaret called after the girls as they left the house.

'All right.'

NEWS FLASH

THIS IS THE BBC HOME SERVICE.
HERE IS THE NEWS ON APRIL 30TH 1945

NEWS HAS JUST BEEN RECEIVED
THAT HITLER HAS COMMITTED SUICICE
IN BERLIN

THAT IS THE END OF THE NEWS

Wolfgang returned to England via the English Channel crossing, docking at Hull. He was anxious to travel to the village of Stylecroft as soon as possible. The train station heaved with travellers, all carrying their heavy luggage, as the porters had more than they could deal with. An ear piercing blast on the hooter warned the passengers that it was time to leave.

'All aboard!' Shouted the guard hanging on the open door with one hand and a flag in the other. Voluminous amount of steam billowed around the engine, making it practically invisible. The conductor looked up and down the line, raised his green flag and blew his whistle. Late comers hastily climbed on board, slamming shut the heavy doors. Slowly the iron horse jerked forward, pulling its hefty load with steam belching out of its funnel as the train gathered momentum.

Wolfgang experienced excitement in the pit of his stomach, as the countryside flashed past the window

I'll soon be seeing my Elizabeth. Never for a moment has she left my thoughts. I'll stop off at Sticklebeck to visit Mr. Grimes. He was so kind to me, while I was interned at camp177

The train slowed as it approached the tiny station, the steam enveloping the engine as it came to a stop. Wolfgang jumped out of the carriage, slammed the door shut and walked to the exit.

'Ticket please.'

'Oh, sorry, I didn't know it would still be needed,' he fished in his pocket for the stub. 'There you are sir.'

'Thank you young man and are you visiting here?'

'Yes I am. I'm calling to visit Farmer Grimes.'
'Ah, Edward and Mabel. Lovely couple.'
'Yes I know. I used to work for them.'
'Well that will be a nice surprise for them both.'
'I certainly hope so. Goodbye.' He waved as he left the station.

He had about a couple of miles to walk to the Fieldhouse farm. As he travelled along the leafy lanes, it brought back memories when they all sweated and toiled in the fields, gathering in the crops, he could still hear his compatriots singing their German songs.

In a way, they were happy times. Not far now I bet this will be quite a shock for them.

He climbed over the style, taking a short cut to the farm. The stone built farmhouse appeared on the crest of the hill, overlooking the valley. He couldn't see anyone about, but as he approached two dogs announced his arrival. He rapped on the faded door and waited. Footsteps sounded on the flagstones and then the door was slowly opened.
'Mr. Grimes!'
'Wolfgang, what a surprise, come in, come in.'
'I thought I would call in to see you both on my way to Stylecroft.'
'Sit down lad and have a cup of tea with us. Mother, put kettle on.'
They sat around the scrubbed table, talking of past times.
'I remember all of you riding on the old tractor,

clinging to its sides, singing your heads off. Wasn't that right Mother?'

'Aye it was.'

'How are things now Mr. Grimes? I know it's been hard for you, with the war and everything. Farmers at home, many have gone, very few of them are still in business.'

'Things here are bad, really bad. Farming has reached an all time low. Now if I could diversify into another commodity, I would. But, it takes money and that's not available unfortunately. Now if I could find someone to come in with me with a little bit of capitol, I would jump at the chance. We would probably break even in the first year. But hark at me I'm daydreaming. Who would come along and put their money into such a venture? They'd be mad to try it.'

'I would.'

'You Wolfgang. I can't believe it. You must be pulling my leg.'

'No, I'm serious.'

The two men looked across the table at each other.

'You mean you'd be willing to work the land, side by side?'

'I would.'

'It wouldn't be a walk over. There's so much prejudice here, wounds are still very deep. It will take years for it to heal, maybe never.'

'I realise it will be a uphill struggle. My Father always used to say 'You never gain anything without working for it first.' 'We hit it off together, when we first met and that meant a great deal to me. The kindness you showed us, under the circumstances, made a real impression on me.'

Mabel Grimes looked from one man to the other, holding her breath not daring to voice her opinion

'I've made my decision Mr. Grimes.'

'Edward, Wolfgang. Edward and Mabel.'

'I've put a bit behind me Edward, before the war. There's nothing to hold me now in my homeland. I made the decision to come back, make my way to Stylecroft and ask my Elizabeth for her hand in marriage.'

'Congratulation lad.' Edward grabbed Wolfgang's hand, shaking it up and down as though he was pumping water from the well. 'Congratulations,'

'My best wishes too,' Mabel said.

'When I ask her it will add a sense of security for her too.'

'Are you certain about buying into the farm? It's a big step.'

'I feel it's right Edward. Let's shake on it,' Wolfgang offered his hand to clench the deal. Edward leant across the table and grasped his hand.

'Now you're a partner in Fieldhouse Farm. How does it feel?'

'It feels as though I have roots here all ready.'

'Another cup of tea Mother to celebrate.' Mabel scurried across the kitchen to put the kettle back on the Aga.

'Never mind the tea Mother. There's a keg of beer in the cellar,'

The barrel was tapped and three jugs of the brown liquid filled the pint vessels and with the chink of glasses the deal was sealed. The smiles all around were a clear indication that each party was more than satisfied with the arrangement.

Wolfgang reached into the inside pocket of his jacket and with drew a large bundle of rolled banknotes. He pulled off the thick elastic band that secured them and started to count.

Edward and Mabel stood transfixed their mouths dropped open in astonishment unable to comprehend that he would carry such a large amount of money with him. They had never seen so much money in one place.

'Did you print them this morning?' Joked Edward pointing to the pile of notes.

'This is my savings Edward, to get Elizabeth and myself a good start.'

He passed over almost half of the bankroll and re-wound the rest of it in the elastic band and dropped it back into his inside pocket.

'This is unexpected lad. I'd have thought that your savings would be back home, not on you,'

'It's going to be a big surprise for Elizabeth,' Mabel said.

'I know. I can hardly wait to tell her. Well I suppose I had better be on my way. I did send a telegram to her saying I would arrive Saturday. Thanks Edward. Bye Mabel. We'll be back soon.'

'Bye lad.'

The two men strolled through the cobbled yard to where the tractor was parked. They climbed on board the machine and with a splutter the engine burst into life. It lurched forward and chugged its way along the uneven track to the main road.

'This brings back memories Edward.'

'Aye, it would lad.'

Wolfgang looked over the fertile land from his

advantage point. He could hardly believe the turn of events. He knew he would always be grateful to Edward, in giving him this chance to make a fresh start.

'Looks as though the bus is late.'

'They sometimes take one off if they haven't the drivers.'

'Oh no. I'll miss my connection.'

'There's an old motor bike in the barn. I still use it occasionally.'

'Thanks Edward.'

The two men retraced their journey back to the farmhouse. In the barn Edward pulled out his old Ariel 1000.

'Ever driven one before?'

'A motor bike? Yes.' Wolfgang replied.

'Well hop on, she'll get you there in time, partner.'

'I don't know how to thank you Edward.'

'Just get yourself to Stylecroft and ask your girl's hand in marriage.' He slapped him on his shoulder.

Wolfgang stood astride the machine and kick started it. With a throaty throb the engine burst into life.

'Safe journey lad.'

'Thanks Edward.'

He opened the throttle and drew away. With a wave of his hand he disappeared around the bend and he was on his way back to Stylecroft.

THIS IS THE BBC HOME SEVICE.
HERE IS THE 9 O'CLOCK NEWS
ON JULY 3RD 1945

WETERN ALLIED TROOPS ENTER BERLIN

THAT IS THE END OF THE NEWS

'How about you girls make a welcome home card for Wolfgang?' Christopher suggested. Scissors, glue, paper and pens were gathered on the kitchen table. The girls busied themselves with the job in hand and silence reigned for about fifteen minutes.

'Mines better than yours,' declared Ruth.
'No it's not.'
'It is, it's bigger.'
'They're the same size.'
'No it's not.'
'Girls, you're not in competition with each other.'
'But Father.'
'No more arguing.'

The local LMS train pulled into the station, it's brakes squealing as it shuddered to a stop. The doors opened and it's occupants alighted. Eagerly Elizabeth scanned over the members of the public. Where was he? Her disappointment welled up and tears toppled down her cheeks. The conductor raised his green flag and blew his whistle and slowly the train gathered momentum, disappearing in a blanket of steam. Leaving Elizabeth standing on the platform alone.

'Didn't they turn up Missy?' The conductor asked.
'No he didn't.'
'Perhaps he'll be on the next one.'

She nodded and turned to leave the station despondency filling her whole body.

Perhaps he's changed his mind.

She was aware of a roar of a motor bike's engine

throbbing, behind her,

Oh dear, someone has missed the train.

She turned to make her way out of the station and walked straight into Wolfgang.

'I thought you were coming by train?'

'I was. But I had the chance of the bike and as my friend had still some petrol coupons left, I didn't hesitate.'

They stood facing one another, their eyes locked in an intimate moment. Elizabeth took a step forward, moved up on her toes, as he drew her to him, imprisoning her with his arms and their lips met with their first meaningful kiss.

A porter pushed along a heavily laden trolley and seeing the couple locked in a kiss, smiled and passed by the couple who was completely oblivious to his existence.

They broke apart embarrassed at their show of their feelings in public. Then they laughed at one another.

'Come on, jump on and come for a spin,' he tickled the carburettor, jumped on the kick start and the engine burst into life. He stood astride the throbbing machine waiting for Elizabeth to climb on. She stood on the foot support, tucked her wide skirt around her knees and sat down on the seat. She hung on as tight as she could around his waist. Wolfgang twisted the throttle and they lurched forward. With a roar they were transported through the village leaving a trail of dust in their wake.

'Mother, Mother, we've just seen our Elizabeth on the back of a motorbike,' Rose and Ruth shouted out, breathless from running.

'No surely not. She's meeting Wolfgang.'

'It was, it was her,' they shouted again.

'Christopher!' Margaret called out down the back garden to where he was working in the greenhouse.

'What's the matter,' Christopher's head popped around the door of the shed.

'The girls reckoned that they have seen Elizabeth on the back of a motorbike.'

'Are you sure?' He addressed the question to them as he wiped his hands.

'We're certain Father,' Rose assured him.

'What's she doing on the back of a motorbike? Margaret asked.

Christopher shrugged his shoulders. 'Goodness knows. She'll be back, so don't worry.' He returned to his garden and the vegetable patch.

My beautiful lawn, all dug up to help the war effort, dig for victory we're told. His thoughts returned to his eldest daughter. *What was she up to now, tearing through the countryside? Who do we know who owns a motorbike? I'll have to have a word with her when she returns. It's not good enough.*

The wind whipped through her hair as she gripped Wolfgang's chest. She could feel his heart steadily beating and she enjoyed the closeness. The exhilaration was breathtaking. She lent forward and shouted in his ear,' Where are we going?'

'Morecambe Bay,' he shouted back.

'But that's more than twenty miles away.' They passed farms where the horse pulled plough was still in use and land girls wearing their brown uniform; headscarves, blouses and jodhpurs, using their pitch forks as good as any man, waved as they passed by. Wolfgang steered the bike expertly, down winding roads, passing the milk churns awaiting collection. Gradually he throttled back down as they approach the qicksands of Morecambe Bay.

As they came to a stop Elizabeth said,' I must telephone home, as they will be worried.' She made the call.

'Hello. Ah, Mother. Yes It's me. Wolfgang came by motor bike instead of the train and we've gone for a ride. Where am I now? We're in Morecambe Bay. That's right Morecambe Bay. All right we'll be back later. Bye.'

'Lets walk along the beach.' He caught hold of her hand and led her towards the sea. They walked along the water's edge, leaving footsteps in the virgin sand.

'I love the sea, in all its moods.'

'What about in the winter when the waves are crashing on the foreshore?'

'I still love it. It holds a fascination for me. Come on we had better make a start back.' They retraced their steps, trying to step into their imprints they had made earlier, but failed miserably. As promised, they arrived back home before dark and walked into the vicarage hand in hand.

'Welcome back to Stylecroft.' Christopher held out his hand in friendship and Wolfgang gladly accepted it. They all sat around the kitchen table swapping stories.

Wolfgang pulled out a couple of photographs from his breast pocket. The first was one of his parents, who were now no longer alive and his sister who still lived on the outskirts of Hamburg. The other photograph was of Wolfgang and his fellow prisoners of war, all dressed in their grey uniforms. The amazing thing was they were all smiling.

'It looks as though they were all happy,' Elizabeth commented.

'They were. It was the end of the war.'

'Ah.'

'Don't get me wrong. It wasn't that hard. We mostly worked on the land. The farmer was kind to us. There was plenty of work to do. Helping with the animals, harvesting, even clearing the snow when it was needed.'

'Now that's all in the past and we can rebuild our lives,' Christopher said.

'I'm so glad you feel that way. I was troubled about our differences. But I felt at home while I was here. I thought a great deal about Elizabeth.' He looked at her with such longing; her parents guessed what was coming next.

'I wanted to come and ask you for your permission for us to get engaged and then marry.' Wolfgang sat next to Elizabeth, holding her hand. They both looked at her parents, hardly daring to breathe.

'We thought you might ask us that. Yes, we'll give you our blessings, with greatest pleasure.' Christopher and Margaret walked over to them and hugged the pair. Wolfgang dropped on to one knee, in front of Elizabeth. The twins watchful eyes were carefully monitoring the event taking place in front of them.

'Dear sweet Elizabeth.' He took hold of her hand and looked into her blue eyes. 'Elizabeth, will you do me the honour of becoming my wife?'

She stood for a couple of seconds, unable to take in what Wolfgang had said. Her eyes danced with excitement, her cheeks flushed as she stepped into his arms trying to gulp back the tears of happiness.

'How I missed you, my little one.'

'Oh. Wolfgang, I thought the day would never come.'

'You haven't answered my question dearest. Don't keep me waiting any longer.'

'Wolfgang, of course I'll marry you.'

He squeezed her so tightly she could hardly draw breath.' You will? That's great, my darling. There's no time for tears.' He gently wiped them away. 'It's time to celebrate.'

'It certainly is. My little girl getting married. That's wonderful news.' Christopher joined in the celebrations.

Elizabeth wiped her eyes and gave both of her parents a big hug.' You've made us very happy.'

'And us,' said the twins jumping up and down.

'That's not the only reason to celebrate, there's other news.' Wolfgang hugged Elizabeth, unable to keep the secret any longer. 'Guess what's happened?'

'I don't know, I can't fathom out what you're talking about.'

'An extraordinary opportunity was placed in my lap.'

'Come on Wolfgang, don't keep us all in suspense any longer.' Christopher said

'Well do you remember Edward Grimes/'

'The farmer you used to work for?'

'Yes that's right. He was so good to me during those troubled times. I thought I'd call back and visit with him while I was here'

'That's a kind thing to do.'

'He was telling me of how hard times had been for them and he was maybe looking for some one to come in and help with the farm.'

'How wonderful a job too.' Elizabeth could hardly contain her excitement.

'But that's not all.'

'No, there's more? Don't hold it all inside you. I'm itching to know,' she pulled at his sleeve with impatience.

'I'm coming to the best bit now. You must let me have my five minutes of glory.'

'Wolfgang!'

'Well it vasn't, sorry, was not only a job he offered'

'What was it then?' her parents asked in unison.

'A partnership. There I've told you.' He sat back his smile spreading from ear to ear.

'A partnership.' Elizabeth repeated. Her jaw dropped open with surprise. ' I don't believe it.'

'Well it's true. I paid him the money before he could change his mind.'

'Oh Wolfgang, I'm so proud of you.'

'Congratulations my boy.' Christopher jumped up and shook his hand.

'Well done. You've well and truly surprised all of us.' Margaret was thrilled that her daughter's future was secured.

'Have you got horses on your farm?' asked Ruth.

'Yes, there are a few.'

'We love horses. Could we ride on them do you think, please?' Rose implored.

'I think we could manage that,' replied Wolfgang.

Bedlam broke loose in the Kelly family and the twins ran riot in their excitement at the thought of riding horses.

'Let's go for a walk darling.' Wolfgang took Elizabeth's arm and steered her outside. He stopped dead in his tracks.

'You will marry me my darling?' His face showed a little tension.'

'Of course I will my love.'

He pulled her to him and their lips met in a deep kiss that only lovers could feel.

'Well really! Kissing in public like that, it's disgusting.' Wolfgang and Elizabeth turned guiltily towards the voice.

'Oh hello Mrs Parker, nice to see you,' they giggled.

'I reckon she should be known as Mrs Nosy Parker,' Elizabeth whispered in Wolfgang's ear. They wandered back into the vicarage, where the family was waiting for them to return.

'I wanted you all to be here when I placed the ring on Elizabeth's finger,' he rummaged in his pocket, his fingers searching for the square box.

'Ah, here it is,' he held it aloft so as everyone could see the red container.

'Isn't it exciting,' Ruth nudged Rose. Wolfgang opened up the case to reveal a solitaire diamond. Elizabeth gasped.

'Wolfgang it's beautiful,' the words caught in the back of her throat. 'Beautiful.' Wolfgang pulled the ring out of the case and placed it on Elizabeth's finger.

'There you are my sweet one.'

There were hugs and smiles and congratulations from all of the family. The twins were pushing one another as to who would see the ring first.

'Now girls, that's not the way to behave, is it?' Christopher reprimanded them.

Pouting they turned away and sat themselves down on a chair, while their Mother clung to her daughter, whispering her congratulations too. They all sat around the table. Margaret took out a cake from the pantry and placed it in the middle of them, along with plates and forks.

'How I missed your cooking Margaret,' Wolfgang said.

'Thank you,' she smiled at the compliment.

I feel so happy for them and yet a little sad too, because I know of the resentment that they will encounter. Sadness too; Elizabeth will be leaving the family home.

How the years had flown. My little girl is getting married.

Her body shivered as she thought about the animosity there was in the village from people who knew them.

If their love is strong enough they will survive. She comforted herself with the thought.

THIS IS THE BBC HOME SEVICE.
HERE IS THE 9 O'CLOCK NEWS
ON AUGUST 6TH 1945

THE USA DROPS THE FIRST ATOMIC BOMB
ON HIROSHIMA KILLING 75,000 JAPENESE
CIVILIANS.

THAT IS THE END OF THE NEWS

The marriage between Wolfgang and Elizabeth was to take place on October 20th 1947. Reverend Christopher Kelly had contacted Bishop Blackburn by telephone to see if he would stand in for him, as he desperately wanted to give his daughter away. The bishop agreed, but not before he had sounded out their feelings about Elizabeth marrying a German.

'Of course I'll marry the sweet child, She'll need all the support she can get.'

Christopher strode into the kitchen with the good news. The girls squealed with excitement.

'Can we be bridesmaids? Please, please can we? We haven't been bridesmaids before.'

Elizabeth dropped on to her knees to be level with them.

'Of course, my little sisters would make wonderful bridesmaids.'

Their excitement exploded and they chased one another around the kitchen, out into the garden and back again chanting, ' We're going to be bridesmaids, we're going to be bridesmaids.'

'Girls, girls. Let's have a little decorum shall we?'

'But Father, we're going to be bridesmaids.'

'My daughter's getting herself married.' Margaret spoke out loud, as though trying to convince herself it was all true.

'Mother I'm going to need your help. There is so many things that have to be done. Book the hall, flowers, the cake, dresses, may be a car?'

'One thing at a time darling. Let's sit down and write out a list. Then we can start to plan from there.'

She won't need me any more after the wedding. It's as though my life is crumbling and I can't do anything to stop it.

Sadness filled her, she was entering another phase in her life, and her centre then would be the twins. Then after they went, it would be just her and Christopher. They would have to get to know one another again. She hadn't given much thought about it before. The sudden awareness her life was about to change too, for some reason filled her with dread.

Margaret went upstairs into her bedroom, knelt down at the wardrobe and pulled open the bottom drawer. She withdrew a brown paper parcel and placed it on the end of her bed. Carefully she unfolded the paper, inside was leaves of tissue paper, which were cosseting her wedding dress. She gently smoothed out the creases and lifted up her gown and held it in front of her. She turned to look in the full-length mirror.

It had been such a wonderful day, the sun shone, everything went off so well. Now it's my daughters turn. I hope she is as happy as we were, she thought.

'Ah! There you are. I thought you'd be up here.' Christopher poked his head around the door.

'Do you think Elizabeth might like to wear it? It's probably too old fashioned for her.'

'I don't think she'll say that,' Christopher took a couple of steps towards her and took her in his arms. 'You're as pretty now as you were then. Come on, let's go and see what she thinks.'

Elizabeth and Wolfgang were busy writing as they came into the kitchen.

'Mother wants to ask you a question.'

'What's that then?'

'Well I was wondering if you might like to use my wedding dress. Just say if you don't want too.'

'Where is it?' Elizabeth asked.

'Upstairs, hanging in my wardrobe. Would you like to see it?'

'Mother, that's wonderful. Why haven't I seen it before this?'

'I'd forgotten all about it until just now.'

'Come on then. We mustn't let Wolfgang see it, or it will be bad luck.'

Mother and daughter climbed the narrow stairs and into the bedroom. The dress lay on top of the bed, spread out, a reminder of the past.

'Mother! It's beautiful. Look at the lace and the seed pearls.' Elizabeth picked up the dress and held it up against her. She stood in front of the long mirror admiring her image.

'Come on let's see if it fits.'

Elizabeth undressed and her Mother helped her into the silk garment.

'Mother it fits perfectly. You must have been the same size as me.'

'I wasn't always this size, I'll have you know.' Margaret said.

'It's exquisite, look how the sleeves taper over my hand. It won't need any alterations at all. Oh Mother, we wouldn't be able to afford any thing like this. That's if we could get it, with the ration on clothing still in force. Are you sure you don't mind if I use it?' Elizabeth asked.

'It's been packed away in the bottom of the wardrobe for years. I'm only too pleased you like it.'

'Like it. I love it. Thank you so much Mother for this gift. It will make it such a wonderful day.'

The two women stood in an embrace, a Mother and daughter moment to be treasured.

'Are you two all right up there?' Christopher called up the stairs.

'Yes. We'll be down in a moment.' Margaret answered.

They quickly folded up the gown wrapped it in the tissue paper and returned it to the bottom of the wardrobe.

They walked down stairs and into the kitchen where the rest of the family sat drinking tea.

'Well?' Wolfgang asked.

'Why couldn't we come upstairs to watch.' Rose wanted to know.

'Because it was a very special moment between Mother and daughter.'

'We're special.' Ruth pointed out.

'And your moment will come too.' Mother said.

'The dress, will it be suitable?' Christopher was just as anxious as Wolfgang.

'It was wonderful, and it fitted as though it were made for me. I couldn't have chosen a better one.' Elizabeth looked at her Mother and smiled.

'And what about us?'

'Well, we'll see how many coupons we can muster up. Then we'll buy some material and we'll make you really pretty dresses.' Mother said.

'When?' they chorused.
'As soon as it's possible.' Elizabeth retorted.

The village buzzed with excitement as the news spread that there was to be a wedding in the village. Margaret and Christopher were stopped so many times by people who wanted to know all the details.

'It's disgusting.' Mrs Walton voiced her opinion. 'Do they really think it will last.'

'Who's to say it won't.' Mabel defended them.

'I bet she's got too.' Mrs Walton's lips tightened into a thin line.

'Mrs Walton! You've gone too far. You don't know that so why make accusations.'

'You don't know either do you?'

'You're just being nasty.'

'Then why is she marrying a German?'

'Love Mrs Walton, plain old-fashioned love. Is that too hard for you to under stand?'

'Then why not pick one of our lads?'

'It's beyond any one's control, who we fall in love with.' Mabel gestured with her hands.

'Bunkum.' Mrs Walton turned and walked away.

'The old cow.'

'Since the petrol is still rationed, we have a problem, there are no cars on the road.' Christopher voiced his concerns.

Mabel had popped in for a cup of tea. Margaret was pleased to see her friend and of course the conversation was about the wedding.

'Let's put on our thinking caps and see what we can come up with.' Margaret said.

'The only suggestion I can think of is a pony and trap.' Mabel

'What a grand idea,' Christopher lent forward and picked up a cup and saucer. 'We could decorate it.'

'That sounds wonderful, we'll suggest it to Elizabeth when she gets back home.'

'I know Farmer Smalley owns a pony and trap. I'm sure he'd be pleased to help.'

'It would certainly provide us with transport. I know we live next to the church, but they could take a trip around the village first, before the ceremony.

'We'll find out first if Elizabeth would like it.' Margaret said.

When Elizabeth returned home from school, they excitedly told her of their thoughts.

'What do you think?' Father asked her.

'I think it's a marvellous idea.'

'You've Mabel to thank for that little gem.'

'I will thank her. It will make it so special. Will you have a word with Farmer Smalley for us?'

'Of course I will, leave it with me.' Christopher said.

As the wedding date grew nearer, the excitement seemed to escalate in the village. Margaret tended her front garden, the autumn colours had always fascinated her, the golds, the yellows, the reds. She loved her summer garden too, but always looked forward to the change in the fall. Her roses were still flowering and she had nurtured pot plants in the greenhouse, which would bring more colours into the garden for the special day.

The twins' enthusiasm could hardly be harnessed. They ran when they should have been walking, screaming when they should have been quiet and squabbling even more than usual.

'My dress is going to be better than yours,' taunted Rose.

'Oh no it wont,' replied Ruth.

'It will. I just know it will.'

'Girls, please be good. We have a lot to contend with and your not helping with all this bickering.'

'Mother she's saying her dress will be better than mine. It wont will it?'

'They will be exactly the same. Now girls run along and find your colouring books and crayons.' Margaret breathed a sigh of relief as they went to find something to do.

'She's pinched my book.' Rose popped her head around the door.

'For goodness sake girls. I'll have to stop your comics, if you're going to continue like this.'

By this time Rose and Ruth realised they had gone as far as they dare and turned to go up to their bedroom. As they did so Rose pulled her sister's pigtail.

'Mother, she's pulled my hair,' Ruth screamed out.

'Right. All comics are stopped for a week.'

'But Mother I didn't do anything,' wailed Ruth.

'Whether you did or not is beside the point. It's still no comics.'

Christopher walked into the room.

'Father, Mother has said we can't have our comics. We can can't we,' She smiled sweetly at him, moving her head to one side.

'If Mother has said no, then it's no.'

'But Father we haven't done anything.' Rose managed to squeeze out a solitary tear.

'You must have been up to something, or Mother wouldn't have stopped your comics. So that's the end of it.'

The two girls looked from one parent to the other, turned and walked away.

'It's not fair,' they chorused.

Wolfgang and Elizabeth sat in the front room discussing their forthcoming wedding.

'Who will you ask to be your best man?'

'I've been thinking about that and I was wondering about asking Edward.'

'That would be smashing. I bet he would be tickled pink. How about we take a trip over there to ask him?'

'What a good idea. We'll do that. Have we enough petrol coupons for the bike? Or shall we go by train?'

'The bike would be easier.'

They made their way through the countryside, heading for Fieldhouse Farm.

'Are you excited?' Wolfgang shouted at Elizabeth on the back of the pillion.

'Of course I am you silly goose.'

They were greeted with great enthusiasm.

'Welcome, welcome. It's so nice to meet the future Mrs Rumfler. Put the kettle on Ma,' Edward shouted over his shoulder.

'That sounds so strange,' Elizabeth smiled coyly.

'You'll have to get used to it,' Wolfgang laughed.

'I know, but it still sounds funny.'

Seated in the kitchen of Fieldhouse Farm, Elizabeth looked around.

To think we are part owners of the farm, it's unbelievable. What luck that Wolfgang had the money. We're so fortunate.

'There's a reason we've come today, Edward.'
'You've not changed your mind lad?'
'Oh no nothing like that. I'm more than happy about our arrangements. No, we've come over to ask a favour.'
'Fire ahead my boy.'
'We're getting married on October 20th.
'Mnn, I heard that.'
'Well, we would like to ask you would you be my best man?'

Edward sat there in silence, his mouth dropped with surprise

' I'm flabbergasted lad, absolutely flabbergasted. Did you here that Ma. Me, to be best man. Can you believe it?'

'Well, I've heard it all now.'

'Of course lad with the greatest of pleasure.' He jumped up took hold of Wolfgang's hand pumping it up and down several times, grinning from ear to ear.

'Ma get the glasses, this calls for a celebration.'

Mabel scurried from the kitchen and returned with four-pint jugs filled to the brim with amber nectar.

'A toast to the young couple. May your way be smooth and may you be blest with many children, unlike us.' Edward gathered Mabel's hand into his, and lifted it towards his lips.

'Silly old devil.' Mabel turned away embarrassed.

'Is it still all right to use your motorbike Edward?'

'Of course it is lad, use it as long as you want. It was only standing in the yard.'

'Thank you. It will help us get around, without having to wait for the train.'

'Yes thank you Edward.' Elizabeth stood up. 'For the motor bike and for agreeing to be Wolfgang's best man.'

'A pleasure my dear.'

'And thank you Mabel, for the tea and the beer, and we'll see you on the 20th.'

'That you will. You can be sure of that.' Elizabeth bent forward and gave Mabel a kiss on the side of her cheek.

'We'll see you soon.' Elizabeth called out as she climbed onto the pillion. Wolfgang kick started the machine and with a wave they disappeared out of the yard towards the main road.

'Imagine me, the best man Mabel. I'll have to dig that suit out from the wardrobe and make sure I haven't put on too much weight and make sure the moths haven't made a meal of it.'

'And I'll have to have a suitable dress to wear. We haven't enough coupons to buy anything else. Perhaps I could find one in my wardrobe and jazz it up a bit.'

'Do you think they will be able to make a go of it Edward?'

'I do. They're so much in love. I'm sure they will be able to rise above all the animosity that there's sure to be.'

'They make a lovely looking couple.'

'Well have to think about that when they come here to live. Where could they stay? It couldn't be with us, there's not the room.'

'Now let's think this out. We've an old outhouse that could be used.'

'But it's a mess.'

'I know. It could be worked on. How about if we did it for them as a wedding present, what do you think?'

'It would be a lot of hard work Edward.'

'I'm not afraid of hard work,' he retorted.

'But do we have the materials to do it?'

'Let me think. Yes, we had put a lot of wood in the hay-barn, that was never used, what do you think?

'I think it is a grand idea.' Mabel agreed.

'Right then, I'll start on it tomorrow'

'Are you going to tell them about it?'

'I wondered if I told them on their wedding day.'

Mabel started to clear the kitchen table. 'But if you leave it till then, they may make other arrangements.'

'That's true. We'll make a start and let them into the secret a little later on.'

'Good idea.'

'I reckon Edward was more than pleased,' Elizabeth shouted into Wolfgang's ear.

He nodded and they made their way back to Stylecroft, once again passing through the green fields of the countryside, with the wind whipping through their hair.

'He was certainly taken aback.' Wolfgang raised his voice.

'I loved the look on his face. One of astonishment, I wish I had had a camera.'

The pair of them leaned to the left as the negotiated a U bend.

'Hold on tight,' Wolfgang called out.

Elizabeth gripped his waist. She loved to feel the closeness and she hoped it would always be so.

THIS IS THE BBC HOME SERVICE.
HERE IS THE 9 O'CLCK NEWS.
ON AUGUST 17TH 1945

TO CELEBRATE
BANNERS ARE TO BE HUNG
TO WELCOME HOME
OUR RETURNING BRITISH ~~SEVICEMEN~~

THAT IS THE END OF THE NEWS

Elizabeth and Wolfgang returned to the village walking hand in hand along the Broad Street their happiness shining like the rays of the sun. Mrs Walton stood in the shop doorway.

'Look at them,' she snapped.

'What?' Mrs Green enquired,

'Those two. It's sickening. What do you make of it?'

'I feel sorry for them.'

'Sorry! Why?'

'They will get an enormous wall of animosity aimed at them, because of the war.'

'Serve him right. He's deceitful.'

'I agree it wasn't very nice. But what would you have done if you were in his place?'

'That's besides the point.'

'But you must have a view?'

'Well I haven't,' Mrs Walton was quite adamant and folded her arms under her breasts.

'I'll be off then, see you another time,' Mrs Green made her way down Broad Street towards the Red Lion.

After collecting as many clothing coupons as possible, Margaret managed to buy a length of pale green shot silk.

'Well done Mother, you've worked wonders. I didn't think you'd be able to do it.'

So the two of them began to cut out the bridesmaid's dresses.

'Pass the pins Elizabeth.'

Margaret pinned the tissue pattern to the material and carefully started to cut around it.

'Is that for us?' The twins rushed into the room.

'Shhh, or you'll make Mother go wrong.'
'But is it for us?'
'Yes, now be quiet, if it's at all possible. You won't want one sleeve longer than the other, will you?'

That seemed to do the trick. Rose and Ruth settled themselves down on the settee to watch.

'There that's job done,' Margaret breathed a sigh of relief. 'Put the kettle on there's a love and well stop for a cup of tea.'

Margaret pulled out the sewing machine from deep inside the cupboard under the stairs. Next she threaded the machine with a pale green cotton to match the material. Slowly she turned the handle and started to sew the garments together.

'Are they nearly done?' Ruth said.

'They'll get done a lot quicker if you're a good girl.' Elizabeth remarked, carrying in the cups of tea on a tray.

'Tea's up Mother'

'All right I'll only be a minute longer.' The dresses began to take shape. First the sleeves were fitted then the interface of the neck-line and lastly the long belts.

The girl's dresses were hanging on hangers by the time they returned from school. With squeals of delight they tried them on. Parading in front of the long wardrobe mirror, twisting and turning, looking at their image from every angle.

'Have you home work to do?' Margaret asked.

'Yes. But, we can do it later.'

'Then hang the dresses back up their hangers and away you go then.'

'But can't we keep them on for a little while longer? Asked Ruth.

'No, get on with your Home Work.'

The village hall was booked for the wedding at two o'clock and the flowers have been ordered. Most of the arrangements had been attended to. It was only left for the invitations to be sent out. Thought Elizabeth

'Is there anything I can help with Mother?'

'Not really pet. I'm just making the cake. You can sit and talk to me if you like. The sugar and butter rations have been saved. Farmer Smalley gave fresh eggs,'

'Everyone has been so kind,' observed Elizabeth.

'I'm using my recipe as it's tried and tested.'

'What are the ingredients?'

'Eggs, butter, sugar and water, then the fruit is boiled for 20mins. Then you add flour eggs and cook for one and half-hours or until it's cooked. On gas mark 2.

'It seems a pretty easy recipe to follow.'

'It is and it never fails. A good result every time.'

'You'll have to let me have it Mother and I can impress Wolfgang with my cooking.' A little later Christopher walked into the kitchen. 'Mnnn that smells delicious.'

'Have you visited old Mrs Harding?'

'Yes, she's not been too well lately, but just as feisty as usual. Is that the wedding cake?' Margaret nodded.

'I hope it will turn out all right.'

'Of course it will Margaret.'

'You know your efforts are appreciated darling,' Christopher gave her a big hug.

'Of course they are.' Elizabeth joined in and the

three of them stood grouped as the twins came in from school.

'What's going on? Is something the matter?' Ruth asked.

'No, nothings wrong. Get upstairs and change and then come down and we'll have tea.'

'But mother we've only just come in.' Rose said.

'Change!'

The big day arrived and the rain clouds hung heavy and rain was threatening at any time. Last minute jobs were undertaken.

The vicarage seemed full of visitors, mostly parishioners and the Mother's Union members and the young wives group, all brought food for the table.

'How can we thank you all,' Christopher received all the gifts with a humble manner.

'Thank you so much.' He looked up into the bluest of blue eyes. ' Pardon me, but don't I know you?'

'I don't think so,' she smiled and covered her marked face with her head scarf and disappeared into the crowd of visitors.

I know her from somewhere, but where?

Margaret disappeared into the peace of the greenhouse, just giving her plants the once over before taking them out to the front of the vicarage.

They look wonderful, even if I say it myself.

She gathered up the flowers and carried them round

to the other side of the building, placing them at each side of the concrete pathway.

There I hope she's pleased with them. They look almost as though they've been painted.

She wandered back into the vicarage with a wide smile on her face.
'Elizabeth have you got a few minutes? I'd like you to see something.'
'All right Mother, coming.'
The two of them walked out into the fresh air.
'Look at them. What do you think?'
Elizabeth stood open mouthed at the scene before her.
'Mother they are wonderful. How did you do it?'
'I've kept them going in the green house, just in case we had frost. I didn't want them to spoil.'
'They're gorgeous. Look at all the colours, they're busy lizzys aren't they?'
'You're right. I've been bringing them on for a few weeks now,'
'Thank you Mother, for making things so special for me and for all the work you've done. It really is appreciated by both of us.'
The two women stood on the stone step hugging one another.

Farmer Smalley brought the ponies and trap an hour early and deposited them on the front lawn, tethering them to a stake he'd driven into the grass. The ponies had little bells attached to their harnesses, which jingled as they moved around. The cart had been left outside the wooden gate to the garden, decorated with coloured tissue paper flowers.

The twins dressed in their pale green dresses, stood before the mirror, looking at their reflection. It was hard to tell them apart.

'We look pretty don't we?' Rose asked.

'You certainly do. You look lovely the pair of you. But I want you to promise to be good today.'

'We will,' they chorused and sat on the bed watching their sister getting ready.

'Everything all right up there?' Christopher called out.

'We're fine.' Margaret replied. 'Elizabeth's concerned about Wolfgang.'

'No need. He's all right. He stayed at Farmer Smalley's and is now on his way to the church.'

'Thank you Father.'

Margaret fussed over her daughter, helping to put her veil on and smoothing out her silk wedding dress.

'I can't believe how well the twins have behaved.' Elizabeth looked at her image in the mirror. 'There that will do don't you think Mother?'

'You look divine,' and she wiped away a tear. ' I'm so proud of you.'

'Thank you Mother. You had better shoot off and I'll come downstairs and wait with Father. Will you take the girls with you?'

'Of course I will. You really do look beautiful. Come on you two.'

The three of them came down the narrow stairs.

'Be careful as you come down Elizabeth,' Margaret shouted back up the stairs.

Christopher was waiting down in the lounge.

'And how are my favourite girls? Look at you, you look as though your going to a wedding.'

'You know we are Father, stop mucking about.' Rose said.

'Who are these young ladies. I don't recognise them.'

'Of course you do, it's us Father, Rose and Ruth., Ruth added.

'But my girls are always shouting and misbehaving.'

'You're pulling our legs Father, you know it's us.'

'You're too grown up. You'll soon be getting married. Mother make another two cakes.' They all laughed at the thought.

'We'll go to the church now. Come along girls.' Margaret ushered the two of them, making sure the picked up their bouquets. ' See you all there,' she called out and made their way outside.

'Oh no! All the hard work for nothing.' She uttered completely dejected.

'What's the matter?' Christopher joined her, to see the ponies had eaten all the heads of the flowers leaving only a few blooms near the gate.

Disappointment filled her whole being.

I had wanted it to be so special for my daughter.

'Never mind old thing,' Christopher put his arm around her shoulder to give her some comfort. 'Don't let it spoil the day.'

Margaret was near to tears.

'Look what the ponies have done.' Ruth nudged her sister

'Well they can't blame us for it, because we wasn't there.'

'Let's go girls,' Margaret ushered the bridesmaids through the gate and headed for the church.

A few bystanders stood by the path, passing complimentary comments as the group passed by.

'Lovely blue outfit Margaret.'

'Oh look at the twins, they look really grown up.'

'This will be the first marriage in the village, since the war you know.'

'I love their dresses.'

Farmer Smalley harness up the ponies and placed them into the trap, their bells tinkling, they were ready for the bride.

Elizabeth snatched a quick final look in the mirror. Satisfied with the result she turned and slowly negotiated down the narrow stairs and into the front room.

Christopher stood in wonderment, how could this alluring vision before him be his little girl.

Her hair compliments the dress, stunning is an understatement.

'I don't know what to say my dearest daughter, you've taken all my words away.'

'It's not like you father to have nothing to say.' Elizabeth smiled.

'If I expressed just how I feel at this moment, I would break down and cry.'

Elizabeth stepped forwards and took her father in her arms. They stood there for a few moments, drawing comfort from one another.

The tinkling bells grew louder as the ponies were getting restless

'Are you ready?'

Elizabeth nodded; she picked up her bouquet, caught up the fullness of the skirt and walked out into brilliant sunshine.

'What's happened to mother's flowers? They were so pretty.'

'Apparently the ponies ate them.' Christopher grinned.

'Oh poor Mother. All her hard work and she wanted it to be so special for me.'

'It was special all right, at least the ponies thought so. They must have thought Christmas had come early.'

'Father you're incorrigible.'

They walked through the gate and Farmer Smalley held the unsettled ponies still, whilst Elizabeth climbed on board, followed by her Father.

'I just knew it would be fine weather.' Elizabeth held on to her Father's arm.

The trap lurched forward and the clip clop of the pony's shoes echoed along the cobbled street. They passed by the church, down Main Street, where people stopped to look at the happiest woman making her way to church.

'Any words to advise me father?'

A friend gave her a wave. 'Who's that?'

Her father was still thinking.

'Never go to sleep on an argument. Always talk it out first.'

'Is that what you and Mother have done?'

'Yes, always and it worked.'

'Then we'll not go too far wrong. Thank you?' She lent over to give him a kiss on the side of his cheek.

They arrived at the church. Farmer Smalley walked to the back of the cart opened the small door that allowed Christopher to climb out. He held out his hand and Elizabeth gathered up her skirt and daintily stepped down on to the road with her Father's help. She caught hold of his arm and together they walked towards the church.

'Thank you for your words of wisdom Father. I'll do my very best.'

'I know you will.'

Organ music reached their ears as they approached the heavy oak doors. The only noise to accompany the Bishop's voice was the tinkling of the ponies' bells.

'Friends we are gathered here today…'

Half an hour later the doors to the church burst open as people spilled out of the building, talking and laughing.

'Wasn't that a lovely wedding?'

'It had me in tears.'

'Are you coming to the reception?'

'She looked perfectly adorable.'

'I noticed the bridesmaids behaved themselves very well.'

Wolfgang and Elizabeth walked arm in arm to the Village Hall followed by their guests. The sunshine peeped through the heavy clouds on the procession of happy people.

The village hall was filled with guests seated along the U-shaped tables decorated with flowers. At the head sat Wolfgang and Elizabeth. Edward stood up and knocked the table with the end of his knife.

'Speech.' Someone called out.

Gradually the hubbub of conversation ceased.

'Ladies and gentlemen. I would like to say what a privilege this is to be talking to you all today as the Best Man.' He looked at Mabel, cleared his throat and carried on.

'It's been a pleasure knowing these two young people, first working with Wolfgang, who is now my partner.' There were gasps from some of the guests.

'I feel very close to them. Now everyone, raise your glasses to this couple setting out on the path of married life. Wolfgang and Elizabeth.'

The guests rose to their feet, raised their glasses of white wine to Wolfgang and Elizabeth.'

'Did you hear what he said?'

'How did that happen?'

'Well I am surprised.'

'Good luck to them. That's what I say.'

'Well done Edward. You speech was just the right length.' Mabel caught hold of her husband's arm. 'I'm very proud of you.'

'Thank you, I was so nervous. My mouth went dry.

I did have a written one in my pocket just in case it all went haywire.' Mabel squeezed his arm. 'You're just an old softie.'

'Don't let everyone know.'

THIS IS THE BBC HOME SERVICE
HERE IS THE 9 O'CLOCK NEWS

On October 2nd 1945

FLOURESCENT LIGHTING
COMES TO BRITAIN INSTALLED
ON A PLATFORM
AT PICADILLY CIRCUS
UNDERGROUND STATION

THAT IS THE END OF THE NEWS

Jessie Lambert, jumped off her bicycle and lent it up against the hedge, and walked to the vicarage and knocked on the door.

'Morning Vicar. You've post this morning and this one's from France,' She handed the bundle of letters to him.

'Thanks for the post Jessie.'

She turned and waved goodbye as she retraced her steps.

I wonder who's sending him mail from France?

She lifted up the heavy satchel of letters over her shoulder, grabbed hold of her bicycle, stood astride the machine and pushed off to her next delivery. Christopher closed the front door and walked back into his den, placing the pile of letters on to his desk. He sat down and stared at the French stamped envelope, contemplating its contents.

Now who could be sending me a letter? It couldn't be any of my compatriots, they wouldn't know where I live, and anything of that nature would come through government channels. I suppose I had better read it and find out.

He picked up his silver letter opener from his desk and slit along the fold of the envelope. At the head of the notepaper was an official stamp. It read.

Dear Reverend Kelly,
I am writing to you on behalf of the Mayer of Dinan, Monsieur Dupont, who would like to invite you to a

gathering we are having on 27ᵗʰ of November 1946. This meeting is to thank people who have helped our town when it was most needed. We hope you will be able to come. Travel arrangements see attached letter.
Yours sincerely
pp. Monsieur Dupont.

Christopher leant back and eased his large frame into a more comfortable position.

How strange, I haven't heard from anyone since I was invalided out of the RAF and for this to come now, most peculiar. Now, can I fit it in with my parish duties?

He leant over to the corner of his desk and lifted up his black diary. He thumbed through the pages to the 20ᵗʰ November.

That's a bit of luck, it's free. I'll have to get in touch with the Bishop and get his permission. There's a lot to organise before then.

Margaret elbowed her way into the study, carrying in the tea for elevenses.
'You look as though you have all the troubles of the world sitting on your shoulders'.
'Your not far wrong.'
'Anything I can help you with?'
He looked up into her kind face, her blue eyes smiled at him encouragingly.
'Not really. I'll explain later.'
'As you please my dear.' She stirred the hot liquid in

the teapot with a teaspoon, then poured out two cups of strong tea through the strainer.

'The girls were argumentative this morning. I'll be pleased when they grow out of the phase. Elizabeth telephoned to let us know how she's getting on at the farm.'

'Mnnn.'

'And I had sex with the milkman too'

'Mnnn.'

'Christopher! You're not listening to a word I've been saying.'

'Oh, I'm sorry Margaret. I've been thinking about the letter I received this morning from France.'

'Who from?' Margaret felt the pit of her stomach turn.

Surely all those horrendous times were not going to start again?

'It was from the Mayor of Dinan. Apparently they have invited a few people there for a some sort of celebration. It should only be for a couple of days.'

'I remember you saying something like that before.'

'But this is different Margaret, the war's over.'

'It may be, but we still feel the effects of it. Food is still in short supply. Clothing is still practically impossible to get hold of..' She shrugged her shoulders.

'I know, but things are improving, gradually.'

'Yes I know. Now about this trip?'

'I'll put things in motion and let the Bishop know about it.'

'When do you go?'

'On the 27th of this month.'

'Right, that gives you just a week. Get your finger out young man, there's a lot to do.'

'Young man, I wish.'

The week flew by and Margaret busied herself with the household chores.

'Mother is Father going away for long?' Ruth asked.

'No, it's only for a couple of days. He'll be back before you miss him.' She ruffled her daughter's curly hair.

'But what if I need help with my homework?'

'Then I'll see if I can help.'

'You usually tell us your busy,' Rose chipped in.

'That's when your Father's here. So, if you get stuck, I'll help.'

'Do you think you would know how to do them? They are ever so hard.'

'Come here you little scamp, come here.'

Ruth ducked under her arm and ran out of the room laughing.

His Bishop had been informed and his case packed, Christopher made his way out of the vicarage.

'Bye Margaret, look after the girls and I'll see you in a couple of days time.' He gave each of them a kiss on their cheeks and with a wave he climbed into the waiting car.

'Where's Father sailing from Mother? Ruth asked.

'I told you from Portsmouth to St. Malo.'

The train journey was uneventful, by the time he had reached Portsmouth Harbour he felt ravenous. He was grateful for the sandwiches Margaret had packed for him.

Home made bread and tasty ham titillated his sense of smell. As he bit into them he could visualise Margaret kneading the dough, covered in flour.

Christopher caught the ferry with only a few minutes to spare. He wandered along the decks and sat himself down at a window seat. Looking through the glass he could see men at work, throwing off the mooring ropes and hastily climbing back on board. He looked around him at other people taking the journey; he noticed a young family watching Portsmouth Harbour gradually disappearing in the mist. He let himself relax and almost instantly fell asleep.

Five hours later the boat made its way into St. Malo docks. He gathered up his newspaper, book and suitcase. Then made his way along the cabin to the exit and walked down the gangplank.

'Reverend Kelly? Bon soir. Welcome to St. Malo. A short smartly dressed young man stepped forward from the waiting crowd. 'I am Colin Dupont. It is with great pleasure and honour to take you to your hotel, then on to the celebration.'

'Thank you Colin. I'm very pleased to meet you.' The two men shook hands and Colin led Christopher to a waiting car.

The hotel room was small and Christopher freshened up before they made their way out again. The car came to a stop outside a brick building, where a reception committee stood waiting for him. As he climbed out of the car a brass band welcomed him with a flourish of trumpets and little children surrounded him waving the French and Great Britain Flags.

What on earth is going on? There must be some mistake.

The music stopped and a portly man stepped forward, wearing a chain if office.

'Monsieur Kelly, I am the Mayor of Dinan, Mayor Dupont.' The crowd of people fell silent and listened to what he was saying. ' Our little town would like to recognise your bravery in saving many of our citizens, during the war with Germany and they are here today to convey their thanks. Familiar faces passed before him, smiling, nodding.

Christopher swallowed hard; he could fell the tears stinging the back of his eyes.

This was the last thing I expected.

'Now mon ami, another surprise for you.' The Mayor stepped backwards and Margaret, Ruth, Rose and Elizabeth moved forwards towards him. Dressed in their Sunday best clothes, the twins looking pretty and very demure. His wife, so smart in a grey flannel suit and Elizabeth in a pretty white blouse and navy skirt.

'But I left you back in England.'

'You thought you did.' Margaret hugged her husband. 'I'm so, so proud of you my darling,' she whispered in his ear. The girls grasped his hands, so tightly as though they would never let go. The crowd clapped and cheered and the Mayor held up his hands for silence. The noise of the crowds abated and the Mayor referred to his notes. He cleared his throat.

'It is with great pleasure Monsieur Kelly, that I have

another duty to perform. It is to present you with the Croix de Guerre for courage and bravery here in France.'

He stepped forward and pinned the medal on Christopher's chest. Then grabbed him by the shoulders pulled him to him and kissed him on either side of his cheeks.

The band immediately played their national anthem, 'La Marseillaise'. Christopher was speechless. Onlookers cheered, waved flags and sung their rendition of God save the king.

'Come mon ami, we have a wonderful meal planned for you,' Monsieur Dupont guided the family into the Town Hall to the civic reception. The square hall was decorated with military flags, in the centre a large oak table set for their honoured guests.

'Madame, Monsieur. I raise my glass to a very special person. One with no thought for his own personal survival. A man who saved many of our citizens and on other occasions halted the German production of warfare. This is a very special person. To the Reverend Kelly, better known to us as David. Raise your glasses to David our very own hero.'

'He's not your hero, he's ours,' the twins chipped in.

'Ah no. I knew it was too good to last,' Margaret sighed.

Stylecroft was buzzing with the unexpected news, that their vicar had won the 'The Croix de Guerre'. When the news leaked out exactly what for, gossip was rife.

'Did you hear about the vicar?'

'It doesn't seem real that the Reverend Kelly did all that.'

'I bet there's more to it, than what we've heard.'
'They only let you know half truths anyway.'
'What is it you've heard?'
'Well it goes like this.'

The Kellys arrived back at the vicarage late Sunday afternoon and were greeted by Bishop Blackburn.

'Congratulations my son,' pumping his hand up and down, 'a wonderful achievement. Did you enjoy the ceremony?'

'It was unbelievable. I had no idea at all what was going to happen. I met old friends and made so many new ones.'

'And the family being there too.'

'That was so unreal. I had left them here at the vicarage and they appeared there. How the girls kept the secret, I'll never know.'

'They were on a promise, that they wouldn't let on about it.'

'Ah now it all drops into place. I remember thinking how well behaved they were, the little devils. Many thanks Bishop for covering for me. I expect you'll need to be about your duties.' The two men shook hands and as Bishop Blackburn left the cottage as Mabel came up the garden path to visit.

'Hello, welcome home. You've certainly stirred up a hornets nest.' Christopher and Margaret looked at one another.

'Have we?'

'You certainly have. Every one is gossiping, making four plus four equals nine.'

'That's Stylecroft I'm afraid.'

'It's because it's so unusual for a Reverend to have been a special agent. It goes to show, you never know everything about a person,'

'You never said a truer word Mabel.' agreed Christopher.

'Well I'll let you get on with your unpacking. I just wanted to say welcome back and to let you know what to expect in the village.'

'Thank you Mabel we'll see you later.' Margaret saw her to the door.'

After leaving the vicarage, Mabel called into the corner shop.

'A pat of butter and a bag of sugar, please Donald. Here's my coupons,' she placed them on the counter.

'I see the Kellys are back.'

'Yes. I just popped in to welcome them home.'

'Trust you to stick your nose in my lady.' Mrs Hardy walked into the shop behind Mabel.

'They say he's been awarded the 'Croix de Guerre'.

'What the hell that, when it's at home?' Asked William as he walked in on the conversation.

'It's an award from the French people for bravery, I believe.' Donald said.

'Now what would they do a thing like that for?'

'William, it's because he was a special agent.'

'How do you know that?'

'Because we were told all about it.'

'By the Reverend himself?'

'No. But I've got it on good authority'

'Then you don't know for certain then do you? It could all be a pack of lies,' Mrs Hardy voiced her opinion.

'Now, now, people, lets keep things in perspective,' Mabel called a halt to the speculations.

'I'm going for a pint, anyone join me?' William said.

'I'd like to, but I've the shop to look after. I'll pop in later on.' Donald said

The Red Lion was packed to the gunnels, everyone discussing the latest news about the Reverend Kelly, so much so, that the proprietor had a job hearing the customers' orders.

'Was that one or two Guinness's, Bob?'

'Two,' shouted Bob above the noise.

'Have you heard the latest Dick?'

'What about the vicar?'

'Yes, what a surprise. The whole village is blathering on about it.'

'I think that's why everyone has come out this evening. I've never had so many people in here at the same time, that's for sure.'

'Come on Dick. You haven't time for chatting. Two pints of you best bitter,' Bill called out.

'Have a heart, there's only me on this evening.'

'What about a lovely young curvy barmaid here instead.'

'You find me one and I'll employ her on the spot.'

'Trust you men. I'll have a half of shandy.' Bob and Mabel joined the group.' Now what's all this about young barmaids?'

'Man to man conversation, you know,' Dick said winking his eye.

'I see, your covering your backs boys. Don't let me spoil your fun.'

Mabel picked up her shandy and wandered over to the table that had just been vacated. Just at that moment Christopher and Margaret walked into the bar.

'Join us over here.' Mabel waved at them.

'Thanks we've only popped in for a quick half.' Margaret said.

'Can I get you a refill Mabel?' Christopher offered.

'No thanks, we'll be going shortly. Christopher nodded and walked up to the bar.

'A sweet sherry and a Guinness, please barman,' and placed the money on to the counter.

'Not in this pub,' stated Dick.

'What on earth do you mean?'

'You're not paying for it in this pub Rev. It's on the house.'

'Well thanks Dick.'

'Let's have three cheers for our vicar. Hip, hip, hooray. Hip, hip, hooray. Hip,hip, hooray. The accolade was unanimous. After several slaps on the back and many people adding their congratulations, they managed to get to their table, sit down and enjoy their drink. The next morning everyone was late getting up. Near panic set in when the twins invaded the kitchen

'Come on girls and help set the table.' Margaret said.

'Why are you so late getting up Mother?'

'Because I never heard the alarm go off.

'Are you going deaf?' Ruth asked.

'No, I'm not. Now come on girls and get moving.'

The table laid and the family ate their breakfast quickly.

'Now run along to school. You don't want to arrive late after the bell.'

The two girls looked at one another. No, they certainly didn't want to arrive late.

'Good bye Mother, Good bye Father, see you at lunch time.'

'They're such good girls Christopher. They're never late for school.'

'I had better start on the sermon for Sunday.' He started to walk towards the library. When there was a knock at the front door. Christopher changed direction, walking along the hallway to the entrance and opened the doorway.

A small boy stood looking at him intently. His blue eyes searching his face.

'Father?'

Printed in the United States
143434LV00001B/1/P